EXECUTION ISLAND

JANICE BOEKHOFF

Lost Canyon Press
P.O. Box 624
Bettendorf, IA 52722

Trade paperback ISBN 978-1-948003-11-7

E-book ISBN 978-1-948003-10-0

Cover by Kim Mesman (mesmandesignco.com)

For Crystal and Mel
The word critique partner(s) does not accurately describe the level of encouragement, joy, brainstorming power, and sanity that you bring to my life. You are both so precious to me.

Introduction

In a world where genetic manipulation is the newest superpower, dinosaurs are brought back from extinction and released on the American population. After several gruesome fatalities, the military hunts down each specimen and transfers it to a sanctuary—the newly formed island of Costa Rica. Contained by an expanded Panama Canal to the south and the freshly dug Nicaraguan canal to the north, the dinosaurs flourish in the tropical climate.

However, the costs required to purchase the land, evacuate the residents to nearby countries, and construct the sanctuary leave the United States saddled with enormous debt. This cost, coupled with an overworked prison system leads to the signing of a new death penalty bill, dubbed by the media as *Jurassic Judgment*.

After four months of accelerated appeals, death row inmates are given a choice: immediate execution or ... exile to Extinction Island.

Wrongly convicted of her best friend's murder, reptile expert Oakley Laveau is sent to the island and survives for three terrifying weeks among genetically modified dinosaurs and ruthless convicts. In that time, she's discovered the truth behind her own genetic manipulation. But the truth hasn't set her free because the man who helped create her is coming to claim her.

Chapter One

THE FACES of the dead swam before her, obscuring the dirty window of the one-room shack. Oakley Laveau pinched her eyes shut to banish them but without success. Her mother. Adler. Daric. Violet. So many that guilt threatened to eat Oakley away from the inside. But to protect herself and those she cared about, she would kill many more. If that made her some sort of assassin, so be it. She'd been created for that exact purpose.

The real question was, could she become more than what she was created to be?

The man fretting beside her would say so. Cane LeBlanc was nothing if not optimistic about human nature. But even the faith-filled pastor showed the strain of the last few hours in the tight lines of his face. Two of their own had been wounded.

In the corner, Neve Torres slipped in and out of consciousness while the only doctor on the island dug around in her back for a bullet.

Not just any bullet. A bullet issued by the FBI. One that was meant for Oakley.

"Why did she do it?" Oakley whispered to Cane. Neve

had taken her place and now fought for her life.

"I wasn't there." He shook his head. "I'd guess she did it to protect you."

Remorse poured through her veins like rivers of regret. Neve, a native Costa Rican and surrogate mother to all those who'd lived in the cave, was the kindest woman she had ever met. Just because Neve never intended to leave Extinction Island didn't mean she deserved to carry around a prisoner's biological tracker.

"Almost there," Dr. Wells Anderson muttered under her breath.

If anyone could find the bullet, it would be Wells. She was a dedicated doctor with a passion for helping others. When Raptor asked her, she'd been brave enough to volunteer to come to the island with the FBI to assist in any way she could. Though originally tasked with replacing Oakley's biological tracker, she'd implanted it in Neve instead, at Neve's insistence.

Taye Turner, who had been staring out the other window, shot a glance over his shoulder. The dark skin on his face wrinkled in anguish, and he turned away again. It had been clear for a while that he was in love with Neve. What wasn't clear was how she felt, or if she even realized it.

Oakley swallowed hard. This was all her fault for not immediately accepting the replacement tracker. For thinking that finding the woman who messed with her DNA ranked higher in priority. What if Neve didn't make it?

To her right, Kaleo moaned, and she went to him. He lay on his stomach with bandages striping down his legs. Her heart ached as she sank down next to his unconscious form. Kaleo Palani had saved her on the first day she'd arrived and many more times since then. Had she gotten him help in time to give him the same chance at life? He had to pull through, but he'd lost so much blood. Life without him would be …

No, she couldn't think about that.

He'd passed out from the pain when Wells was stitching up the backs of his legs, and the doctor hadn't had a chance to rub any painkiller into his wounds before Neve arrived in even more serious condition.

Oakley rummaged through one of the bags and found the tube of homeopathic cream—Neve's special concoction of herbs. As gently as possible, she peeled back the tape from the bandages and smoothed a thin layer across Kaleo's torn flesh. Red Grizzly had shredded the outer skin, but Wells said the underlying dermis was pretty much intact.

Oakley worked her jaw. She'd make that overgrown *Utahraptor* pay for this.

He stirred until she finished with the cream and replaced the bandages. Then, he fell completely unconscious again— his body's way of dealing with the trauma and blood loss. *Please let him heal.*

"Got it." Wells held a small object pinched between her first two fingers. So tiny and yet so destructive.

Wells tossed the surprisingly intact bullet to the dirt floor of the shack, then pressed a cloth to the wound. "She's not coughing up blood, so I don't think the bullet hit her lungs. There's not enough blood for it to have hit her liver or kidneys. Without an operating team, I can't be positive, but chances are she's going to make it."

Oakley blew out a breath and put a shaky hand over her heart.

Taye dropped to his knees beside the cot, grasping Neve's limp hand. She didn't open her eyes.

"Thank you, God," Cane said as he placed a hand on Wells's shoulder. "Can I help clean up?"

"Sure." She handed him a few bloody rags to wash out in a nearby bucket.

Oakley should help also, but she couldn't move. Couldn't function. They were only in this shack because of her. In her desire to find answers from her past, she'd led the director of

Asperten International—Lumas Verret—straight to the cave hideout. Every self-centered step she made had put others in danger. Not just those in the cave. But her brother, Eric, too. Just before Adler Calais died, he'd whispered Eric's name. He must have taken him on Lumas's orders and brought him to the island. Lumas would use Eric to get to her. He wouldn't stop until he forced her and Cane to deliver Penna, the woman who helped create the genetics program, and her daughter, Teagan. If Oakley ever got her hands on the director again, she'd show him the full wrath of her special ability that he prized so much.

———

THE NEXT MORNING, a familiar high-pitched whistle bleated through the thin walls of the shack. A transport ship was approaching the coast. Oakley went to the window, even though she'd never see through the miles of jungle.

When the bleating continued, her gaze searched out Cane's. His expression was flat. She raised her eyebrows in question. Should they go meet the prisoner transport ship as he and Neve had always done?

She couldn't do much right now to search for her brother. Her only lead to Eric's whereabouts was the bunker owned by Asperten International. Her former boss, Ogden "Raptor" Greene, had access to portions of the bunker, but he'd disappeared after dropping Neve off. Until he returned, she had no chance of finding Eric.

Cane gave a slight shake of his head. He was probably right. It was too dangerous. Special Agent Glaser had probably figured out he'd shot the wrong person. He would still be looking for her.

But the memory of her first arrival on the island pressed into her mind like a hot branding iron. Cane had tried to rescue her from the Cazador gang; he'd just been a little too late. At the time, he'd known Kaleo would take care of her. But since Kaleo was here, any woman coming in on that ship would be at the mercy of the violent members of the gang. She shifted on her feet. Maybe there wasn't a woman onboard this time.

But what if there was?

She gave a firm nod to disagree with him, and without waiting for a reply, grabbed a bow and arrow set from the corner. Cane would follow. He always had her back. On the way out, she smoothed a hand over Kaleo's forehead. He mumbled something without waking.

Outside, her heart gave a little hiccup. Was her brother out here alone? Adler would have hidden him somewhere. The bunker was the best-case scenario. She shook her head to corral her focus. The jungle was no place to be caught unaware. She surveyed the foliage as both Kaleo and Cane had taught her. All was still. The sounds were normal. A far-off screech from a startled dinosaur. The twitter of birds. The undisturbed flow of the wind through the leaves. No threats at the moment.

Cane joined her, and they began walking in the direction of the coast.

Her feet took up a steady rhythm as her mind wandered again. If Adler's whispered confession meant he had brought her brother to the island, it would have been for Lumas. Eric must be in that bunker.

Where was Raptor? Maybe they would run into him on the way. He'd said he needed to call some other FBI agents. But she'd scoffed. More FBI wasn't likely to fix this mess.

Again, she reined her mind back to something she could control. The ship couldn't wait. If they didn't get there first, the Cazador gang would kidnap anyone who disembarked.

An hour later, they neared the landing pad where the prisoner transport ship would dock. The massive steel door had already been lowered to the concrete pad. Were they too late?

"Stay here," Cane whispered. "You're just my backup. If the guys from the gang see you, they'll kill us both."

She reluctantly nodded. The members of the gang thought she was dead, and it needed to stay that way.

Cane stepped out of the jungle with his bow in his hand and quiver on his back while she crouched behind a bush to watch. Someone wearing a pair of leather boots clomped down the gangplank, the same boot brand she'd been given upon her arrival. Jean-clad legs became visible, then a bright yellow sweatshirt—not the best color for blending into the jungle. A man in his midtwenties with russet-red hair and freckles stepped to the concrete. He had enough bulk to be substantial, but he couldn't have been more than a few inches taller than her short stature.

No one else disembarked. So, no women were aboard. Time to go and leave this new guy for the gang. But that wouldn't happen. There would be a snowball's chance in the jungle before Cane would abandon someone out here. No matter who they were or what they'd done.

He spoke in a soothing and gentle voice. "I'm Cane. I can take you somewhere safe."

Shuffling sounds came from the opposite end of the clearing. Members of the gang were on their way. They would steal all the newcomer's supplies, then force him to their resort compound. If the new guy played by the rules, the compound could be a safe place. If not, he would suffer jungle justice, especially if Kaleo wasn't there to stop it. But who knew what this guy had done. Maybe he deserved it.

"You have to come with me now," Cane said.

The newcomer took a step backward toward the ship. Not the right move.

Cane eased in her direction as the leaves at the other end of the clearing rustled. Wyatt, the gang member who normally guarded the front door, came into view. His brown hair hung in greasy waves around his ears. He held a spear in one hand and a rifle slung across his thick chest. Ammunition was scarce on Extinction Island, so he wouldn't likely use it, and he wouldn't have to with five more gang members emerging from the trees.

The newcomer's eyes had gone wide with fear and confusion. He'd frozen in place.

Get out of there, Cane. She couldn't help him without exposing the fact she was alive.

Wyatt tensed his legs to run at Cane, but then a five-foot-tall dinosaur leaped from the jungle and landed in front of him. Its skin was a mottled gray-green color. When it turned its head, its jaw displayed several long, sharp teeth sticking out to the side, preventing the animal from closing its mouth.

Ice water pooled in her veins. *Fangtooth.* This was the dinosaur that had come with them on the boat from the research lab, the one that seemed a little too intuitive. She scanned the trees. It never traveled alone.

Wyatt didn't seem concerned about this relatively small dinosaur. He thrust his spear at the creature's stomach. Fangtooth dodged expertly as if it was familiar with Wyatt's fighting style.

Cane slowly backpedaled in her direction. Even the newcomer headed her way, obviously determined to avoid the dinosaur fight.

Wyatt swiped his spear toward Fangtooth's chest.

Another quick, evasive maneuver.

Then the real attack came. A huge dark blur topped with red—the *Utahraptor* they called Red Grizzly. It was twice as large as Fangtooth and almost as smart. It picked off one of the gang members at the rear of the group. A bewildered scream. A sickening crunch.

Cane reached her, and they took off into the cover of the trees. She glanced back to see the newcomer following. *Great.* What would they do with him now?

Chapter Two

A HUNDRED YARDS AWAY, Oakley slowed her steps. Red Grizzly and Fangtooth were probably occupied with their meals and wouldn't track them. She gave a shiver at the thought of someone she knew from the gang being eaten. But it was reality out here.

They had to travel quietly now. Other hunting dinosaurs were their more immediate danger. Surprisingly, the new guy walked light on his feet, like an athlete. Cane moved around her and took the lead, leaving her back with ... whoever he was.

"What were those?" the newcomer asked.

She put a finger to her lips. He gave a shaky nod and glanced at the impinging trees.

After ten minutes, it was clear that Cane was leading them to the tree house. The gang members knew of its existence, but Kaleo didn't let many of them go there.

Twenty minutes later, they were climbing the rope ladder. She let the new guy go up before her. As the last one up, she gently closed the hatch while keeping one hand on the knife tucked into her waistband. Her bow and arrows wouldn't do much good in close quarters like this.

"What's your name?" Cane asked.

"Hudson Kale."

"Okay, Hudson, you're safe here. Make sure you stay until we come to get you," Cane said.

Cane hadn't asked what he'd done. Curiosity niggled at her, but it was probably better not to know. Most of the people here were murderers.

"Why?" Hudson asked.

"Well, the dinosaurs for one. Red Grizzly and Fangtooth are only two out of thousands. And you don't want to run into other convicts. Not to mention the traps out there."

"Traps?"

"Ones built by the convicts. If you see a splayed-out carving on a tree, like an asterisk except with a symbol in the middle, stay away from it until you learn the different markings."

The newcomer twisted his hands for a minute as he looked around the wood-paneled space. Then he went to the window. Carelessly, he swung the shutters wide, trapping a wandering gecko's tail between the slats. The tail pinched off, and the gecko scampered away.

"Poor thing. Why did you do that?" she asked.

"I didn't see it." He looked mystified. "Won't it grow back?"

She frowned. "Yes, it will, but it still probably hurts to have your tail cut off."

His gaze settled on her. Not in a lustful way exactly. His expression held awe.

"You're Oakley Laveau," he whispered.

She didn't respond. How could this man know her?

He took a step closer. "Youngest woman sentenced to Extinction Island."

Wonderful. She had a convict groupie.

"I know everything about you. Five feet two. Dark brown hair. Amazing blue eyes. Middle name Acadia. Your

9

mother is dead, but not your father. You have one half brother."

She whipped out the knife and advanced on him. "What do you know of my brother?"

He scrambled back, stumbled on a cot, and fell to the floor. "Nothing really. Just that you have one. It's part of your bio."

She kneeled and, with trembling fingers, pressed the knife to his abdomen. "Bio?"

"Everybody on the island has one. It's public information. Yours is the most popular." He scooted a few more inches until his head pressed against the wood paneling. He gave her a shy smile. "You look just like your pictures."

She moved the knife up to point at his chest. "What pictures?"

"Lots of them." He shrugged. "I'd guess many of them were taken from Monica's stuff, since your dad doesn't seem like the kind of guy to share."

A cold prickle ran up her spine at the mention of her dead best friend. This guy knew way too much about her. It was time to go. She stood and turned her back on him.

"Most of your hardcore fans think you're innocent," he said. "You know, your dad has been seen at FBI headquarters. I think he's trying to prove your innocence."

Maybe. But the last time she'd talked to him, he told her to accept that she would spend her life on Extinction Island. "Was this recently?" she asked over her shoulder.

"Yeah. The tabloid reporters broke the story just before I got on the boat."

Perhaps he was trying to get the FBI to find Eric.

Without turning around, she went to the trap door and descended the ladder to the forest floor. Let Cane try to acclimate the crazy, stalker dude.

Five minutes later, Cane joined her at the base of the tree house.

"Harmless or murder-suicide obsessed?" she asked.

"Harmless … I think."

"I don't suppose you'll leave him to fend for himself?"

"No. We can have Kaleo evaluate him later."

At least Kaleo would make it obvious that she belonged to him. "Where are we going to put him permanently?"

"Either he'll live with the Cazador gang or possibly at the cave."

She nodded rather than state the obvious. Lumas Verret had seen everywhere she had been because of the camera he'd implanted in her right eye. Even though it had been removed, the cave still wasn't safe to return to. Unless they got rid of Lumas.

The thought drew an icy finger down her spine. When had she gotten so comfortable with murder? Whether she blamed her genetic makeup, this island, or just circumstances, there was no denying that, little by little, her moral compass had twisted until it pointed well south of pacifist.

They walked in silence for forty-five minutes. Then Cane took one solid footfall and stopped. She halted behind him.

At nearly the same time that she planted her foot, a loud crack sounded ahead of them. It could have been the crack of a whip, similar to a swinging *Brachiosaurus* tail, except there wasn't any accompanying disturbance in the trees. Kaleo used a whip, made of old seat belts, to deter smaller dinosaurs, but this had sounded louder than that.

Cane pointed up. She nodded. As the better climber, she would scramble up and try to get a look ahead. While she quietly pulled herself onto a limb, Cane swung his bow off his shoulder and nocked an arrow.

About fifteen feet off the ground, she peered around from the far side of the tree. Still too many branches and leaves to get a good look. She climbed ten more feet and peered around again. A small break in the foliage gave her a clear view of a twenty-foot-long dinosaur munching on a similar-sized dinosaur not quite twenty feet ahead of them.

It took her mind a few seconds to register the whole scene. Something was off. The body of the fallen dinosaur lay at the mercy of the predator's munching teeth, but its head lay more than ten feet away. The neck had been severed, not with knife-like precision but with enough compression to rip the tendons and bone so that they hung in equal lengths from the scaly skin. A small circle of blood darkened the leaves, though surprisingly little.

Somehow, this predator had swiftly decapitated the other animal.

The predator raised its head. It looked somewhat like a *Dilophosaurus* based on the two yellow ridged crests above its eyes, but with the unusual addition of long, praying-mantis-like arms that folded underneath its body when it bent down to feed. Its skin had scrolling markings of blue and green, almost like a peacock. It turned its head and scanned the area, then looked up. Sharp mud-brown eyes focused on her. She held in a gasp.

It tilted its head back and forth several times. The crests on top shifted as if they weren't bony protuberances but more like sensing organs. Slowly, it lowered its head back to its meal.

On nimble, nearly silent feet, she climbed back down. Not willing to risk speaking, she tapped Cane on the shoulder and led him far around the kill zone. When they got back to the shack, she'd have to find a way to tell him about the newest genetic monster Lumas and his protégé, Auburn, must have created.

———

IT HAD BEEN silent in the stuffy room since ten-year-old Eric Laveau had arrived. Silent except for his own crying and shouts. How long had he been here? He couldn't count on knowing from the times he'd slept. Those were only short naps, taken when he got too tired to yell. He scratched at the metal door just to hear some sort of other sound.

A tear leaked out of the corner of his eye. What if no one ever came? He would probably go to sleep one day and never wake up. That was why he didn't sleep long. It might be the last time.

The small table contained four water bottles and eight granola bars from the package of a dozen. He'd almost drank four bottles of water already. He hadn't touched the dried meat in the plastic yet, but all the chips were gone. Food wasn't really the problem; he wasn't all that hungry anyway. He stared at the last swallow of water in the bottle on the ground. He'd been trying to drink just a little at a time to make sure he had enough to last, but he was so thirsty. And his throat was raw.

He scooped up the bottle, ripped off the cap, and finished it. The water burned his throat but eased the tight knot in his stomach.

The lights flickered. He yelped as darkness overwhelmed him, but the lights came right back on. Maybe today was the day that his dad would come. It was getting harder to believe that. He put his head in his hands and tugged at his messy hair.

What could he do except wait? He'd tried to escape a hundred times. There was no way out of this room. *Please, Dad, come find me.*

Chapter Three

THE WIND WHIPPING at Auburn Verret's hair eased as her father, Lumas, slowed the boat for their approach to Extinction Island. The tall trees of the jungle waved in the breeze. Inviting as if it were paradise, but hiding deadly secrets. She rubbed her arms as a shiver came over her.

She'd been here only one other time—to visit a peninsula on the opposite shore where her father said this had all started. Her adoptive mother, Penna Gallardo, had re-created the first dinosaurs there in a lab housed in an abandoned prison building. She'd experimented with their genetic code in the same way an artist varies brushstrokes and color tone. No matter how Auburn had tried to imitate her efforts, it came out to little more than counterfeit replication. Sure, the notes on gene manipulation Penna had left behind worked, but Auburn hadn't been able to create anything original. The most she could do was tinker with what was left to her. All fine, except Dad wanted her to expand the program.

Auburn's true talent lay in manipulating computer code. DNA was a type of code in itself, but it could be affected by everything from environmental factors to random mutations to ultraviolet radiation. Outside factors were always an issue.

Not so with a computer. It reacted a certain way solely because the code told it to. It was logical, predictable.

She unhooked her laptop from the charging cord and checked it. Full power. She would need to conserve the battery life until they reached the bunker, but she couldn't help taking a peek at the kill switch computer code, disguised in a folder labeled Failed Gene Modifications. Her father would never open a folder of failures. The program would be safe, just so long as Glen, her father's computer expert, didn't find it. In the last week, looking at the code had become almost a ritual to perk herself up whenever the pain of Adler's death tore at her heart. At any moment, if she saw fit, she could kill the one who'd killed him. And eventually she would, once Oakley confessed to the crime.

The boat slowed to a crawl as they approached the protected docking area. She'd only seen this location through Adler's eye implant. It was a sea cave formed from a lava tube. A metal ladder connected the dock with a tunnel that naturally led almost a mile inland. Her father had expanded the tunnel to run directly underneath the bunker. It would be a long but easy walk.

Dad motioned for her to loop the rope over the piling. She flipped her laptop closed and set it down.

"Is the tracker still active?" he asked.

Of course, he would assume she'd been looking at the status of Oakley's tracker. More than likely, it was still in the same spot. "Yeah. Aren't you worried about the FBI being here? Someone had to install the tracker after all."

He shrugged. "It's a big island."

Running into the FBI would mean answering a lot of questions about why they were here. Only inmates and biologists, like Raptor Greene, came here. Visiting Extinction Island was illegal, probably to keep people from stealing eggs or juvenile dinosaurs, or even taking dinosaur parts for souvenirs. Of course, Cane had residence on the island by claiming the pastor's exemption.

Perhaps Dad would just say they were on company business. But tracking Oakley wouldn't be the kind of company business the FBI would approve of. If they only knew of Dad's other plans for an enhanced peacekeeping force. That had to be kept confidential. Genetic enhancement was frowned upon for quite logical reasons.

The porcupine-like quills at the base of her neck tingled. She'd used them once in a while to put down small dinosaurs at their floating research lab in the Gulf off the coast of Louisiana. If they ran across larger dinosaurs, would her poison be much of a protective measure?

The tunnel provided a dank, shadowed, and musty walk to the bunker. When she emerged from a submarine-like hatch into an air-conditioned computer room, she smiled in relief. This was her kind of place—climate-controlled and full of terabytes.

She threw her backpack onto the floor and, within minutes, had hooked up to the wireless internet. Time to download all her programs and get this place ready for surveillance. Neither Oakley nor Penna would come to them, so Auburn would have to help Dad find them.

The lights flickered. "I'll check the generator and gather some supplies," he said. "We aren't staying."

She waved a hand at him over her shoulder. The blueprints for this place showed it had plenty of rooms to keep him out of sight of her computer, but still she brought up the interface for her kill switch program first in case he came back quickly. It had a range of five miles. She should be close enough for it to work now. She typed in Oakley's identification number, then the kill switch code. Her fingers brushed the top of the key needed to execute the command. She could push Enter. It would be so easy. Adler's hazel-green eyes flashed through her mind. The way his hair always did its own thing, refusing to be controlled. His huge cocky grin.

She raised both hands off the keyboard and into the air as if she were putting them up for the police. It wasn't time yet. She took several deep breaths to regain control of her emotions.

The lights flickered again, and the screen rebooted. *Sheesh.* Hadn't Dad found the generator yet?

A muffled thump came from the hall.

"Dad?"

No answer. Another thump, like some guy hitting his head against the wall. She left her chair and went to the doorway of the room.

Everything was silent.

She was about to sit down again when the thump sounded to her right. The narrow corridor stretched past three solid doors in that direction, ending in a wide door with a small window at the top.

A long moment went by while she waited to hear the sound again.

Thump.

It came from the door on the left, closest to the end of the hall. She slid her feet down the slick tile floor. Was she the girl in the horror movie about to meet a grisly fate because she went into the unknown by herself?

That was stupid. This was Asperten's bunker, her dad's bunker.

At the door, she lifted to her tiptoes and peered inside. It was a bunk room with one bunk on the far side and a small table with food and water on the other. A thump hit the door and made her jump back. What in the world?

Somebody or something was hitting the door. But she couldn't see who or what it was from the window.

She stood on the tops of her toes to get a better view. A set of feet, smaller than her own, was visible. A kid was in there … alone.

The lock on the outside looked just like the ones on the security doors back at the floating lab. She tried the same code that would open those.

With a hollow pop, the door lock released.

The door swung open just a few inches. She pulled it the rest of the way.

"Oak—" A boy no more than ten years old jumped up and stared at her with frightened eyes. The name he'd tried to say died in his throat. Despite their similarities, he could tell she wasn't Oakley.

"I'm not going to hurt you." This had to be Eric, Oakley's brother. She'd seen him once a couple of years ago with his father at the lab. Technically, he was her half brother too.

"Who are you?"

Your other half sister. But it was better not to go into that now. He was freaked out enough already. "That's not important. How long have you been in here?"

His brow furrowed. "I don't know."

Pounding footsteps came from behind her. Eric retreated to the bed and curled into a ball.

She spun around. Dad came to a stop in front of her.

"Why is he here?" she asked.

Her father didn't look surprised. But he hadn't visited the island for almost a year. Adler had been the only one to come here. Maybe she should have monitored his activity more often.

She swallowed down her additional questions. Dad didn't divulge answers until he was ready. She tried to ignore the little boy behind her as she focused on the next logical course of action. "We need to change tactics. Oakley is surrounded by other inmates right now. At least seven other biological trackers are in close proximity to hers."

As the words left her mouth, Dad gave her a slow grin.

He'd already planned for this. She'd been wrong in thinking they would have to go hunting. Oakley would come looking for them.

———

THE OTHERS in the shack had heard several loud cracks, which they described as halfway between gunshots and snapping whips. Oakley told them the sound was neither and described what she saw.

"Another new dinosaur," Taye mumbled. "And this one doubles as a guillotine."

Not for the first time since coming to this island of death, her thoughts turned dark. *Maybe they should have just executed me.*

"You haven't seen this animal before?" Wells asked.

"No," Taye answered, then glanced at Kaleo, who was still asleep. "And I'm confident he hasn't either."

After brushing a lock of hair off Kaleo's forehead and caressing his cheek, Oakley leaned against the window frame. "Either they are bringing more genetic monsters to the island or these creatures are moving toward us for some reason."

"Maybe it's both," Cane said. "We know they are bringing small ones here because Fangtooth hitched a ride with us when we returned a couple days ago. But this one is large. Plus, it seems like too much of a coincidence that we keep running into them. What if by bringing our unique"—he gave Oakley a cryptic look, and she shook her head—"scents together, we are creating an irresistible draw."

"You mean, they can smell all the humans in one place?" Wells asked.

Oakley bit her lip. That wasn't what he meant, but none of them could predict how Wells would react if she knew the truth about their modified DNA and the complications that it brought. It would be best to send her back to the mainland none the wiser. However, the fiery look that came over her every time she glanced at Cane meant she wasn't likely to leave him anytime soon. Maybe it could work out. Wells had expressed many times how inhumane it was to send prisoners here. She did everything she could to help them. In that respect, she and Cane had the same mission.

Cane gave Wells a quick nod.

A surge of protectiveness hijacked Oakley. Spiritually, Cane was an open book, but he hadn't yet revealed to everyone what his body had been created to do. If he told Wells his greatest secret, she'd better be worthy of the honor.

Unfortunately, Cane was probably right. The pheromones they both secreted were an attractant for these dangerous dinosaurs. It had been the case for sure with Camocroc, and Demon Dragon had always seemed to find her easily as well. Individually, they might only draw the dinosaurs located in the vicinity, but what if, collectively, their pheromones were drawing the dinosaurs in from other areas?

"I need to find Raptor anyway, so there will be one less … human here," Oakley said.

"You can't go by yourself," Cane protested.

Again, he was right. The dinosaurs weren't the sole threat to her. She grunted in frustration.

"I'll go with her," Taye spoke up from the corner. "Neve isn't likely to wake up for several more hours. I can track him for you." He paused for a moment to gaze at Neve's sleeping form. "I can't just sit here and do nothing."

Oakley nodded, grabbed her bow and quiver, and handed them to Taye. He'd be better with that weapon than she could hope to be. She looked around for another weapon. Kaleo's whip lay folded under his cot, likely retrieved by Taye at some point after the last dinosaur attack. But the whip had never been natural for her.

In the corner, a five-foot-long metal pole rested against the decaying wood wall. The ends were darkened with rust, but it was in good shape overall. What had it been used for before the evacuation of Costa Rica? Maybe to keep the roof clear of branches and leaves? Or to prop open the slatted push out windows? It was a good conductor and would at least provide her some protection from smaller dinosaurs.

She hefted it in her hand and almost laughed at the simplicity of it. Would it stop the hinged, crab-like arm of a dinosaur intent on decapitating her? Probably not. "Better than nothing."

Before she left, she bent down and pressed a kiss to Kaleo's cheek. He awoke briefly and said, "Care, Hook," which she took to mean *Be careful, Hook.*

She smiled at the use of his nickname—a reference to the two missing fingers on her left hand, taken by an alligator during her day job prior to being sent to the island. Amazing that he could transform the traumatic event into a badge of honor for her.

"Let's go," she said to Taye.

Outside, Taye whispered, "Do you know which direction Raptor might head?"

"He didn't say, but I think he would have gone back to the FBI camp to see if Glaser returned there."

Taye flashed her a brilliant smile, transforming his normally stoic face into something akin to an ebony jewel. "I'll find him."

She nodded. Taye was the best tracker in the jungle. "I have no doubt."

He made a wide circle around the shack, then took the lead in a northeasterly direction. She followed, keeping a close watch for any movement in the jungle since Taye would be concentrating on the trail.

Fifteen minutes later, he dropped back, and gave a disappointed grimace. Not enough of a challenge for him. "You're right, he went to the FBI camp."

She stepped around and led him farther into the jungle. After another ten minutes, she paused and crouched down to listen. They were fifty yards from the camp. Any closer and they might be spotted.

Voices drifted on the slight breeze. One of them had a deep timbre with a slight southern accent—Raptor. She couldn't identify the other voice.

Still in a crouch, she crept forward until the words crystallized.

"You need to talk to Brooks," the unidentified voice said.

"I'll call, then," Raptor replied.

A pause. Presumably Raptor was calling someone, though she couldn't see him.

"Yes, sir," Raptor said. "Reporting on those two previous issues. Dr. Wells Anderson is alive and well. And Oakley's tracker is now active as you can see in the Extinction Island database. However, there is an additional problem."

Another pause.

"I wasn't referring to that, but I appreciate you looking into it. I meant that Agent Gabe Glaser has become a problem." Raptor cleared his throat. When he continued, it was in a grave tone. "He is intent on harming Oakley Laveau."

A longer stretch of silence.

"He blames Oakley for the death of his partner." Raptor listened for several more minutes before continuing. "If you think that's the best plan, then I understand, sir. Please communicate the info through the proper channels to Agents Glass and Dalmon."

Several voices spoke in low tones farther away. Perhaps he'd moved to speak to other people. She waited rather than reveal herself to the other FBI agents. Glaser wanted her dead. They might share the sentiment.

Minutes later, Taye tapped her on the arm and pointed to their left. A gentle rustling came from over there. It was barely audible over the jungle sounds, but after having been trained by Cane and Kaleo, she heard it too. Raptor wasn't being stealthy. He knew they were there.

She gave a low whistle as they intercepted his path. When he came into view, he held a finger over his lips and pointed away from the FBI camp. They walked about a hundred yards before stopping under the protection of an elephant tree. She leaned the metal pole against the rough bark.

"You disappeared from the shack," she said.

"I had to try to find Glaser."

"And?"

"He came back to camp before I returned, cleared out his supplies, and took off again."

Her stomach somersaulted. "So, he's still out here trying to kill me."

"We will all be looking for him, including the other FBI agents. Plus, Agent Brooks is on his way to the island."

"What? Why?"

"In his exact words, 'It's all going to crap down there, and I've got the shovel.'"

She crossed her arms over her chest. "Uh-huh. Those were his words."

"Well, maybe not his exact words."

She rolled her eyes and steeled her fear into a locked cage. "I don't care about Brooks or Glaser. I need to find out if my brother is safe."

"That was my first call." Raptor ran a hand through his shaggy hair. "Yes, he is missing. Marcel is also on his way to the island."

"You talked to my dad?" She hadn't truly spoken to him for two weeks, when he'd arrived on the visitor's boat and refused to answer her questions about her mother and Asperten International.

"No, I spoke to Felice."

A pang of bitterness shot through Oakley's heart. Felice hadn't been any kind of mother to her, much less a step-mother. But that didn't matter now.

"Apparently, they looked for Eric at the lab before

assuming he was brought here. She wanted to come as well, but of course, it's illegal."

Family members of convicts couldn't set foot on the island. They had to visit solely from the visitor's boat. But if questioned, her dad might be able to convince the FBI he was on company business since he worked for Asperten.

Hopefully, it would be a moot point, and she'd find Eric before her dad arrived. "We need to check the bunker. If Adler brought Eric here, it would be the safest place to hold a child."

Not that Adler would care so much about Eric's safety, but the bunker would be the easiest place to keep someone prisoner.

She grabbed the metal pole, and she and Taye trailed behind Raptor as he led the way. A half mile from the general area of the bunker, a shuffling in the bushes froze them all in their tracks. Raptor pulled a long knife from his belt. Taye nocked an arrow in his bow. She held the pole sideways in front of her.

A small green head popped above the low foliage and squeaked a soft greeting. She relaxed her stance. "Cody. I've missed you, buddy."

Her pet *Coelophysis* bounced to her side and pushed his head into her hand. She rubbed his small patch of white downy feathers. More squeaks came, followed by a series of clicks from deep in his throat.

"Okay. Quiet down now."

They resumed their walk, and Cody fell into line behind them. She glanced back once to see Taye patting him on the head. Cody had a way of softening even the toughest warrior.

The Asperten bunker was carved into solid rock on the side of a hill. Raptor tapped in the entry code and spun the submarine-style handle. After she and Taye slipped inside, Raptor turned to speak to Cody. "Dino-free zone, little guy. See you later."

The animal gave a frustrated squeak as the door shut. Oakley took in the space ahead of her. Smooth metal walls and metal floors patchworked into tiles from some sort of thick sheet metal. Her pole clinked against the floor as she set it down. A long hallway stretched out, punctuated here and there by plain metal doors, a few chairs, and a couple cots. The whole place resembled a landlocked submarine.

Raptor slipped around them and headed for the first door. He opened it and searched the room for anywhere that a child could hide. She moved to the next door and did the same. It was a bunk room, probably Raptor's, with one coat hanging on the back of a chair. In a small closet, a few pairs of shorts and shirts were folded on a shelf. No one hiding in there or under the raised bunk.

The three of them quickly searched the half dozen rooms off the hallway. After the last one, she joined Raptor at a secure door that had a keypad entry panel positioned at chest height.

She waited for him to open it, but he just stared at her.

"Problem?" she whispered.

"This is the part of the bunker that Asperten has never let me see."

The windowless door was massive and made of steel. She tapped on it to judge its strength. Solid. "How do we get in there?"

"We don't."

Something about Raptor's voice drew her attention to him. He frowned and brought up his right hand, which had been hidden from her view by his body.

He held a piece of paper out to her. "This was stuck to the door."

Her breath caught in her throat as she read.

Let's trade. Bring Penna and the girl to me tomorrow at the place where this all started. She will know.

Chapter Four

LET'S TRADE. The note had to be from Lumas. It confirmed her worst fears and had her insides twisting like the coils of an angry serpent. Lumas had Eric. Could she believe that he was safe? She didn't exactly have a choice. What was it they asked for in the movies? Proof of life. Lumas wasn't about to give her that. Plus, she had no way to contact him to even ask for it.

She'd stood at the secure door, banging and yelling for several minutes, but no one came. The truth slowly seeped in. This would be the safest place for Eric, but they wouldn't have kept him here knowing it was the first place she'd look. If he had at one time been in there, Lumas certainly had taken him to the meeting point, wherever that was.

She swiped stray hairs off her face. "I need to talk to Penna."

Raptor gave a grim nod. "I'll keep trying to get in."

He walked them to the door, and she gave him a quick hug before retrieving her pole and stepping outside. As soon as the door closed behind her and Taye, Cody came running up. He skidded on the leaf cover and slammed into her knee.

"Hey, now." As she bent down to rub his head, something buzzed by her ear at high speed.

"Run!" Taye yelled.

Blood drained from her face. Someone was shooting at them!

She followed Taye on a dead sprint toward the surrounding trees. Dirt and leaves popped up behind her like miniature geysers. The bullets were close. This was someone who knew how to shoot.

They reached the edge of the small clearing and darted into the tree cover. A chunk of bark broke off the nearest tree and flew into her cheek. She didn't dare look back.

For a few minutes, they crashed through the underbrush until Taye stopped on a dime in front of her. Despite her fear and panic, she had the good sense not to tear around him to keep running. She halted against his back, then peered to the side of his shoulder.

A female *Therizinosaurus* crouched next to two sleeping babies. It raised one of its claw-tipped arms and eyed them anxiously. Then it slammed a foot onto the ground. This was one of the plant-eating dinosaurs the gang hunted for food. They also used its three-foot-long claws as projectiles for wooden spears. Just one of those claws could do a lot of damage.

Taye lowered himself slowly to sit in the dirt. She followed his lead.

The gesture didn't seem to calm the animal. Maybe it didn't like that Oakley was hidden. She moved carefully out from behind Taye to make herself more visible.

The *Therizinosaurus's* head darted in her direction. Its nostrils—mere slits in a bony snout—flared as it sniffed deeply for several seconds. Then it settled itself next to its sleeping children. Finally, a dinosaur that didn't want to kill her because of how she smelled.

Running footsteps pounded somewhere beyond the

animal. Taye flattened himself on the ground. She did the same.

The footsteps slowed on the other side of the *Therizinosaurus*. The mother lifted its head to stare down the newcomer. As long as the shooter stayed on the opposite side, the dinosaur's bulk would block them from view. But if that person looked over top, she and Taye would be sitting ducks.

Oakley held her breath for a long moment. *Please let him move on. Please let him move on.* She chewed on her lip and furrowed her brow. Who had she been talking to in her head? God? Maybe Cane was having more of an effect on her than she realized.

The shooter stepped along the length of the *Therizinosaurus*. The mama dino shook its head and gave a soft warning grunt. The footsteps receded quickly.

When Oakley couldn't hear the shooter anymore, she breathed in deep and let the air out. First time she'd ever been saved by a dinosaur, unless she counted all the times Cody had inadvertently helped her situation.

Where had he gone anyway?

Taye touched her arm and pointed down to encourage her to stay low. In that respect, he was in more danger than she. At his height of six feet, he would be seen long before anyone would see her.

As they slunk away from the mama dino, Cody came barreling into her from the side. They rolled together down a small embankment. She held in her gasp for the sake of silence.

Thankfully, there weren't any logs or rocks to stop their roll. She slid to a halt unharmed at the bottom of the slope. But when she released Cody, her fingers came away slick with blood.

"Taye, he's hurt," she whispered.

They both searched for the source of the injury. About midway down his tail, blood seeped from a sharp gouge.

"He'll be fine," Taye assured her. He scanned the forest with narrowed eyes. "I just need the right tree."

He ripped several leaves from what looked like a Eucalyptus tree, then pulled down a section of vine from another one. Using a little water from a nearby puddle—to activate the leaves, he said—he layered them on Cody's tail like a fan and then wrapped the vine around to hold them on.

"That will prevent infection."

"Thank you."

He nodded and turned to walk, but then he turned back. "Glaser?"

Boiling hot anger churned in her midsection again. "Had to be. Hardly anyone else here would use a gun."

"How did he know where we'd be?"

"Good question. Probably took a chance that I'd come back to see Raptor."

She stuffed the anger down. No time to worry about Glaser. She had to get Eric back.

Taye took off in the direction of the shack. She needed to get to Penna as soon as possible, but of course, she couldn't ask him to stay away from Neve for too long. And this latest attack had convinced her not to go out alone. Maybe Cane would go with her. `

———

SPECIAL AGENT GABE GLASER growled in frustration as he stomped through the jungle. He'd lost them. If only she hadn't bent over at just the wrong moment.

She deserved to pay the ultimate price for what she'd done. His partner, Jack, had been just weeks from retirement. Gabe hadn't even had the heart to tell Jack's wife of his death yet. What a wonderful conversation that would be. *Sorry, Sharon, instead of traveling to exotic locations with the love of your life, you'll be facing retirement alone.*

This might have been his only chance to shoot the person who actually deserved the bullet. He still wasn't clear about how the other woman ended up with her tracker, but Oakley's manipulations had to be at the root of it.

Waiting for her to visit Raptor at the bunker had been the perfect setup, but now he was back at square one. And without any help. He'd purposely avoided returning to his colleagues at the campsite to keep them from being accessories to anything he'd end up doing.

His phone buzzed in his pocket. He glanced at the screen. Special Agent Noah Brooks, his boss, was calling ... again.

He silenced the call. No reason to talk to him until he could rightfully claim Oakley Laveau was dead. Then, he'd find some way to explain why he'd shot the wrong woman. Assuming, of course, anyone ever found out. The woman couldn't be a convict since she only had one tracker active in her body—Oakley's tracker. So who was she? Maybe she'd run away from the mainland and come to the island. Maybe her family had long ago given up on her. The tracker still registered as active on his phone, so she hadn't died yet.

He spun around and doubled back to the bunker. He had a plan. Oakley would avoid the bunker from here on out, but she'd find another way to meet up with Raptor.

He pulled from his backpack a plastic bag with a material that looked like thin filaments of insulation. Microcomputers were a revolution unto themselves. He scooped up a leaf about the size of his palm and approached the door of the bunker. After inspecting the seam, he shook his head. It was too tight, probably a soundproof airlock. That explained why Raptor hadn't come out during the shooting.

He had to find something smaller. After searching in a nearby embankment, he finally found a thin, flat wisp of a mineral that had crystalized out of the basalt. It was rigid and just thin enough to hang on the seam in the top of the door. He positioned it so the door would likely open before it fell, then he placed six or seven filaments on top. One of them should find its mark.

———

SEVERAL HOURS LATER, Oakley and Cane approached the old Lankester Botanical Gardens building where they'd left Penna and Teagan two days before. It had been easy to convince him to come with her because he wouldn't let an innocent child suffer. But he seemed unsure about a confrontation with Lumas. Even though Lumas was his biological father, the man twisted and warped every life he touched.

Leaving Kaleo in his injured state was hard, especially since they would have to be gone overnight, but she had no choice. Wells said Kaleo was doing well, and she promised to take good care of him. At least he'd been awake so she could talk to him before she left.

Cane double-tapped on the door in spots that formed a large triangle—the signal Penna and Teagan would recognize. After a loud thunk, the door swung open.

Penna greeted them with a bolt of wood in her hands. Apparently, they had barred the door. Good thinking.

"Where's Teagan?" Cane asked.

"Hunting for breakfast."

Oakley frowned as she leaned her pole against the wall. "But we didn't have any weapons to leave with you."

Penna gave her a rare smile. "We are vegetarians. She's gathering berries and roots." She put a hand up. "And before you complain about how safe she is, Teagan can take care of herself. She's been raised on this island, and she has more of a weapon in her head than all of us."

No doubt. The fifteen-year-old was beyond intuitive. To the point where it was uncanny. "She's genetically modified, right?"

Penna nodded.

"What did you modify in her?"

Padding footsteps sounded at the door. "I'll let her tell you."

Teagan entered carrying a blanket full of berries, with her long brown hair tangled around her shoulders. She smiled at them, then dropped the berry-laden blanket on the small table in the corner. "Tell them what?"

Penna gave her a pointed look and a nod.

Teagan wiped her hands on a towel. "Oh, you want to know about my genetics."

Weird, how she always knew things she shouldn't. That had to be part of it.

Teagan locked eyes with her.

It was like looking into the mirror and really seeing every pore, every cell, every detail of yourself. Teagan's eyes seemed to reflect understanding and sympathy and scrutiny all at the same time. Like Cane's, except on steroids.

"You already suspect," Teagan said.

Could this young girl really sense what she was thinking? "But how?"

"My mom would use lots of big words regarding my basal ganglia. I only know that I can read biological signals as if I'm body surfing them."

"Body surfing?"

"That's what it feels like inside my head. The biological signals, *bi-sigs* as I like to call them, rush at me in a wave. I piece them out into categories, almost like streaming them into different types of waves—small ones, crashing ones, cresting ones, subsurface ones—so that I can pay attention to the ones that matter."

Oakley was speechless. This was above and beyond what anyone had ever done with a human brain.

"You can read minds." Cane's flat voice spoke to his shock as well.

32

"Not really. But kind of."

Spoken like a true teenager.

"In a sense, I know the direction of thoughts." Teagan picked up a berry and popped it in her mouth. After she finished chewing, she continued, "I can also … well, I guess you'd say that I can influence the direction of flow."

"Excuse me? What?" Oakley sat down on the ratty couch the women used as one of their beds.

Penna answered for Teagan. "Biological signals are merely the flow of electrons between nerve cells. Teagan's neurons detect and interpret that flow. She can also add electrons to the stream." She waved a hand in the air. "It's not a Jedi mind trick like implanting thoughts. A person's brain is too complicated and a single, specific thought is likely to be misinterpreted by the receiving neurons. However, she can direct waves of electrical signals at a person to give them a certain feeling or desire."

Whoa. Teagan could make people do things? Truly a power Lumas would kill to possess and then use to kill once he possessed it, if he knew about it.

"No," Teagan said as she turned to Oakley. "I can't make people do things. And I'm better at interpreting than sending, probably because I do that more often."

"A person's free will and sense of morality are always governing their actions," Penna said. "Though we haven't explored the extent of her ability, what Teagan can do would most accurately be described as planting suggestions while the host is in a suggestible state, similar to inducing hypnosis."

A strong sense of purpose enveloped Oakley. It was time to get down to business. She opened her mouth, then closed it again and pointed at Teagan. "Don't do that. Use your words if you want to know why we came."

"Sorry." Teagan dipped her head for a moment. When she looked up, she gave Oakley a side-eyed glance. "But I already know why you're here. You're afraid, and it has something to do with my father."

"He has my brother. He wants me to bring both of you to him in exchange for my brother's life." She related the events of the afternoon.

"*At the place where this all started*," Penna whispered. "He must mean the old laboratory we had on a small island between the Nicoya Peninsula and the main coast of Costa Rica. It used to be a prison. I've never gone back there for fear he might still be looking for me."

Teagan shuddered. Was she feeling the intense fear her mother had of Lumas? What would it be like to have that sociopath for a father? Her gaze darted to Oakley, and pain flitted through her eyes. Uh-oh, Oakley had made her struggle worse. Maybe it was time she learned to control her wayward thoughts.

Of course. That was it. In light of Teagan's unexpected influence, thoughts were the key to beating Lumas. The outline of a plan began to form. "Obviously, we aren't turning you both over. Hear me out."

She described her idea in detail, down to the placement of participants and the timing of events. Hopefully, it would be enough to rescue Eric.

Both Penna and Teagan agreed to the plan, but Oakley didn't need special abilities to sense the atmosphere of fear in the room. Lumas was unpredictable at best, deadly at worst. Tomorrow they would find out if her plan could match his.

Penna and Teagan lay down on their couch beds in the main area, whispering back and forth. Oakley and Cane went to the back room where the floor was cleaner than the main area and laid some blankets down. They stretched out with their heads next to each other and their bodies pointing toward opposite sides of the room. As they settled in for the night, a heaviness weighed on her bones. Cane, too, was somber. Come to think of it, his usually peaceful countenance had been subdued ever since Adler's death. As if he carried the weight of it alone even though Oakley was the one most responsible for it.

"Are you okay?"

His sigh came out pinched. "I keep thinking about yesterday. How could I have helped to kill someone?"

"You were protecting us."

"This wasn't self-defense. We planned to kill him, and I went along with it."

His words hit too close to the sore spot she'd worn into her own heart. "Because you knew he would kill all of us if he could. There's more than one way to defend people."

"Proactive defense is a nice synonym for premeditated murder. And isn't that what Lumas likes to say? He wants us for peacekeeping, to *defend* people."

"There's a difference."

"How?"

"Lumas is lying."

He twisted the blanket between his fingers. "When Adler said he killed my mother, I'd never felt such rage. I wanted to kill him with my bare hands. Even with God helping me, I couldn't control the anger. What if there comes a time when I let loose on someone else?"

"You're not going to do that."

"How do you know?" His voice broke on the question.

"Because you have good inside you. That is what matters." Time to give the gift of his strengthening words back to him. "You are more than the sum of your choices."

He gave a slow nod. "You're right. Wells told me something similar. She said, 'God is helping you, but you are not God. You won't always be perfectly calm and in control.'" He cleared his throat. "That's why I need God. To forgive me when I blow it."

"You're always talking about grace," she said, "but what

does that forgiveness mean if you insist on carrying the guilt anyway?"

A small smile lingered on his face, barely visible in the moonlight when he turned his head. She smiled back at him. There was the man who had floated through life as light as a feather in this place of death. Though his concepts of mercy and forgiveness didn't make sense to her, she needed this version of him, needed to know that some type of freedom was possible ... for him at least.

Chapter Five

MORNING SUN GLINTED of the luxury yacht as it pulled away from the makeshift dock. Its crew was under orders to return to open sea and wait for communication. Lumas Verret scowled at the man standing on the wooden planking, billionaire explorer from Australia, Quincy Ness.

Lumas's trigger finger itched on the pistol he carried. "I said only you."

Ness gestured to his companion. "This is my bodyguard. Doesn't do me any good to get the girl if a dinosaur kills me before I can leave. I'm the one taking all the risks here. It's illegal for me to set foot on this island. If you're caught here, you'd merely say you were checking on your creations or some other nonsense."

Lumas bit the inside of his cheek before responding. "That's why I had you come to the other side of the island. No one docks in this area."

"I can see why." Ness shuffled his feet across the weathering wood.

Lumas turned his back on the man and began walking into the jungle. If only he could have invited one of his more civilized contacts for this purchase. But those men wouldn't have come to the island. They would have sent their employees to collect Oakley. As an outdoorsman, Ness had agreed to come on his own, which meant fewer people in the loop for the transaction and greater secrecy. Plus, he'd also agreed to the exorbitant sum of fourteen million dollars, assuming Lumas could provide proof of her genetic ability.

At least Ness and his bodyguard were in good shape and wouldn't slow him down. They had to get back to the original prison lab before Oakley showed up. It was too risky to attempt an exchange at the bunker, given the presence of the FBI, so he'd left the note and then spent half the night traveling with Auburn and Eric through the tunnels and the other half rowing across the gulf to the island lab where this journey had all started.

"Do you have the tranquilizer?" Ness asked from behind.

Lumas nodded while holding a finger to his lips. Though he had searched for threats through this part of the jungle on the way, things could change quickly here.

Despite the two bags of luggage, they made good time to the other side of the peninsula, where the ocean came inland and created the Gulf of Nicoya. He climbed down into the well of the large rowboat. If he had more occasion to be on this side of the island, he would have shipped in a speed boat, but this would have to do. Fortunately, he now had two others to share the several miles of rowing to get to the lab. San Lucas Island in the gulf was now an island within an island, though when he'd first met Penna here, Costa Rica wasn't yet Extinction Island.

At the time, she'd been working at a secret genetics lab with a pompous man, who hadn't understood her brilliance. Then Lumas took over. Inside the abandoned prison, they made their first dinosaur together—a tiny *Dilong* with DNA taken from preserved bone marrow. It took perfect conditions to preserve ancient bone marrow, but scientists had been finding soft tissue in fossils for years before Penna used it to re-create a species.

Many years and many species later, he built her a new floating lab in the Gulf of Mexico, which she'd fled without a word. His dreams had vanished along with her. Was he really about to see her again? The glimpse of her he'd gotten through Oakley's eye implant had stimulated his heart and his mind. If he could find her, he'd make sure she couldn't leave him for a second time.

He put all his anxiety and excitement into rowing the boat. When they docked, he nearly jumped out. Auburn and Eric were waiting for them inside the crumbling remains of the lab. But first he had to hide the boat. Otherwise, Oakley might destroy it and leave them stranded.

After stashing it behind a dilapidated stone wall that used to be part of a guard shack, he hurried down the path, leaving Ness and his bodyguard to carry their own luggage. The familiar stone structure seemed to carve out its own break in the jungle via its imposing size. Though this was an old prison, he'd never kept Penna prisoner here. Back then, she wanted to explore all the avenues he offered. They could be that way again.

It would all come together today. He'd have Penna, and maybe even the young girl who followed her around. There was something special about that girl. Then he'd finally resolve the situation with Oakley. He would give her one more chance to embrace her true self. If she wouldn't work with him, he'd cut his losses.

⊏⊐

OAKLEY'S ARMS burned from constantly rowing. The boat Lumas had obviously left for them barely held four, but they couldn't have left anyone behind. They were all vital to the plan. Penna had to keep Lumas talking. Teagan had to persuade. And Cane was their backup. Once they got Eric, they would find a way to squeeze him into the boat.

"Let me." Penna took over rowing. "I know where to drop him off."

Cane would sneak into the jungle and set up a bow and arrow sniper's nest facing the dock where Oakley, Penna, and Teagan would tie off the boat. Even though Lumas hadn't said where on the island he'd be, the dock was the logical place to meet him and also a better place to force a confrontation than inside the old prison-turned-lab.

If Lumas didn't hand over Eric, Cane had instructions to shoot him. Whether or not he would actually do it was a wild-card at best.

After Cane set out into the jungle on the southeast side, Penna steered the boat toward the eastern dock. When they were twenty yards out, Oakley shifted restlessly in her seat. The area was deserted. At least they had time to get out of the boat and be ready to confront Lumas.

They pulled the boat alongside the weathered boards and tied off. If only they would have had room for her one weapon —the metal pole. Oakley stepped carefully onto the creaking planks. Would they dump her right into the salty water? Penna and Teagan joined her, and by unspoken agreement, they trod on different boards to distribute their weight.

At the end of the dock, she hesitated. Penna came up behind her and pointed due west. "The lab was this way."

Okay, but they didn't want to engage Lumas indoors on his turf. She waited a few more moments on the dock, then sighed. They might not have a choice. Maybe she could draw him out once they reached the lab.

She and Teagan followed Penna along an overgrown, grooved path.

"You started everything here?" Oakley asked.

Penna shot her a grimace. "Yes. I wasn't that young, but I was naive. I won the intelligence lottery, and what did I do with all of it? The equivalent of buying twenty sports cars just because I could."

A shiver ran down her back. If Penna hadn't initiated her genetic tinkering, would Oakley even be here? Perhaps her mother wouldn't have gone to work at the same company as her father. Or maybe she would have decided not to have children at all. Cane believed it all happened for a reason. So that she could be here. Could she come to grips with the fact that the only way for her to be here was for her to be a genetic freak?

She couldn't exactly reassure Penna that none of this was her fault, so she stayed silent. Hopefully, Cane was following them and would find a good vantage point to see where they were headed.

The smothering jungle suddenly opened to a clearing that was dominated by a large limestone block building. Ivy crept up the cracked walls, and trees hung over the roof.

Still no sign of Lumas.

Penna began to walk toward the structure, but Oakley put a hand on her arm. "Stick to the plan. He wants us to approach."

Penna stopped and took a protective stance in front of Teagan. The teenager could interpret Lumas's thoughts from a distance, but she'd have to be closer to influence them. They didn't plan to get closer.

As they waited, Oakley's chest tightened in gratitude. Penna was willing to risk herself and her own child to help get Eric back. Whatever complicated mix of hubris and logic defined this woman, she was also brave.

Oakley took a step toward the building, angled herself in front of them, then stopped. Even though Penna had started this, it was Lumas who'd taken it to dark levels. Penna didn't deserve to be abused and used by him any more than Eric did. She'd find a way to force Lumas's hand and get Eric back.

Penna shifted on her feet as if she'd rather go in on her own and leave Teagan out here.

"No closer," Oakley said. "Make him come to us."

A familiar voice crept through the trees like a snake winding its way among the branches. "Wonderful to see you again, my dear."

His covetous words weren't meant for her. Lumas stepped out of the trees with his gaze fixed on Penna. A greedy, lustful smile parted his lips.

Penna's lower lip trembled slightly before she responded, "You've been busy since we last saw each other."

"Nothing compared to what I could have done with you. And now that we are reunited, our potential will be limitless."

Lumas appeared to be unarmed and was distracted by Penna. Oakley slid her feet in his direction.

She'd made it three feet before he turned his laser-sharp gaze on her. "You're probably wondering where your brother is. Don't worry, you'll see him soon. But first, I'd like you to meet someone else."

On cue, a stocky man wearing a bucket hat stepped from behind a tree. He carried no weapons either, but a man who carried a rifle stepped out as well, hovering beside the other man's shoulder.

"This is Australian adventurer Quincy Ness and his body-guard, Erman."

Oakley's heart rate picked up. Just when it seemed she'd figured him out, Lumas was always changing the rules. "What are they doing here?"

"They are here to see you."

Cryptic. The man mirrored Lumas's lustful countenance, except he was looking at her.

Lumas cleared his throat. "We will get back to them. You wanted to see your brother." He let out a loud whistle.

The door to the lab opened, and Auburn and Eric descended the stone steps. As they came to stand on the other side of Lumas, Auburn looked at Ness with open curiosity.

Now Auburn, Lumas, and the weird new guys formed a semicircle in front of Penna and Oakley. Teagan was still hidden behind Penna. Being half-surrounded was nerve racking, but only one of them had a visible weapon, so Oakley kept the corner of one eye fixed on the bodyguard.

"Oakley." Eric's soft voice came out as a whimper.

"It's okay, buddy."

He moved toward her. Auburn grabbed the back of his T-shirt and held him fast.

Teagan whimpered as well. Without looking back, Penna reached around and put a steadying hand on her arm.

Oakley glared at Lumas. "What do you want?"

He finally focused on her. "Well, I can tell you I have no use for normal unmodified Eric over here."

Not a surprise. Lumas had said he wanted a trade. He might not know what Teagan could do, but it was a safe bet her DNA was modified.

Lumas stretched both arms out, simultaneously pointing at Auburn and Ness.

Auburn released Eric, and he ran toward Oakley. She absorbed the weight of his hug as he wrapped himself around her stomach.

At the same time, someone grabbed her right arm—Erman. She'd lost track of the man in her excitement at seeing Eric. At least Erman kept the gun pointed at the ground. But it would have been better if the one man with a weapon had stayed farther away from them. More chance Cane could take him out.

"I want Penna and the girl, so I'm going to let you take Eric and go," Lumas said.

Ness scowled and opened his mouth.

Lumas put up a staying hand. "I just want one thing from you first."

She patted Eric's head as she squinted at Lumas. "What?"

He gave her a wide grin. "I want you to embrace who you are and what you're capable of."

"Meaning?"

"Use your power to kill Erman."

Beside her, Erman's hand tightened around her bicep. She looked into his face. He was scowling at Lumas in confusion. Clearly, he didn't know what she could do or he wouldn't be holding on to her in the first place.

"That's hardly necessary," Ness protested.

"You wanted to see her in action. Go on," Lumas insisted. "Kill one person to save another."

She shook her head as Erman—finally realizing something bad could happen—loosened his grip.

"It's who you are, who you were created to be. Don't be ashamed of it." Lumas's voice soothed and placated. "You have the power to choose. There's nothing wrong with that. If you were a tough, strong man, no one would think anything about you defending yourself or your brother."

In a way, he was right. She had the ability to kill when most women of her small size couldn't, no different from the men of the world. The men who took what they wanted. Without her power, she and Eric were only victims. And here she was with Eric in her arms and the only man holding a weapon within reach. She could save them both right now, and yet she hesitated. Did that make her noble or foolish?

Auburn and Lumas had crept closer. Oakley tried to take a step back, but Erman wouldn't allow it. He raised the gun to chest level, pointing it intermittently at them and away.

Teagan slid over and placed a hand over Erman's. She closed her eyes.

The man's mouth gaped, and a myriad of emotions flew

across his face. Then, his brow settled into a leathery line, and his eyes went wide with fear. He stepped back from Oakley, which caused Teagan to lose her grip.

As soon as her hand fell away, the anger returned to Erman's scowl. He grabbed Oakley's arm again. Okay, they had tried to do this the easy way.

She took both hands off Eric, then sneaked her left hand under her arm and seized Erman's fingers. She gathered up her anger and her fear for Eric, for Penna, and for herself, and pushed the emotions from her core. A tingle spread from her chest to her hand. Eric might feel her lower body warm a few degrees, but he wouldn't be hurt.

Erman stiffened as the current flowed from her hand and into his muscles. The veins stood out on his neck. The gun let out a shot and bucked in Erman's grip.

Eric yelped.

Ness startled as the bullet sailed over his shoulder, and then he fled into the trees.

Lumas lunged for the weapon. He grunted as his fingers closed over the barrel. It must have shocked him because he let go immediately.

When Erman's eyes rolled toward the back of his head, she released him. He slumped to the ground and moaned.

Soft sobs came from Eric, who had buried his face in her stomach. She bent to look into his face, but he was suddenly snatched away from her. Lumas had picked up the weapon and now held it to Eric's head.

She put one hand up toward Lumas and another toward where Cane would likely be watching. Cane couldn't shoot Lumas now without risking Eric's life. "Don't hurt him."

"Finish him." Lumas nodded toward Erman.

Why was he so intent on making her kill someone? It wouldn't prove anything other than what she already knew. She was a killer.

Ness came creeping back out from the jungle. What a coward.

Movement from the right caught her attention. Penna and Teagan had taken several steps backward as Auburn advanced on them. A strange concoction of awed anger twisted Auburn's face.

The zing of an arrow brought Oakley's head around again. A thunk sounded as it found a mark—Ness's right arm. He fell to the ground, crying out in pain.

Cane's shot created the distraction she needed. She reached for Eric.

Lumas backpedaled, and her hands closed on empty air. He raised the gun, pointing it first at Oakley and then at Penna.

"No!" Auburn yelled.

Auburn stepped in front of Penna as another arrow whizzed down. It stuck into the carpet of leaves a few inches in front of Lumas's foot. Cane was missing on purpose, trying to give them time to get out of here. But she couldn't leave without Eric.

Except she couldn't get to him. Lumas was already at the steps leading to the lab, still dragging Eric with him.

Penna tugged on her arm. They had to go. Any second, Lumas would be inside where he could shoot at them from the cover of the lab.

She ground her jaw. If she couldn't take Eric with her, she had to take some leverage to force Lumas to give him back later. As Lumas and her brother disappeared into the lab, Oakley spun around and grabbed her sister's arm. She delivered a relatively minor shock, causing Auburn's muscles to lock. Oakley couldn't kill her with her electrical power, but it stunned her enough that the three of them could drag her to the boat.

They lowered her in first because once Cane joined them she'd have to ride scrunched up on the bottom, then they all jumped in, and Oakley began rowing. As they came around to the southeast side to pick up Cane, the enormity of what happened hit her. Her shoulders slumped. Defeat dragged at her limbs. She'd been so close. Eric had been in her arms. And then she'd lost him again.

Chapter Six

ON THE SEEMINGLY ENDLESS hike through the jungle, Auburn stomped her feet behind Cane. She had trouble keeping up because she'd never had much stamina for exercise, plus her muscles were still fatigued from Oakley's electric shock, but she wouldn't let them see her struggle. The other women trailed her, perhaps to ensure she didn't run off. But where would she go anyway? Extinction island was unfamiliar, and she had no way to defend herself. She let her fingers graze the quills along the hairline at the bottom of her neck. Well, she had one defense mechanism but had never used it outside a lab.

With each crunch of leaves beneath her feet, Auburn released some of her frustration and anger. This wasn't how it was supposed to go. Things were reversed. Rather than coercing a confession from Oakley and exacting revenge, Auburn was the captive. She needed to clear her head if she had any chance to escape. But the thought of escape wasn't the sole issue clouding her mind. Seeing Penna alive had affected her more than expected. Penna was the only mother she'd ever known. For a brief moment, Dad had pointed the gun at Penna, but that had to have been an act. Dad wanted her for his research. He would never kill her. And what was with that Australian guy? He acted like he was there for Oakley. But why?

Perhaps Dad had given up on convincing her to join them. If so, he might not care if Auburn killed her. But would Oakley's death further their common goal? A global peace-keeping force with their genetic abilities could save lives. Maybe the best revenge would be forcing her sister to support the mission.

She glanced at Cane in front and Oakley in back. Something had changed between the two of them since they'd come to the floating lab last week. There, Cane had been starry-eyed when he'd mistaken Auburn for Oakley. Now, his pheromones were subdued, almost blocked. She could sense the two of them communicating but not in the robust way they had before.

Cane was a puzzle. Did he know about his other ability? Probably not. Auburn wouldn't have known either except that she'd read his DNA. Or rather both sets of his DNA.

He halted in front of her, and she knocked into his back. She would have snapped at him if not for the pheromones streaming off him in waves of fear. The jungle had gone silent. The only sound was the gentle tussle of leaves in the breeze.

The young girl swept up next to Cane. She pointed in front and to the right. Cane swiped his bow from his shoulder and nocked an arrow.

Like a spear, Oakley held out the metal pole she'd picked up once they'd reached the shore.

Several tense seconds ticked by. The hairs on Auburn's arms stood at attention.

Then, a huge dinosaur head burst through the leaves. The mouth was full of three-inch-long snapping teeth. She sidestepped in the nick of time. A tooth grazed her thigh and drew blood.

The dinosaur was a large *Utahraptor* with a red crest on its head. Momentum carried it past her. It disappeared into the encapsulating jungle.

"What was that?"

"Red Grizzly," the girl whispered.

The girl swept past her again, moved to Oakley, and turned Oakley's shoulders ninety degrees. The rear attack came from that exact position.

A smaller, gray-green *Velociraptor* broke through the foliage with a mighty snap. *Wait.* She recognized that dino. She'd created it with one of Penna's last DNA modifications. *Oh no.* It probably had genius-level intelligence.

Oakley jabbed the pole into its mouth, and it pulled back with a yelp. She must have electrified the metal.

A thrashing came from beside Auburn. The red dinosaur had made a U-turn and was attacking again.

Cane swung his bow around and let the arrow fly, but he likely couldn't see the target for the leaves. He notched another arrow. The dinosaur would be on her before he could get a second shot off.

She reached below her hairline, grasped the rounded base of one of her quills, and tugged it free. If she was going out, the dinosaur would go out with her.

When the piercing eyes of the reptile appeared, she took aim, then flicked her wrist as the rest of the animal charged through, whipping the quill at its chest. She didn't have to hit it anywhere vital. If the poison got through the thick skin, the red raptor was as good as dead. It just might eat her before that.

Suddenly, the *Velociraptor* gave another yelp, this one less out of surprise and more plaintive. Red Grizzly responded by dodging to its left.

Her quill missed its body by a half inch. How had she missed?

But Cane didn't.

As Red Grizzly switched course, it slid into the base of a nearby tree. Cane buried an arrow in its shoulder.

After a hard thunk into the tree, it righted itself and ran off, grunting in pain.

The *Velociraptor* looked like it would attack them all to avenge its friend, but then it locked gazes with the young girl. They entered a tense staring contest that lasted close to a full minute.

Apparently, she won. The *Velociraptor* ran off on the same trajectory as Red Grizzly. But that *Velociraptor* was more than just intelligent. It was intuitive in a way that was matched by the girl. Understanding washed over Auburn like a frigid rain. What she had copied and given to a dinosaur, Penna had given to an embryo, approximately fifteen years before.

⊏⊐

THEY CAME at the Lankester Botanical Center building from the rear this time. Oakley breathed a sigh of relief. Guarding the back of the group the entire way had been exhausting. Only one creek crossing to go, and then she could rest and plan their next move to get Eric back.

A set of weathered *Triceratops* bones blocked the artistic, curved bridge over the creek. Rather than wading through the muddy water and spending the night drying their shoes, they picked their way past the horns, through rib bones, and along the tail bones, which were as slippery as walking on Lincoln Logs.

After she finally shut the door behind Teagan, she sagged against it. Teagan and Penna both sank onto the couches. Cane leaned against the wall. Auburn floated out in the middle of the room, arms wrapped around herself, looking over the accommodations with disgust.

"Everyone okay?" Cane asked.

"They were coordinated in their attack," Auburn said.

It was similar to what Penna would say. Both of them were trained scientists, except Auburn must have trained herself.

"Most dinosaurs don't attack that way," he said.

"I recognized that one. The smaller one."

"You should." Oakley couldn't keep the bitterness out of her voice. "You created Fangtooth."

Auburn dropped her gaze at first. Then, she spun in a circle until she faced Penna, but she still didn't make eye contact. "I made him using a partial DNA strand I found buried in your Extras file on your computer."

Penna sucked in a breath. Oakley raised her eyebrows. Why was that important?

Auburn shifted her gaze to Teagan. "That means you made the dinosaur go away."

Gooseflesh broke out on Oakley's arms. Fangtooth was just like Teagan. Why hadn't she made the connection before?

"Not exactly," Teagan said. "I pushed into its mind more of the fear it already had."

Penna spoke up to interpret. "Mirroring a biological signal is easiest for Teagan because the exact neurons involved in the emotion or action are already activated. She directs energy at that area to magnify the effect."

"Teagan." Auburn sounded as if she was testing the name out. "She didn't have to touch the creature to do that?"

Teagan let out a humph. "I'm right here. I can speak for myself. It works better if I can touch them, but I don't have to if the signals are strong enough. That dinosaur was intense. It's bi-sigs felt like a tsunami."

"As fascinating as this is," Oakley said, "we underestimated the draw that four of us with pheromones would create. We have to be more careful."

Auburn glared at her. "What are you going to do? Kill me off so there's only three of you out there next time?"

If Oakley hadn't been leaning on the door, she would have stumbled backward. She'd barely met her sister. What had she done to deserve such hatred?

"Everyone around you dies." Auburn turned to Cane. "Watch your back."

Oh, this was about Adler. Auburn must have seen the footage of his death.

"I'm just as much to blame as she is," Cane said.

Without taking her eyes off him, Auburn responded, "You didn't spark the bomb that caved in Adler's chest and exploded his heart. She's evil."

Oakley bit her lower lip. She couldn't say anything to that. It had been her fault. Maybe she should regret it more, but Adler would have killed her and the others. She regretted only that Adler hadn't told her where Eric was before he died.

A twinge of unease ran through her gut. Following that logic, she should hunt Lumas down and kill him because he also would kill her if she didn't go along with his plans. But if she decided to do that, there would be no chance of a relationship with Auburn. Should it matter? They were only connected by blood, not shared experience.

"Being made for evil purposes is not the same thing as being evil," Cane said.

Auburn let out a long sigh. "Just take me back to the main bunker, okay? I can contact Dad from there."

"No one's stopping you from leaving. Go ahead." It was a total bluff. Oakley wouldn't let her only leverage against Lumas walk out the door. But Auburn's battle with fear was evident in her shaky hands and dilated eyes, not to mention her pheromones. Maybe in this vulnerable state, she would open up. "Why do you support a man who is a kidnapper?"

Auburn stared at the high ceiling. "That's not normal

behavior for him. He just needed to find Mom." She gave Oakley a quick glance. "Penna, I mean."

"Would he kill Eric?"

A split second of hesitation. "No, of course not."

"So then, I have no reason to turn Penna over to him if he won't really kill Eric." Oakley scoffed.

Auburn just rolled her eyes.

"You have to admit," Oakley said, "that a man who crosses the line to kidnapping will continue to cross the line to get what he wants."

A sneer crossed Auburn's face. "You're one to talk."

She ignored the all-too-accurate jab. "He ordered Adler to kill Cane's mother. And Monica, my best friend."

"You have no proof of that. And I have no reason to believe you. You killed Lillian, your own mother. *Our* mother."

The truth of her words hit Oakley afresh. Every time the stranglehold of guilt and pain lessened, a reminder would come, and the noose would tighten all over again. But how did Auburn know about that? Lumas must have suspected it.

"Did he tell you what his plans are?" Cane asked quietly.

"No, and I wouldn't tell you if he had."

Oakley pushed off and advanced on her. "Are you completely blind?" She pointed out the door. "That was a transaction. He was selling me to that creeper from down under. And you'd be okay with that? You don't strike me as a human trafficking kind of girl. Or is it acceptable because I'm a genetically modified human? I'm not really a person, I guess. In that case, he'd sell off Cane too, or even you."

Auburn lifted her gaze to the tattered roof again and kept it there.

At least she seemed conflicted about her *father*. Oakley folded her arms over her chest. "Tomorrow, we're going back to the bunker. You can contact Lumas to swap you for Eric. If you love *Dad* so much, you two can have each other. Just get off my island and leave us alone."

She swiped a hand down her face. When had she started to think of this as *her* island?

Auburn snapped, "Or what?"

Oakley spoke without much thought. "Or he'll meet the same fate as Adler."

Chapter Seven

STRANDS of dark hair curtained Auburn's face when she woke. Her mouth was a scratchy cotton ball. She must've forgotten to brush her teeth last night before bed. She brushed the hair from her eyes and sucked in a startled breath.

Oh yeah. She was on the floor of an old botanical center. Her head rested on a folded jacket for a pillow. A threadbare blanket protected her from the grungy floor. Cane and Oakley must be in another room. The only people in the front area were Mom—did she deserve to be called that?—and Teagan, both of whom slept peacefully.

She pushed up on one elbow. Penna looked younger in her sleep, less world worn. Had being on the run taken its toll, or was it the horrors of this island? The familiar questions crept into her head. *Why did you leave? Why didn't you take me with you?* Her gaze shifted to Teagan. Was she the reason? Had Mom left to protect her biological child?

It shouldn't matter. Auburn's life with Dad had been fine. He'd taught her the value of discipline, logic, and above all, controlling emotions. With great might came a great burden. She had an obligation to use her ability to benefit others.

Did he miss her? Was he worried about her? With her

gone, he might not have been able to activate his newly installed implant like he planned.

She couldn't get back to him just yet. No one needed to guard her in this place. She wasn't capable of navigating the dangers of the jungle on her own. Their close call yesterday had made that clear.

A quiet cough came from the doorway to the adjacent room. Cane held up a bowl of something as an invitation. In response, her stomach grumbled.

She dragged herself off the floor and joined him in the other room so as not to wake Penna and Teagan. The back area had apparently been a small exhibit hall, but now it housed only empty wooden shelves.

Cane motioned to Oakley who lay on the floor with her back to them. "She's awake, just refusing to get up yet. Want some berries?"

Auburn was a grumpy morning person too. Perhaps they shared other traits defined by their similar DNA. At least they weren't identical. She couldn't have stomached that.

She took the bowl and devoured several berries eagerly. "Thanks," she said around a mouthful of blackberries.

As usual, his calm, curious gaze unnerved her. He presented himself as a centered, faith-filled man. But most pastors didn't conspire in murder plots. "Why did you agree to help kill Adler?"

His eyes pinched tight for a moment. When he opened them, the peace had been replaced by resignation. "He wanted to hurt us. There was no reasoning with him."

"So, you claim self-defense for murder. Nice." She squinted at him and lowered her voice. "You did it for Oakley, didn't you?"

He barked out an uncomfortable laugh. "No. If anything, it was more for Teagan. She doesn't deserve to be hunted down, then used, for just being herself."

Interesting. In the lab, he'd seemed under the sway of

Oakley's charms. Now, he spoke about her dispassionately. Something had definitely changed between them. Maybe she could use that to her advantage. "You could say the same about Adler. He didn't deserve to have you hunt him down and kill him for being himself."

Cane's eyes hardened. The man had a backbone after all. "Except Teagan isn't trying to hurt anyone else." He drilled her with a long stare. "Adler's intentions should matter more to you than they seem to."

She gulped down another berry, then handed the bowl back to him, about half empty. He had a point. Adler definitely kidnapped Eric and brought him here. Maybe he had done some of the other things Cane and Oakley accused him of. Or maybe not. She'd never get the chance to ask him. The familiar ache of loss pierced her rib cage. She pushed it away with deep breaths.

Her gaze moved from Cane's face to his hands holding the bowl. Hands that could kill at will. Adler hadn't possessed the same type of power. And yet, they'd killed him for the potential threat he posed. These two probably couldn't be trusted to be responsible with their powers any more than Adler. Her kill switch could end it all, but would using it make her just like them?

She returned her gaze to Cane's face, full of kindness and compassion once more, albeit with a few more lines than when they'd started the conversation. He rubbed his thumb over the webbing between his fingers. Again, she wondered if he knew about his other ability. He searched her face questioningly. *Oops.* He could feel the confusion and distrust in her pheromones. Perhaps she should tell him. Dad had waited too long to tell her of her ability—she'd accidentally killed their cat with a poisonous barb by then.

"You had a twin," she said soberly.

He nodded. "Penna told me. A girl who must have miscarried before I was born."

Auburn hesitated. She could let the conversation die. But he deserved to know the whole of who he was. "Yes … and no."

"What?"

"She died, technically a miscarriage, but she never left the womb."

"I don't understand."

"I tested your DNA. You have two distinct profiles."

She waited while he thought about that. Waves of confusion pulsed off him, as if the static from an empty television station was vibrating through her cells.

"You're a chimera, Cane. Your twin either died during implantation or shortly thereafter. Your embryo absorbed her cells."

He went completely still. The room was silent for several minutes. Eventually, he whispered, "What does that mean?"

"It means you probably have another ability. I'm guessing you know nothing about it."

He swallowed hard. "What ability?"

She narrowed her eyes. "Take me back to my father right now, and I'll tell you."

He swiped both hands through his hair. Twice, he opened his mouth, but no words came out. Finally, his voice squeaked as he said, "I absorbed my twin, and now I have whatever her power was supposed to be? That's disturbing."

She shrugged. "Penna experimented with all kinds of adaptations found in nature."

"She should have left well enough alone," he said. "Humans don't need more ways to wreak havoc on their environment or fellow humans."

Oakley rolled over on the floor. "He's right. Lumas didn't create us to be a peacekeeping force."

Auburn shook her head to disagree, but her gut tensed in protest. Oakley had been right about something she said last night. Ness had come to the island for a reason, and it wasn't to see dinosaurs. Had Dad tried to sell Oakley to someone who wanted to use her abilities?

No. There had to be another explanation. She pressed her lips together and turned away from them.

As she entered the front room, Teagan sat up on her couch-bed. The girl peered deep into her eyes, then quickly dropped her gaze.

"What?" Auburn asked.

"The truth cannot be misinterpreted. You take the truth and twist it into what you want it to be."

"Uh, we were talking about my father."

Teagan lifted her gaze. "I know, but I'm talking about you."

Auburn bit her lip to keep from snapping at her. On her way by, she kicked the leg of the couch-bed where Penna was still sleeping. "Let's get going, okay?"

AS RAPTOR PUSHED the bunker door open, something small hit his head and bounced onto his backpack. Probably just a leaf. He filled his lungs with the fresh morning air, closed the door, and set out for the janitor's shack where Cane's group congregated. Hopefully, Cane and Oakley were there with Eric. Somehow, she would find a way to outsmart Lumas.

Raptor had spent a long night tossing and turning at the thought of Eric being held captive. He would have gone with them to find the boy, but Oakley insisted he stay at the bunker in case Lumas came back.

At the shack, Wells let him in, and he examined the features of each face. No Oakley or Cane. Certainly, no little boy. Where were they?

Before he could ask, several sharp knocks sounded on the front door. Raptor pulled it open to reveal Special Agent

Noah Brooks tapping his fingers against the back of his cell phone. This wouldn't be good.

Agent Brooks pushed his way inside and immediately stopped short. He pointed at Wells. "I recognize you from your driver's license photo, Dr. Anderson." A fast scan of faces. He shook his phone in the air. "None of you are Oakley Laveau. And yet, her signal is coming from this location."

Raptor ran his tongue over his teeth. Give the truth? Or a creative explanation?

Brooks crossed his arms. "Care to explain, Raptor?"

No creative explanation came, so he went with the truth, mostly. He explained how Neve took Oakley's tracker— leaving out the part about Oakley escaping the island— because she was in danger from Lumas Verret. Somehow Raptor convinced Brooks that Lumas was obsessed with Oakley because her father worked at Asperten. Brooks said something about that scenario matching the financial records he'd found. Raptor merely nodded and finished his explanation with Special Agent Gabe Glaser shooting Neve in the back.

"What would cause Glaser to do this?" Brooks asked as he leaned over Neve's sleeping form.

"He blames Oakley for Special Agent Jack Fischer's death. He used the location tracker and must have thought Neve was Oakley from behind."

"Did Oakley have anything to do with Fischer's death?"

Raptor hesitated for a fraction of a second.

Brooks picked up on it. "This would not be the time to lie to me, Mr. Greene."

Wells spoke up. "Some of Oakley's convict friends kidnapped me and Agent Fischer."

Brooks glanced around as if trying to determine if any of them were in the room. "To try to help Oakley avoid the tracker?"

"Yes," Wells said. "But they didn't kill him. We were

attacked by a *Carnotaurus*. The convicts told Agent Fischer to stick with them, but he ran off. The *Carnotaurus* pursued him."

"Did Oakley know about the kidnapping?"

"Not until after it happened," she answered.

"I see. Where is Oakley now?"

"I don't know," Raptor responded. "But we can go back to the bunker. She might show up there."

Of course, she wouldn't go there after Glaser had tried to shoot her by the door, which meant it was the safest place to stash Brooks while Oakley concentrated on finding Eric. Maybe Brooks even had access to the secure part of the bunker, and they could check there for clues.

Brooks nodded and prepared to leave. At the door, he turned back to Wells. "You're staying here?"

"For now," she said.

"Don't go anywhere. I want to be able to find you," Brooks said as he preceded Raptor out the door.

Raptor gave Wells a little shrug before he firmly closed the door to the shack behind him.

They walked for a half hour in silence. At least Brooks had some experience at being light-footed in dangerous territory. His footfalls were nearly silent.

Not far from the bunker, clear evidence of a trail came into focus, and Raptor slowed his pace. He'd already planned on checking the perimeter before approaching the bunker. No way would he let Glaser set up another ambush. But even Glaser wouldn't have been this careless. The narrow pathway and the height of the disturbed leaves on the bushes were obvious and definitely made by a person.

He raised a hand to bring Agent Brooks to a halt, then he crept forward, peeling the foliage back layer by layer until he reached something not a part of the jungle—the faded yellow of a T-shirt.

But this person was no threat.

Raptor cleared his throat.

Marcel whipped around with terror written on his face. He just as quickly relaxed. "I'm glad I found you. Can you get into the bunker?"

"Some of it."

Marcel stood with drooping shoulders. "You haven't asked why I'm here, so I gather you know about Eric."

He gave a slow nod and moved aside. "This is FBI Special Agent Noah Brooks."

"I know," Marcel said.

At Brooks's narrowed gaze, Raptor gestured to the bunker. "Yes, there's a bit more to tell. I'll fill you in when we get inside."

He led them to the door in the hillside and punched in the code. Once inside, they sat on folding chairs with Raptor facing both Brooks and Marcel. He filled them in on Adler's dying declaration and the note from Lumas.

"Do you have any direct proof that Lumas Verret kidnapped someone?" Brooks asked. "The unsigned note only mentioned a trade and said to meet, correct?"

"Yes, but—" Raptor started.

Marcel interrupted, "My son disappears at the same time that Lumas comes here. That's not a coincidence, Agent Brooks."

The hard note in Marcel's tone was uncharacteristic. His friend was under considerable stress after Oakley's conviction and now Eric's kidnapping. Not to mention the fact that Brooks was the one who had mistakenly informed Marcel of Oakley's death a few weeks ago. To his credit, Brooks didn't rebuke him or threaten to arrest him for setting foot on the island.

"Okay, let's work with that assumption, then," Brooks said. "If Lumas kidnapped Eric, where would he hold him?"

"Only Penna knows where they are supposed to meet. But this bunker is a likely option for hiding someone. We've searched the entire main area." Raptor swept his hand toward the secure door. "I don't have access to the rest."

Agent Brooks went straight to the keypad. "I've got the bypass code."

Raptor stood by with his arms crossed as Brooks typed in a long series of numbers. He hit Enter and stepped back.

Nothing happened.

Brooks repeated the same sequence.

Again, nothing.

Finally, he spoke in a quiet voice that was as dangerous as any weapon. "Somebody changed the code without informing the FBI."

"Believe me now?" Marcel asked.

Raptor rolled his eyes. On its own, the change in the code didn't prove Lumas was up to anything illegal. But Oakley wouldn't lie about what Adler said or about how Lumas had held her and Cane captive when they'd visited the floating laboratory. Even so, Raptor couldn't mention that. If Agent Brooks found out she'd gone off the island, he'd be obligated to carry out her death sentence immediately.

An uncomfortable pause filled the room until Agent Brooks spoke. "It's time for me to figure out what's going on with Asperten."

Chapter Eight

KALEO WOKE to the familiar ache in his lower extremities. Wells had said the slashed skin would burn and itch before it healed completely into stiff, thick scars, but he was lucky to be alive. Alive and alone.

Oakley had left two days ago on a search for her brother. If only he could be helping her. Or just as important, he should be hunting down Glaser for what he'd done to Neve.

Instead, he would concentrate on taking small steps around the room with his legs heavily bandaged. If he could convince Wells he could walk in a somewhat normal fashion, she might let him out of here. This would be his practice run while she searched for more herbs.

He lowered his feet to the dirt floor.

Taye, who had been sitting next to Neve so he could hold her hand while she slept, looked over at him. "Every marathon starts with one step."

Kaleo snorted. "Not exactly profound. And I won't be up for marathons anytime soon."

He lifted himself off the cot with a grimace and took slow steps while Taye filled him in on Agent Brooks's arrival. He'd slept through the whole thing apparently.

As he lowered himself to the cot again, he asked, "Hey, have you been to check on the compound recently?"

"Yes, early this morning. I told them you were injured and couldn't return. Wyatt seems to have taken charge in your absence."

"Hmm." Not a surprise but not the guy he would have chosen. Wyatt had killed twenty people from a highway overpass to land himself here. But then again, the only person Kaleo would have chosen to take over was with him—Taye. "What about the newcomer Cane and Oakley collected?"

"Still in the tree house. I gave him some dried meat and berries for now."

"What was his name again?"

"Hudson." Taye raised his eyebrows. "He seems to be quite a fan of Oakley's."

"Join the club." People generally had strong reactions to her. The last guy who'd come to the island hated her. "I really need to meet this guy and set him straight."

"What are we going to do with him?" Taye asked.

"I'd rather take him to the compound, but he's seen Oakley. Do you think he would keep quiet about her being alive?"

"I think he would if he understood it was to protect her."

Kaleo let out a heavy sigh. "Is it better to have him ruin things at the compound for us or to risk giving him access to Cane's people?"

He and Taye said in unison, "Take him to the compound."

"I think Oakley would agree," Taye said.

"Can you handle that, my friend?"

Taye nodded, kissed Neve's hand, and stood. "No better time than now."

After Taye had grabbed his spear and left, Kaleo coaxed his legs into a few more small steps. His list of those deserving retribution was growing: Glaser, Lumas, even Red Grizzly. But he couldn't muster up any anger. At the moment, with legs that still propelled him forward, all he felt was gratitude.

GABE GLASER CHECKED his phone one more time, then shut it down in order to preserve the battery. Plus, if he kept his phone on, other FBI agents would be able to track him while he was tracking Raptor. The agents stationed on the island were loyal to him, but eventually, Special Agent Noah Brooks would send someone else to the island to find him. He'd missed at least ten calls from Brooks in the last two days alone. Better to miss the calls than to say something that might incriminate him later. As soon as he found Oakley and exacted justice, he could return to the States with a story about how she'd refused the replacement tracker and he'd had no choice but to carry out her sentence. True enough. Having the tracker implanted in someone else was pretty much the same thing.

One of his agents spotted him at the edge of the clearing that comprised their camp and halted him with an upraised hand. He waited for the man to come to him. Agent Weber slipped him some food and a note, then tilted his head toward the trees.

Gabe faded into the jungle. Once at a safe distance, he unfolded the paper. His stomach dropped at the hastily written words.

Brooks is here looking for you. Catch her soon.

The boss himself had come to lead the hunt. But was he hunting primarily for Oakley or both Gabe and Oakley? Either way, Gabe had to find her first.

AUBURN SPENT the walk to the bunker sandwiched in between Penna and Teagan. She matched their pace, but her huffing and puffing brought glares from Oakley. The march had been silent except for Auburn's heavy breathing and a few yelps from curious dinosaurs that cleared out after a zap from Oakley's metal pole. But one dinosaur she hadn't zapped. It seemed more like a pet with the way it rubbed on her leg. Oakley patted its head a few times, then it ran off, probably to forage among the trees.

They circled around a wide area several times before coming to a spot where they peered out at a large metal door constructed in the hillside. It had a circular wheel for a lock and a keypad. This must be the bunker's above-ground entrance. She had only ever entered from the underground tunnel.

"What are we waiting for?" Auburn whispered.

"We can't get in without Raptor," Cane answered.

Whoever that is. "Oh, is that the behaviorist guy? Never mind. I bet I can get us inside." Then maybe she could escape to the secure portion of the bunker.

A metal clank came from the door. It creaked open, and two men came out. One of them was Special Agent Brooks, whom she'd met once at Asperten's headquarters. The other person was a man she'd only seen through Oakley's implanted eye camera.

"Who's with Raptor?" Cane asked. "He looks military."

The man did have a strong bearing, and his clothes were camo. "FBI," Auburn answered. "That's Agent Brooks."

"Uh-oh." Cane looked at Oakley. "We can't let him see you."

That was a new development. Brooks was probably here looking for Eric, right? But then, why wouldn't Oakley want him to see her?

This could be helpful. Maybe if she screamed, Oakley would be forced to leave her here alone. She opened her mouth when a warbling cry came from some animal in the distance. She clamped her lips shut. Then again, screaming in the middle of a jungle full of predators wasn't a good idea.

"But what if Lumas is in there with Eric right now?" Oakley asked.

Cane put a hand on her arm. "I'll take Auburn in. If we can prove Eric is in there with Lumas, then he will be forced to give Eric to the agent."

Oakley squinted at her, so Auburn plastered on a completely passive look.

"You don't know if Brooks is loyal to Glaser," Cane insisted. "You can't take the chance."

Glaser? Was that another FBI agent?

Finally, Oakley nodded. The men had already closed the door and were moving toward the jungle.

Cane quickly stepped out. "Raptor."

After a quick shove from Oakley, Auburn followed behind him. It might be better for her situation to simply point at Oakley and turn her in to the FBI, but Dad probably wouldn't want that.

Cane explained to the men her connection to Asperten, leaving out the part about her being Oakley's sister. Agent Brooks peered at her with suspicious eyes. She obviously looked too much like Oakley for him to accept her credentials blindly.

"Your name is Auburn Verret?" Brooks asked.

"Correct," she answered. "You and I met sometime last year at headquarters. You know, the floating lab."

Brooks slowly nodded. Off to the side, he fired questioning glances at Raptor. "Do you know why the code to the restricted portion of the bunker was changed?"

"No." Dad had only told her the new code, not why he'd changed it. Over the years, she'd learned not to question him.

Raptor opened the outside door for them. She stepped in first, then stopped short. Marcel stood in the small hallway that led to the main room. He blinked at her, apparently just as stunned to see her.

She shook off the surprise. He might be her biological father, but in reality, he was nothing more than a sperm donor. Both of her biological parents had agreed to give her up in favor of keeping her sister. Nice family lineage. Her biological mom had been the worst one. According to Adler, she'd flipped out and tried to kill Oakley.

Up until Auburn was ten years old, she only remembered meeting Marcel twice. Both times, he was introduced as her uncle. Dad told her the truth on her sixteenth birthday. It hadn't changed her life much. She didn't know Marcel. She knew her dad.

Or did she? Dad had done things on this trip she couldn't explain. This business with Eric. Asking the Australian guy to come here. But Dad deserved the chance to defend himself. She wouldn't listen to Oakley and Cane without hearing his side of things.

"Auburn?" Marcel rounded his eyes with hope, like a puppy dog.

Ridiculous. If he'd cared about a relationship with her, he never would have agreed to give her up. She shifted backward, putting Agent Brooks between them.

Brooks swiveled to look at her and Cane. "Have either of you seen Oakley?"

Auburn looked to Cane for direction, but he didn't acknowledge her glance. "Last time I saw her, she was with several other people in the old botanical gardens. But I don't know if she's still with them or not. She tends to run off."

"Where's that?"

"Not far."

"You will need to take me there later," Brooks said.

Auburn lowered her head, slipped around Brooks, and moved farther into the bunker until she came to the secure door. Was Dad back there even now? What would Brooks do if they found him with Eric? It wasn't worth the risk. She had to warn him.

Cane pushed past the other men. "Can you open it?"

"I think so." She stepped up to the door, balanced on one foot, and pressed her other foot onto a raised depression in the floor right next to the hinges. The bunker was soundproof, so none of them would hear the thirty second panic alarm. She groaned and bent down to rub her calf for about that much time. "Sorry, cramp."

When she straightened, they all looked at her expectantly. She blocked the view of the keypad with her body and typed in the twelve-digit code.

The lock gave a click, and she opened it.

The men entered ahead of her. They didn't find anyone. All three rooms in this portion were empty. If Dad had been here, he'd escaped in time.

Agent Brooks asked, "What is this flashing light?"

"A system issue. I'll fix it." She sat down at her father's computer and cleared out the panic alarm.

Before she could close the laptop, Agent Brooks snatched it from her. "I think this will help me figure out what's going on around here."

She held her hands up, palms flat. Better that they take Dad's computer instead of hers, hidden in a folded-up drop-down desk. The embedded kill switch program was obviously illegal, assuming the FBI techs could figure out what it was for.

Chapter Nine

OAKLEY CLENCHED the shaft of her metal pole until her knuckles were white. Every minute Eric spent with Lumas put him at risk. And Cane and Auburn were taking too long.

A crawling sensation crept under the surface of her skin, right along her shoulder blades. This was more than just nerves. Teagan put a hand on her arm. Her eyes were round, her mouth open. She felt it too.

Oakley leaned in where both Penna and Teagan could hear. "If we get separated, head northeast to the small janitor's shack near the abandoned school."

The words had barely left her mouth when a rush of wind from above knocked her back.

"Get down!" she screamed.

Teagan had already begun to hunker down before Oakley yelled, but Penna made the move a little too late. Something long and green and stick-like clipped her in the shoulder. A glancing blow, then the green stick hit the ground with a thud. Penna merely grunted in pain.

No, not a stick. This was a leg. One of the long legs of the Mutant Mantis dinosaur she'd seen feeding on a headless corpse two days ago. The leg retracted in the direction from where it had come.

If only she could get a fix on the rest of it, but its body was hidden behind a row of bushes. Teagan reached out and touched the retreating appendage before Oakley could stop her. The leg stopped moving.

"This is strange. I can't get to its head," Teagan said. "I can only move the leg."

A high-pitched squeal came from the bushes, then the appendage began to slide sideways. The bushes parted and a large dinosaur head with moving yellow crests broke through, diving straight for the ground. Teagan's manipulations had essentially caused it to trip.

"Run!" Oakley yelled. "Go to the shack!"

Penna and Teagan took off toward the northeast. Oakley gave the creature a strong shock to the leg with her metal pole and then ran in the other direction. After a few minutes, she doubled back to make sure the creature would follow her pheromones instead of Teagan's.

Mutant Mantis had righted itself. It swung one of its long limbs at her head. She dropped to her belly while holding her metal pole upright. The creature's leg snapped off the top foot of the pole, sending a flying disc of metal into the jungle.

As soon as the appendage passed overhead, she jumped to her feet and ran again.

Mutant Mantis flipped its leg around and slammed it down vertically, trying to smash her to the ground. She darted to the left just in time.

The leg landed on a sapling tree and split it down the middle. No roar of pain came. The creature lifted its leg as easily as if it had stepped on a twig.

Did it even have pain sensors in its legs? Time to find out. She shifted course and darted under the creature's belly, swinging her pole as she dove at its stabilizing leg. The pole hit with a satisfying crack.

A dinner-plate-sized portion of something flaked off and fell to the ground. It looked like a crustacean's shell. But the dinosaur gave no sounds of pain or even an acknowledgment of injury. Mutant Mantis lifted its leg and swung at her again.

She rolled to the side, then jumped up straight into a run. Several levels of stomping feet pursued her. How was she going to outrun it?

About twenty yards ahead, honking, snorting sounds permeated the brush. A herd of something big. Her only way out of this might be to hide in the herd.

At a full sprint, she broke through into a clearing full of mother and baby *Apatosaurus*. With no time to stop her momentum, she planted her pole in the dirt and vaulted over the nearest baby *Apatosaurus*.

Her pole thunked to the ground as she landed on the other side. She scurried under the belly of another baby. Carefully avoiding the feet of the mothers, she weaved her way through the herd.

Frustrated grunts echoed from the edge of the clearing. Mutant Mantis must have lost her trail. One of the mothers squealed and arced her long neck and huge head in that direction. The other mothers seemed to agree on the threat and joined in, forming a veritable wall of heads and necks.

Thanks to these mothers, she was safe for now.

―――――

OAKLEY TOOK several extra minutes to circle back to the bunker, and even then, she approached it from the other side of the clearing, staying hidden in the foliage. Close to the entrance, a soft chirrup, followed by clicking noises made her stop.

"Here, boy," she called quietly.

Cody bobbed out of the bushes. She gave him a quick once over. The leaves Taye attached to his tail had fallen off, but the flesh had scabbed over nicely. He'd be left with a divot in his tail and nothing more. She smoothed his small patch of feathers down, then returned her attention to the bunker.

Raptor was just leaving with Cane. The man who exited behind them made her heart leap. *Dad!*

Agent Brooks wasn't anywhere around, so she took a chance and stepped out.

Dad noticed her immediately. "Oakley!"

Tears moistened his eyes as he ran toward her. He spun her in a circle to look at her. The comfort of his arms around her soothed her more than she could say. But this was no place for him. "You shouldn't have come."

"I had to."

"I'm working on getting Eric back," she said.

"You've seen him?"

"Yes. In fact, we need to trade Auburn for him. Where is she?"

"She's in the secure portion of the bunker with Agent Brooks," Cane said while pointing at the door. "Eric isn't here."

"But Lumas will come back here," she said. "He's not an island dweller. He will seek the safety of this place."

"Agreed. But he could have stayed at the prison lab."

"Maybe, except he wants Penna. Staying at the lab only gives us a chance to get reinforcements and overpower them. But if he keeps us on the move looking for them …" Oakley pursed her lips. "Where's the one place on the island that's relatively safe and connected to Penna?"

"You're thinking the old sanatorium."

It was the place where Penna and Teagan had lived for fifteen years. "He would have seen it through my eye implant, and it's somewhere Penna might go."

"Speaking of Penna," Cane said, "where is she?"

"You found her alive?" Dad gaped at her.

Oakley nodded. "Hopefully, she's at the shack with Teagan. We ran into that Mutant Mantis creature."

Dad's eyes went wide, and he gawked at the surrounding trees.

She'd probably looked much like him when she'd first arrived. "It's a modified dinosaur. Kind of a mean disposition." Nothing would be gained by freaking him out.

"Auburn might not agree to come with us," Cane said.

"She will," Oakley responded. "She wants to see her *father* as much as we want to see Eric."

"I'm coming too." Dad folded his arms across his chest.

"Not a great idea," she said.

"If you can hack it out here, so can I."

"I have ways to protect myself." She'd alluded to her newly discovered abilities before but had never directly told him about her mutations. Would he accept her despite who she was created to be? He had to suspect it already, given the suspicious way her mom died.

"I'm going," he said firmly.

Raptor stepped forward to put a hand on his shoulder. "I'll come and guard his back."

Dad gave him a thankful look.

"Okay. You guys go get Auburn. I'll wait here."

"You are a hard woman to find," the deep voice came from behind Raptor.

She leaned around slowly. *Busted.* A man in his thirties wearing camo stood with muscular arms crossed over his chest. An FBI man if she'd ever seen one. She blew out a breath. "Special Agent Brooks, I presume."

"Come inside. We need to have a chat."

She could make a run for it. Brooks might be in good shape, but he'd never catch her. She shifted her weight back and forth. No, if she didn't address this now, it would only compound her problems later. "Quickly. My brother needs me."

As Raptor had done, Brooks insisted on Cody staying outside because the bunker was a dino-free zone. After they sat in opposite-facing chairs, he asked her to start at the beginning with her friend Monica's murder. She shook her head. That would take too long, and the whole story involved special abilities she refused to divulge to the FBI. "All you need to know is that Lumas Verret has my brother. He's using Eric as leverage to either kidnap me or sell me to someone else. He has access to your tracking system, so I can't get tagged again because then he'll know exactly where I am. When he is no longer a threat, I'll happily let you implant more tracking junk in my arm."

And then it hit her, Lumas would always know how to get to her because he knew the people she was close to on the island. She wasn't safe anywhere.

She brought her focus back to Brooks. "For right now, I need your help in finding Lumas and proving that he's done these things."

"First Glaser. Now him. Why would he target you?"

Ugh. How to put a vague spin on this? "I think he's interested in me because I look a lot like his daughter."

Brooks furrowed his brow. He wasn't buying it, but he didn't argue.

"I think I know where he might be," she said.

"How do you know?"

He would never believe the truth. "It was something he said to me."

Brooks ran a hand through his dirty blond hair. She was asking for a lot of faith, considering he probably knew she hadn't been completely honest. He glanced at the bunker door and then back at her. "There were some things I wanted to check out here, but I'll do it later. I'm coming with you."

"That's not necessary. I'll return here."

His gray eyes turned as hard as flint. "I'm not letting you

out of my sight until you get another tracker. I won't allow you to go missing again."

"Fair enough." She shrugged. Depending on how things went, Mr. FBI might get more information than he bargained for.

Brooks went to a nearby table and picked up a laptop. "I need to put this somewhere safe, and then we can head out."

Oakley nodded at Cane. He went to get Auburn, who would go with them in the hope of seeing her dad again. Tension coiled in Oakley's gut. They might be only hours from recovering Eric, but what if she was wrong? What if Lumas came back here instead? Someone would have to stay just in case.

———

KALEO TENSED at a frantic knock on the shack door. They weren't expecting anyone just now. Taye had recently returned from attempting to take Hudson to the compound, except Hudson had refused to go. He insisted he would only go where Oakley went. Maybe it was better that way. If Hudson wasn't at the compound, he wouldn't be able to let any information about Oakley slip. The men at the compound could never find out she was still alive, especially Wyatt, who was known to take revenge and had access to the few guns at the compound. If the secret got out, Wyatt would probably hurt Misty first, an older woman Kaleo had protected for the last year. He couldn't let that happen. Except for her poisons, which she'd used to murder several husbands, Misty was completely defenseless.

Taye had finally decided to leave Hudson in the tree house by himself. The man was going to be a problem.

With a knife in his hand, Taye removed the wooden plank barring the door and cracked it open. Kaleo grabbed the hilt of his whip next to him on the bed. Despite his injured legs, he would defend the people here.

Several seconds passed of whispering between Taye and what sounded like a woman. Taye eventually relaxed and allowed a woman and a young girl to enter. The girl kept her head down, but her eyes scanned the room.

The woman spoke first. "I'm Penna Gallardo, and this is Teagan. Oakley sent us here."

Taye had grabbed the wooden plank to replace it, but the door swung open again. A short, stocky man with reddish hair and pale skin stepped inside. Taye held the board up, ready to pummel him.

"Wait. I just want to see Oakley."

Taye grunted. "Hudson, I told you, she's not here."

So this was the serial killer groupie. "How did you find us?" Kaleo asked.

He pointed at Taye. "I saw which direction he went. Then, I found a dried blood trail that led here."

That trail had likely been left by himself after Red Grizzly's attack. Well, now was as good a time as any to set this guy straight. "Let him in."

"Uh, I'm already in."

Kaleo rolled his eyes. "I'm the guy who decides if you get to stay. What's your reason for stalking Oakley?"

"I wouldn't exactly call it stalking." He gave a lopsided grin. "Though I can see why it would look that way."

A long silence draped over the small room. Kaleo was just about to motion for Taye to remove Hudson when he spoke. "I just want to protect her."

"You don't even know her."

This time, Hudson rolled his eyes. "She's only been here about a month. I know everything about her life before, and you don't have access to that info, so I probably know her better than you."

Kaleo suppressed a growl. He opened his mouth to

comment on how much Extinction Island could change a person, but he snapped it shut. He had no reason to explain anything to this random guy.

Hudson pointed at him and then at Taye. "You, him, me, we were always going to end up here, but she doesn't belong here."

"What did you do to get here?" Taye's quiet question hung in the air for a moment.

Hudson shifted his weight. He didn't want to answer. Finally, he spit the words out fast, like they were burning his tongue. "I electrocuted women in their bathtubs." He took a breath and continued in a calmer tone. "Only despicable women. Some had beat their kids. Others robbed people or cheated on their husbands. One even convinced local kids to carry drugs into their school for her."

Kaleo's jaw tightened. So, this stalker was a copycat, reen-acting crimes similar to Oakley's except he victimized people he thought deserved it. Kaleo sought out Taye, who gave a subtle shake of the head. They were on the same page. This guy was too unpredictable to allow around Oakley. What if he decided she wasn't as innocent as he thought?

He scowled at Hudson. "We are already protecting her. You don't have anything more to offer."

Hudson gave an exaggerated blink and focused on Kaleo's bandaged legs. "I can see that. You're barely walking, and she's not even here."

"She has protection with her," Wells said. But her words of confidence came with a furrowed brow. Obviously, she was worried about Cane.

"Uh, actually, Oakley's on her own," Penna said. "Agent Brooks was there, so only Cane and Auburn went into the Asperten bunker. We waited outside until we were attacked by"—she let out a heavy sigh—"one of Auburn's creations. Oakley told us to come here and said she would meet us after she distracted the creature."

What? Why hadn't Penna mentioned this right away? Oakley might still be on her way, but what if she hadn't escaped the dinosaur? He nodded at Taye. "Go find her."

Taye scooped up a bow and quiver. As he reached the door, Hudson shadowed him. "I'm coming with you."

Taye shrugged as if to say, *Whatever*. They both disappeared out the door, and Wells replaced the wooden plank to lock it.

"What if they can't find her, Mom?" Teagan whispered.

Penna didn't answer. Instead, she gently rubbed her daughter's shoulders.

Kaleo pounded his fists on his knees. He should be out there looking for her. Not shut up in here like an invalid. What if something bad had happened to her?

Chapter Ten

ON THE ROAD to the abandoned sanatorium, Oakley's nerves were stretched taut. She'd never traveled with six other people in the jungle, unless she counted the gang on the first day she'd arrived. At least those guys had known how to avoid detection.

When Taye and Hudson had shown up at the bunker with news of Penna's and Teagan's safe arrival, Raptor and Dad were in the midst of an argument about who would stay in case Lumas returned with Eric. Oakley suggested Dad, but Raptor made the point that if Lumas came back to the bunker, Dad would be no match for him. Thankfully, Taye made the issue moot by volunteering to stay. He had the skills to overpower Lumas and even the bodyguard if necessary.

Auburn had been strangely silent on whether she thought Lumas might be at the sanatorium. Oakley took that to mean it was a strong possibility.

Another stick cracked under someone's foot, sounding as loud as a gunshot on this deserted, overgrown road. Three of their party—Marcel, Hudson, and Auburn—had no experience in stealth. It had forced them to a slower pace in order to keep the noise level down.

Oakley kept a wary eye on the surrounding trees and vine curtains. Too many dinosaur attacks had come as a surprise lately. So when Cane abruptly stopped, she almost ran into his back.

They were here. From the front gate, she stared in the direction of the creepy building, with its reddish roof rising almost to the treetops. Built at the turn of the twentieth century as a hospital for tuberculosis patients and also used as an orphanage, the sanatorium had been labeled one of the most haunted places in Costa Rica before it became Extinction Island. From the cracked windows, peeling wood siding, and mismatched doors, it was easy to see why. Cane's hesitation came out in his pheromones and crept through her bones. If only she could turn off that connection between them.

He focused on her face as if sensing her frustration. "We need to think this through."

She agreed. "If Lumas is holed up in there with Eric and that Ness guy, then they have the bodyguard with his gun. And just because we didn't see Lumas with a gun before doesn't mean he doesn't have one. So the best play is to make a peaceful exchange. Auburn for Eric."

"This time, it would be better for you to be the one sniping at a high vantage point," Cane suggested.

She frowned. "Why?"

"Your presence will only complicate the transaction. If you're not there for Ness to drool over, things might go smoothly."

He had a point, but it stung. Everything became more difficult when she was involved.

"Okay."

"I'll go with Oakley," Raptor announced.

"No," Agent Brooks said. "I'm going with her."

Both Raptor and Brooks had tranquilizer guns. Brooks also had a handgun, but he wouldn't use either weapon unless a life was threatened. Raptor, however, would sense the threat level since he'd already seen what Lumas was capable of.

He opened his mouth to argue, but she put a hand on his forearm. "Help get Eric back. Please."

He gave a tight-lipped nod.

"I'll go with her too," Hudson said.

The five of them, even Auburn, raised their eyebrows at him. Auburn's pheromones were just as easy to read as Cane's. *Why is he here?*

Oakley had no answer.

"Give me twenty minutes to set up." She took Cane's bow and arrow and started to move south, but then she turned back to Cane, intentionally ignoring Auburn even though this might be the last time they saw each other. "Don't trust Lumas. And don't go inside the sanatorium."

Cane scrunched his mouth to one side. He'd made no promises. Well, she couldn't make any either. Perhaps she'd shoot Lumas the second he popped his head out the door. Auburn gave her a dirty look. She must have sensed her aggression. But Auburn didn't have a clue. The crumbling building ahead had been Penna and Teagan's home for fifteen years because of Penna's fear of Lumas. The man was dangerous.

Oakley led the trio into the trees. The topography appeared higher in that direction, but she would have to hunt to find the right vantage point through the canopy.

Though three doors were situated across the structure, Cane would approach the door all the way to the left because the two other doors rested three feet above ground, the steps having long ago weathered away.

Fifty feet up the hill, she found a grouping of dark boulders sticking out of the ground. She climbed up on the highest one. The angle was right, but the branches of a tree ten feet away blocked her view.

She climbed down, broke two branches off the tree, then

climbed back up. Perfect. She grabbed a small blanket from her pack to make a more comfortable platform on the rough rock. She lay on her stomach with the bow held in the open space in front of her. Brooks sat silently on a boulder to her right.

Hudson shifted on a rock on opposite side of her. "Did you ever think you'd end up here?"

"Shh," she whispered.

He lowered his voice, even though she'd actually meant for him to stop talking. "I mean, I worked hard to get here, but you? You must have been destined to come here. Don't you ever wonder why?"

All the time, but discussing it with him was not going to happen. "Be quiet, Hudson."

He grinned at her. "That's the first time you've used my name."

She glared back as she grabbed an arrow and nocked it. Through the opening in the trees, Cane came into view, followed by Dad and Auburn. Raptor brought up the rear. He had one hand wrapped around Auburn's bicep, and the other on his holstered tranquilizer gun.

They all stood five feet from the building for a long minute. The place was eerily still.

Cane approached and rapped once on the door.

It slowly opened. The person's face was hidden in the shadows. But the gray button-down shirt and khaki pants gave him away. Lumas.

The fury she'd tried to keep under wraps began to bubble over. Her hands shook. This man had ordered Adler to steal her brother from his bed. He'd brought Eric to an island where anyone—including the dinosaurs—could kill him.

She could easily shoot him through the opening, but three things stopped her: Eric might be standing just inside the shadows as well. She couldn't take the chance she'd hit him. Plus, Agent Brooks sat on a boulder next to her. Committing cold-blooded murder in front of an FBI agent sounded pretty stupid. Finally, Lumas was technically Cane's father. If she took him out this way, Cane might never forgive her.

With a deep breath, she kept control and steadied her hands. Behind her, she heard the quiet ripping sound of Hudson picking grass from the ground at the base of the boulders. Apparently, he was bored.

Cane and Lumas talked animatedly for a few minutes. Lumas gestured to the interior.

Cane shook his head.

Raptor removed his tranquilizer gun from his holster, keeping it pointed at the ground. He also kept his grip on Auburn.

Lumas gestured more insistently.

Cane continued to shake his head.

Lumas fisted his hands at his sides and planted his feet.

Cane looked to Raptor and shrugged.

Auburn had already slipped closer to the door, subtly dragging Raptor with her. Oakley's forehead broke out in a sweat. If they disappeared inside, she couldn't protect them.

But then Lumas began to close the door on them. Auburn's arms shot out from her sides, and her voice carried on the breeze, too faint to make out the words but her frustration was evident.

Slowly, Lumas reopened the door.

Dad rushed to it. Auburn tugged in that direction while Raptor held her back, uncertain. Then, he followed Dad as well.

Cane stayed outside.

No! She pounded her fist against the rock, then cringed in pain. Lumas was getting exactly what he wanted. He'd probably send the goon with the gun out for Cane any minute. At least she could take care of him if he dared to try anything.

Time ticked by as Cane stood alone in the unkempt lawn of the sanatorium. Oakley could only protect him at this point. What if Lumas slipped out the back with Eric? She'd never see them go.

Sweat began to collect between her shoulder blades. What were the chances her dad and Raptor would be able to convince Lumas to give them anything?

Heaven help her. Her only hope lay in Auburn convincing Lumas that he didn't need Eric ... or the rest of them.

———

AFTER TEN LONG minutes of waiting, Cane couldn't take it anymore. He had to get in there. He went to the center door, one that was raised off the ground. They wouldn't be expecting him to come in that way. Though it would be hard to reach, it would be easy to kick in since the wood was bleached and cracked.

He dragged over an old tire and part of a wooden planter box. Standing on top of the pile, he wobbled and grabbed the side of the building for support. The door had a knob, but the wood connecting it to the doorjamb had all but weathered away. Cane braced his shoulder and shoved. With a hard creak, it swung open a few feet. He placed both hands on the floor and hoisted himself up.

Unease tightened his gut as he quietly stepped into the deserted entryway of the sanatorium. The place was too quiet. No sounds of a joyful reunion. No voices at all.

Cane kept an eye out for the men Lumas had been with yesterday. He came to the stairs to the upper level where Penna and Teagan had lived. Lumas could have locked Eric away in one of the bedrooms upstairs, but the doors on those rooms hadn't seemed secure. The lower level was a better bet.

At the bottom of the stairs, he hesitated. He hadn't been in this part of the building before. Most of the doors along the hall were closed. But this had to be the place. Soft voices came from behind one of the doors on the left.

As he approached, he recognized Marcel's soothing voice. A rusty sliding bolt barred the door from opening. He was about to call out to them when a circular jab to his shoulder stopped him cold.

The barrel of a gun.

"Hold on there, mate." It was Ness with his slow accent.

Cane let out a grunt, then turned around. This man had wanted Oakley, but did he know what Cane could do? If it came down to it, would Lumas offer him two for the price of one?

"Outside," Lumas said, appearing from over Ness's shoulder.

As Cane moved past them, he shot a look at the woman behind Lumas. Auburn flattened her lips and shifted to stand closer to her father … his father. Did Lumas know? Auburn had scrutinized his DNA. Had she told Lumas? He had to at least suspect. The big question was, did it matter to him? Or would he sell Cane to the highest bidder without a second thought?

He shook off the thoughts of himself. "Let Eric and Marcel go. You don't need them anymore."

No one responded to him as they led him out the back of the sanatorium, across an expanse of unruly grass, and to an enclosure with a six-foot-tall wooden fence and an iron gate. It looked like the kind of pen where Penna might have kept a dinosaur version of livestock when she and Teagan had lived here.

He could use his poisonous gas to overpower Ness, but either Lumas or Auburn would warn Ness before the poison had a chance to work. Ness shoved him inside the pen and closed the gate. A metallic click sounded as Ness turned a lock on the outside.

The enclosure smelled like a mixture of feces and rotting hay. The feces scent probably came straight from the soil. The rotting hay sat in a pile in the back of the gas-station-sized pen.

Auburn hadn't spoken a word or looked at him once on the way to his new jail cell. Now she turned her back and followed Lumas dutifully. She was her father's daughter.

Chapter Eleven

STUPID, Raptor chided himself. They were trapped because of him. He'd followed Marcel into the room, lured in by Eric's soft sobs, which allowed Lumas to shut the door and lock them in. He should have been smarter than his emotions. He shouldn't have counted on the fact that he still had his tranquilizer gun. What good did the weapon do him now?

He held his frustration in check so he wouldn't scare Eric even more. Marcel, who had been on his knees with his arms wrapped around the boy for several moments, now stood and frowned.

"Maybe if we both try it together," Raptor said.

Marcel patted Eric on the chest to tell him to stay put, and then they both threw their shoulders into the wooden door. It groaned but didn't give. They tried again with the same result.

The dank room resembled a cell more than a sanatorium hospital room. Then again, maybe they used these basement rooms as makeshift morgues when their patients died of tuberculosis. He staved off a shiver.

Marcel went to the small, high window. Raptor took a few steps in that direction, but he'd already checked it out. It was sealed shut and too high for him to get a good angle to punch through it. The room contained no furniture or accessories, so there was nothing to throw through the window either.

"Dad, when can we go home?" Eric choked back another sob.

"Soon, my little goose."

Raptor's heart squeezed. Though he hadn't seen Marcel and Eric as often as he'd seen Oakley, *little goose* was a nickname he'd come up with after hearing Eric sneeze once. It had sounded just like a goose's honk. Apparently, the nickname stuck.

"Give me a minute to talk with Raptor, okay?" Marcel said.

Eric nodded, and the two men moved to a far corner.

"We have to get out of here," Marcel whispered. "I have my phone, but the only people I'd call to help are the ones who are already outside."

Raptor tapped a finger on his lips. "If I lift you on my shoulders, can you punch through the glass?" He was too heavy to get on Marcel's shoulders.

"Probably not." Marcel sighed.

Raptor sighed. "Even if we broke it open, the only one who could fit through is Eric. Assuming he wasn't cut during the escape, he'd be on his own in the jungle until Oakley could get to him. Not a good situation."

"Lumas won't stop until he gets what he wants," Marcel said.

Raptor raked a hand through his hair. "Oakley and Penna."

Suddenly, the door swung open. Marcel dashed to Eric and stood protectively in front of him. Raptor fisted the tranquilizer gun. As Lumas walked into the room, a stocky man with a real gun stood watch at the door. Raptor relaxed his grip.

"You didn't bring Penna." Lumas blew out a long breath. "A pity. That could leave us at an impasse. However, I'm growing tired of dragging this kid around the jungle"—he pointed at the other man—"and Ness wants to find Oakley. Here's my only offer. I'll let you take Eric home if you give me Oakley. I know she's here somewhere. Will you agree to lure her out?"

"No," Raptor said.

Lumas raised both eyebrows. "I wasn't talking to you, Mr. Greene." He returned his attention to Marcel.

Raptor grabbed Marcel's arm. "Don't sacrifice her. We'll find another way."

"Eric and I aren't safe here." He shook Raptor's hand off. "I can't protect both of them."

Fury boiled in Raptor's veins. "Is that what you told yourself when you decided between Oakley and Auburn?"

Marcel swiveled to him, standing chest to chest. "The past is the past. Eric need a future. Oakley is better able to take care of herself."

"Daddy." Eric tugged at his jeans. "Will Oakley be all right?"

Marcel lifted him into his arms. "Of course. More importantly, she will be happy to have us safe and leaving the island."

Raptor turned away from him. How could he be so willing to give up his daughter? Worst of all, he wasn't wrong—she'd probably agree with this plan.

———

AN HOUR PASSED while Cane studied the confines of his new prison cell. Tall wooden walls with the metal gate as the one way in or out. At least it was outdoors, though not as clean or sweet-smelling as his cave. A pang of churning emotions hit him: something akin to regret mixed with shock. The last time he'd been in the cave, he'd killed someone.

An image, a snapshot of the scene, nearly stole his breath.

Wells hanging from the ledge of the cave about to fall to her death because Chubs clung to her legs. She'd defended Cane, truly saved his life. He'd returned the favor when he'd pulled her up from the ledge. She was brave and strong and beautiful with her untamed hair and dark intense eyes. Her heart was as wild and free as her platinum curls, and she gave of herself with no thought for her own comfort or safety.

If he didn't make it back to the shack, would she miss him?

Something scratched at the gate of the enclosure. Auburn twisted a key in the lock and quickly ducked inside the cage. Hope flared inside him, until she reached her arm out to lock the cell again and pocketed the keys. She hadn't come to let him out.

He squinted at her. She couldn't be harmed by his poisonous gas, but he was still taller and stronger. He could take the keys and escape without hurting her. But first, he'd hear what she had to say. He leaned against the wood fence, inviting her to break their silent standoff.

"You shouldn't have killed Adler."

He hung his head. Even though they'd already talked about this, she needed more answers. He understood, but answers rarely healed a broken heart. "I know. I was defending my friends."

Such a copout. That wasn't all of it. Adler had snuffed the life out of his mother just because Lumas had told him to. That made killing him a lot easier.

"He was a hard man to love. But I did love him. He wasn't all bad."

She was right. Cane had wielded his justification like a shield. But she'd turned it into an arrow that pierced his heart.

God made him. The small voice in Cane's spirit might as well have announced the truth through a bullhorn. God had made Adler, and he hadn't made him evil. He'd given him the same choices they all had. And Adler had chosen evil.

But how much of a man had to be corrupted before he deserved to die? It wasn't Cane's place to judge. He should have sought the path of peace.

"I wanted revenge." It hurt to admit the truth. He took a deep breath and blew it out. "Here's what I know, and it's not much. The anger you're still harboring over Adler's death is the same anger Oakley carried over Monica's death, and the same anger I still carry for my mother's death." He ran both hands through his hair. "The cycle of anger just keeps repeating and more people die."

She shrank away from him, her back hitting the bars of the cage. "I could kill both of you."

The certainty in her voice sent a chill down his spine. "What do you mean?"

"I could get justice for Adler."

He rubbed at the start of a headache in his temples. "It doesn't work like that. I see it now. When revenge is delivered as justice, it's like playing God. I take an eye for an eye, and it only leaves us both blind."

"What else is there?"

"The opposite of anger," he said. "Mercy and grace."

She snorted.

He wasn't getting anywhere with her. "Is Eric here? Is he okay?"

"Yes to both questions. Dad said Eric preferred the boat ride and hiking through the jungle to sitting in the old prison."

That was a relief, but they'd taken such a risk with the young boy's life. "Why am I here, Auburn? What is Lumas going to do with me?"

Her gaze flicked around the dirty cage. "He said he wouldn't give you to Ness because you're his son."

So he did know. Perhaps Lumas wanted to get to know him. But Cane didn't feel any family ties to the man who ordered his mother's murder. "He'll want me to kill for him. Like Adler did."

"Only to help keep the peace …" Her robotic voice trailed off. She cleared her throat and started again. "Your mother was going to ruin the whole program."

After everything she'd seen, she couldn't possibly still believe Lumas's lies. "And what about him kidnapping a young boy? You have to stop making excuses for him."

She crossed her arms over her chest. "If you were to get out of here, would you kill him?"

Eighty percent of him wanted to say yes, that Lumas would pose a threat to everyone until he was dead. The other twenty percent couldn't imagine killing his own father. More than all the percentages added together, he'd had enough of killing. Chubs's face still swam through his nightmares, mouth open in a gaping scream as he fell hundreds of feet to his death.

He answered truthfully. "No. I'm done with killing unless it's to protect someone in the moment."

Thumping footsteps drew their attention to the cage door. Raptor appeared with the bodyguard behind him.

Erman furrowed his brow at Auburn. "Everything okay?"

"Fine."

"I'm supposed to put this guy in here with him."

She moved to open the door. As Erman shoved Raptor in, Auburn slipped out. Cane's gut pinched. He'd missed his chance to get the keys from her.

⸻

"WHEN IS that dude coming out? Or any of them?" Hudson asked.

Good questions with a frustrating answer. Oakley sighed. "I don't know."

Over an hour ago, she'd caught a glimpse of Cane's dirty blond head disappearing through the center door of the sanatorium.

"They've been in there awhile. Seems pretty dumb to me." Hudson stared at her as if his follow-up comment deserved more attention than the other grumbling he'd done.

Agent Brooks gave a grunt that seemed akin to an eye roll.

She had to agree. Maybe she should send Hudson to the back of the sanatorium to see if anything was happening there. Nah, he would do something stupid.

She scraped stray hairs off her face and refastened her ponytail. Putting her out of reach of Lumas seemed like the right decision before, but she'd give anything to be in there looking for Eric right now.

Hudson stomped around in a circle.

"Could you not do that?" she asked.

"Not walk? Why?"

"Because you're making too much noise. I won't even hear the dinosaur that's going to eat you until the first crunch. And the crunchy popcorn kernel sound is not how you want to be remembered."

She smiled as he nearly tripped over his feet.

Movement at the sanatorium captured her attention. Lumas stuck his head out the leftmost door, looked around, then stepped into the grass. She nocked her arrow again. She could take him out now. Her guide finger trembled.

While he continued to scope out the surroundings, Lumas drew a gun from the small of his back and pointed it at the door behind him. Dad walked slowly out with something stuck to his hip. As they cleared the door frame, the shape became distinct. Eric clung to the loops of Dad's jeans. His terrified face nearly stopped her heart.

"Oakley, we've made a deal." Lumas's raised voice carried easily over the fifty yards separating them. He scanned the trees in her direction. Somehow, he knew her general location. "I'll let them go if you come to me."

She suppressed the urge to curse. Where were Raptor and Cane? This was exactly why she hadn't wanted them to go inside. But Dad had found Eric, and he was okay, if a little terrified. Question was, would Lumas honor that deal? If she turned herself in, could Dad and Eric both go home?

She placed the bow and arrow set on the blanket and jumped from the rock.

As her feet hit the ground, Agent Brooks grabbed her elbow. "No negotiation. Men like him don't honor deals."

"I have to do something."

He released her arm. "Let us help you."

She bit her lip. Could she trust these two? She didn't have much choice.

Brooks must have taken her silence for agreement. "You head straight at them. Hudson and I will come around from the east and surprise him."

It sounded like as good a plan as any. She nodded and began her descent. She stopped in front of the rocks, and Lumas met her gaze. She scowled at him before she moved into the trees, blocking her from view.

Hudson and Brooks disappeared into the jungle on her left. She stomped through the low brush and swept branches out of her way rather than duck under them. Hopefully, the noise would mask the approach of the men.

Partway down the hill, the foliage broke again, giving her a clear view of the sanatorium, probably the last one she'd have before confronting Lumas. Auburn looked down at her from one of the rooms on the second floor. As usual, her face was an impassive mask. Surely, she could see Lumas for what he really was now. But she made no move to help. In fact, she made no move at all. She watched with the plastic gaze of a mannequin in a store window.

The leaves closed Oakley in a temporary cocoon again as she moved farther down the hill. Two steps later, she froze at the telltale click of a gun. Out of habit, she scrolled through the names of people she was hiding from who might have a gun: Agent Glaser, who was a total wild card. Wyatt, who'd come so close to catching a glimpse of her when they'd collected Hudson from the boat. And pretty much anyone else from the compound. Lumas would have been on the list, except he was in front of her.

"I learned how to sneak around in the Queensland rainforest, bird." Quincy Ness stood to her left, feet spread wide.

How could she have forgotten him? The electricity in her blood sparked. This rich punk was full of surprises. Maybe this time he'd let her touch him just for a second.

She took a step toward him. He backed away, keeping the gun trained on her. Guess not.

"This way." He pointed the gun toward the south.

They weren't going to join the others? He gave her a wide berth as she walked past him. Sunlight hit her face, and she craned her neck to see down below.

Agent Brooks stepped up with his weapon drawn. He spoke in a loud, authoritative voice. "Lumas Verret, put the gun down."

Shock registered on Lumas's face, diametrically opposed to the relief evident on Dad's face.

"Walk," Ness ordered from behind.

She put her hands up and took a step. From below, Hudson saw her and yelled, "No!"

Both Brooks and Lumas looked up at her. Her dad took the opportunity afforded by the distraction. He hoisted Eric into his arms, then darted past Brooks and into the cover of the trees.

"Go. Now!" Ness insisted at her back.

Her last image of the scene was of Brooks and Lumas squaring off with their guns trained on each other.

Chapter Twelve

GABE GLASER SWALLOWED his growl as he tracked Oakley and the stocky guy who had just kidnapped her. He was forced to track them the old-fashioned way since only Raptor had the GPS trackers on his body. When Raptor had met up with her, there were too many people for Gabe to step in. After that, she'd been guarded by Agent Brooks. As soon as she'd been left alone, Gabe had moved into position to take her, but this guy with the Australian accent had gotten to her first.

Both this man and the one whom Agent Brooks had confronted seemed to want Oakley alive. Too bad that conflicted with Gabe's desires.

With his gun out, he followed them across a ravine and up another hill. Rustling came from a distance behind him. Had Brooks decided to save Oakley rather than arrest the other guy? If so, Gabe would have to make his move soon to keep from being discovered. With a little luck, Brooks would conclude that this kidnapper had gotten frustrated and killed Oakley.

He timed his footsteps with the pair ahead but stretched them out to gain on them. When he finally caught glimpses of the Aussie's back, he said in a low voice, "Stop."

The man whipped around, leading with his Beretta. Gabe blocked his arm with a forearm, halting the turn, then Gabe smashed the butt of his Glock into the Aussie's wrist. The Beretta dropped to the forest floor, sliding through dead leaves and grass.

Gabe shoved him to the ground.

Oakley shifted to run, but Gabe grabbed her shirt and swung her in an arc toward him. She lost her footing and fell to her knees. After scrambling around to face him from the forest floor, she pinned him with a fearful but uncomprehending look. Of course, she wouldn't know him.

"You killed my partner." His voice was a rough growl.

She shook her head and opened her mouth, but he wouldn't listen to her lies.

"Jack Fischer died because you didn't want another tracker implanted."

That stopped her head shaking. He'd hit the truth, and she knew it.

A rustling came from behind again.

He had to do this fast and get away. Brooks was coming.

Keeping his eyes on Oakley, he raised the Glock.

The bushes parted to his left. A low rumble sounded from the throat of a leggy dinosaur. Not Brooks at all. He turned away from Oakley, his full attention on the creature.

OAKLEY HELD HER SCREAM INSIDE. She scrambled backward until her back hit a tree trunk, while staying on the ground. No sense in making herself a bigger target for either the dinosaur or human predator. She didn't know this man, but even if he hadn't mentioned his partner, with his gun and military crouch, he could only be Agent Gabe Glaser. How did he keep finding her?

Wisely, he didn't make any sudden moves. Mutant Mantis

twisted its head and sniffed the air. Was it searching for her? Then it lowered its snout and peered at them with beady black eyes.

When it focused on her, it blinked several times rapidly and tilted its head. Surely, she didn't look like a better meal than the muscular FBI agent.

Oakley jumped at the blast of a gunshot as Glaser unloaded a round into Mutant Mantis's chest. The bullet passed through and came out its shoulder.

Not only was the animal not cowering from the injury or running away, it now looked quite ticked off. Where was this creature's heart located anyway? Before Glaser could fire another round, Mutant Mantis swung its right front appendage in a half circle faster than a Cy Young pitcher. It hit Glaser's gun hand with a sickening crunch that had to mean broken bones.

The weapon flew into the jungle beyond them. When Mutant Mantis pulled back, Glaser's wrist and forearm were angled in an unnatural direction.

Oakley slid along the base of the tree, trying to put the trunk between her and the dinosaur. Mutant Mantis flicked its gaze to her but then quickly refocused on Glaser.

Another head reared up on her other side—Quincy Ness searching for her again.

His eyes rounded as the fearsome dinosaur directed its attention to him.

Glaser took the opportunity to escape by spinning around another tree. He was probably hoping the dinosaur would finish her off. She could try to shock it, but escape would be better.

She shifted away.

Ness kneeled and grabbed her arm, anchoring her to her spot. A small trickle of blood eased from the bullet hole in Mutant Mantis's chest. The wound looked too high in the chest to have caused much damage.

Ness tugged her in his direction until she was almost free of the tree trunk. Maybe she could run then. Even though Ness had found his gun and was pointing it at her, he'd soon be too busy trying to fight off the angry dinosaur.

Thrashing came from the bushes near where Glaser had disappeared. Agent Brooks broke through the trees with his weapon out, followed closely by Hudson.

"Whoa—"

Agent Brooks clamped his other hand over Hudson's mouth. But it was too late.

The introduction of more people threw Mutant Mantis into a tirade. It let out a honking screech that sounded like a car squealing its tires and backfiring at the same time. Both of its front legs came up in a blur of powerful strokes, whipping out like two ends of a pliers.

The creature's blow was aimed in her direction. Survival came down to her or Ness.

She pivoted around the base of the tree, ending up behind the man.

A thump and rolling sound almost drew her gaze back. But she refused to look. She'd seen so much death on this island. No need to carry the image of Quincy Ness's fate with her.

From the other side of the tree, Agent Brooks frantically waved for her to come to him.

The dinosaur let out another fearsome screech. She had to move.

She shifted around the back of the tree just as Mutant Mantis slammed one of its deadly legs down where she'd been crouching.

She dove at Agent Brooks, accidentally knocking his gun away. Brooks grabbed her hand and tucked her behind him. Hudson wrapped an arm around her.

The creature's other leg swept through and caught Brooks on the thigh. He grunted, even as he pushed her away from the monster and down the incline. Perhaps the gangly front legs would make it difficult for Mutant Mantis to follow them.

No such luck. She glanced back to see the dinosaur sliding on bent back legs while holding its front legs out horizontal to the ground, like an imitation of Elvis sliding onstage to please the crowd.

When it came close to them, it swung its legs erratically, just trying to hit someone. The breeze of its swiping arms chased the three of them as they ran awkwardly downhill.

***

"HERE YOU ARE." Dad's voice made Auburn turn from the window where she'd stood like a statue, watching events unfold, powerless to change them.

"Is Oakley gone?" she asked.

"Probably."

"Did you sell her?" she asked on a whisper.

"Of course not."

Was it the truth? She'd never been able to tell when he was lying.

"Ness will tutor her, help her control her powers. And what do you care? If anything, you can look at this as revenge for what she did to Adler."

Good point. Why did she care? Days ago, she'd been ready to execute Oakley with the kill switch program. Now, things were more complicated. Perhaps Oakley was caught up in all this in the same way she was. Her dad had just held a gun on an FBI agent. That wouldn't be swept under the rug.

"Ness will get her counseling to figure out why she doesn't want to use her abilities to help people."

That didn't sound right. Though it was usually ugly, Oakley used her power to protect the people she cared about … at any cost. The same thing Dad claimed to be doing.

A stray question pricked at her mind. "Did Adler try to kill Oakley in the tree house?"

Before they'd left the lab, Auburn had reviewed all of the video from Adler's eye implant. She'd needed to see the world through his eyes. Then, when that wasn't enough, she needed to see *him* alive. She'd scoured the video from Oakley's implant and found a few seconds where Adler held a gun pointed at her. He'd seemed intent on pulling the trigger, but then he'd fled.

Dad folded his arms over his chest. "Yes. One of many instructions he ignored. She was blindfolded, so he thought I wouldn't know."

"That was why he ran, because her blindfold slipped off. Then, you didn't tell him to kill her?"

"No."

It sounded like the truth, but how would she know? Dad had spent a lifetime feeding her half truths.

He shoved his phone into her hand. "I need you to install the app for my pod, so I can control the dosage."

"Maybe that's not such a good idea." The concoction of testosterone and adrenaline she'd cooked up and inserted into a pod in his arm was a temporary measure and would come with a price if used too often.

"Agent Brooks would have taken me down if he hadn't been forced to go after Oakley."

He didn't understand. "The excess adrenaline will weaken your blood vessels and elevate your risk of a heart attack. The excess testosterone could increase mood swings and cause angry outbursts, along with anxiety."

"You gave me this for a reason. I have to be able to protect myself … and you."

She'd given it to him because he'd begged her to. The same reason she did anything for him.

But at least he hadn't left her, like Penna had.

Dad jiggled the phone in front of her because she hadn't

taken it. With all the modified humans running around, she did want him to be able to protect himself.

"Fine, but don't administer the dose more than twice a day." She installed the app on his phone and typed in the passcode to give him administrative access. She handed it back. "Tap here to administer three milligrams of adrenaline and a thousand nanograms of testosterone."

After pushing the button, Dad set his phone on the windowsill. A few seconds later, he took a deep breath and sighed. "Thank you." Then, his expression turned serious. "Tell me what you know about the girl and about the FBI being here."

She told him about Teagan, then related the run-in with Agent Brooks in the bunker and how he'd quizzed her. She ended with explaining she'd given him Dad's computer.

At her last admission, his jaw dropped. "You gave him my laptop?"

"He didn't ask. He took it. What's the big deal? The FBI knows we're doing some tinkering with dinosaur DNA. All the proprietary gene modifications are on *my* laptop, not yours."

Dad growled and pushed a hand through his salt and pepper hair. "You had no right." He glowered at her. "We will have to go get it."

"How?" Another hike through the jungle sounded grueling.

"There's another tunnel entrance near here." Dad pounded a fist on the plastered wall, causing a cloud of flakes to drop. "You'd just better hope that he hasn't taken any evidence from it."

A tremor of fear quaked in her insides. Not fear of what he might do to her. He'd never physically hurt her. This was a deeper, more invasive fear. Dad still wasn't being honest. He'd certainly exploited Eric's kidnapping, if not orchestrated it. And he'd forced Oakley to go with Ness, if not outright sold her. Each of those might be explained away. Together, they were not the actions of an innocent man just trying to set up a powerful peacekeeping force. And now he was obviously worried about incriminating evidence on his computer.

First, Adler, then Dad. How had she gotten to the point where she made excuses for all the men she loved? She'd convinced herself she knew them, but their actions had proven her wrong.

A seed of rebellion took root in her mind. With a shuddering breath she disguised as a cough, she pocketed his cell phone.

Chapter Thirteen

THE LENGTH of the downhill trek had kept Oakley, Agent Brooks, and Hudson from becoming Mutant Mantis's next meal. They'd traveled faster on the slope than it did, even with its strange sliding maneuver. By the time they'd reached flat ground, they were ten yards ahead. Then, they'd lost the dinosaur in an all-out sprint for thirty yards.

Once they were able to slow down and she caught her breath, she grabbed Brooks by the forearms. "What happened to Eric and my dad?"

"Marcel fled as soon as you distracted Lumas." He opened a Velcro flap on the side of his pants and pulled out a phone. "I'll check." He continued walking while he tapped on his device.

His pace slowed, and a pronounced limp caused him to tilt to the side with every step. She'd forgotten about his injured thigh. The adrenaline must be wearing off.

A few minutes later, Brooks gave an answer that helped her relax. "Marcel is almost back to the bunker. I can only assume Eric is still with him."

Thank God.

She gave a startled shiver. Had she really just thanked a higher power? Cane was definitely influencing her.

"Raptor's phone still says he's located at the bunker, but I think he must have left it there."

She stopped in her tracks. "He didn't come out of the sanatorium?"

"No." Brooks stopped too, leaning on his left leg. A small circle of blood had darkened the right leg of his jeans, not enough to cause concern, but the hit had been hard. His leg was probably broken.

"What about Cane?" she asked.

He shook his head.

Both Raptor and Cane had been taken. "We have to go back."

"No thanks," Hudson said.

Agent Brooks twisted his lips to the side and stared at her as if *she* were a new species of dinosaur he didn't know how to classify. Hudson offered no further input, though he glanced fearfully back from where they'd come.

A deep rumble sounded several yards behind them. Not Mutant Mantis but still a threat. The sun was going down, and the blood from Ness's body would call more predators into the area.

"Let's get somewhere safe for the night," Brooks said. "I've got another weapon at the bunker. We'll come back for them in the morning."

She frowned. What would Lumas do with Cane and Raptor overnight? But Brooks needed medical attention, and the desire to make sure Dad and Eric were safe burned like fire in her chest. She pushed out a sigh, then nodded. Surely Cane's God would watch over him for the night, and hopefully, Raptor too.

THE SUN HAD SET by the time Auburn finally had a chance to sneak out to see Cane again. Her dad and Erman sat drinking in one of the bedrooms. Erman supplied the whiskey and told stories of the many adventures he'd had with Quincy Ness. The man's body had been found, minus his head. As she slipped out of the room, Dad asked Erman how much money it would take to hire him. Funny how Erman no longer seemed to care that Dad had ordered Oakley to kill him.

The phone she'd swiped from Dad burned a hole in her pocket. She only needed it for a brief minute, but if he missed it during that time, she'd have steep consequences to pay. Fortunately, the single dose from the pod had kept him satisfied to this point.

She gently swung the back door open and closed, then tiptoed across the overgrown lawn to the animal cages. Darkness cast deep shadows along the iron bars of the pen. She heard mumbled chanting as she approached. Cane jumped up immediately, and the sound stopped. Had he been praying? His green eyes seemed to radiate in the darkness, and his expression was peaceful. Those eyes held her immobile for a moment. So wise and yet somehow so innocent. As if he looked for the best parts in everyone. If only he'd seen the good in Adler.

Raptor came up behind him, suspicion coating his gaze.

"It's time for you to go." She pulled the phone from her pocket and swiped the screen on. A map appeared with their location marked as a blue dot. Several orange lines ran throughout the landscape. She tapped the one nearest to them. "These are underground tunnels that lead back to the main bunker. This one is a quarter mile to the east. If you follow the brook"—she pointed over her shoulder where the sound of water could be heard—"it will take you to this rock outcrop." She indicated it on the map. "Look for a storage door flush with the ground. It should have a keypad embedded in it. The code will be 5975."

"Why are you helping us?" Raptor asked.

"The boy." She swallowed hard. "He shouldn't have had to suffer. Marcel took off with him on a heading toward the bunker. Go find out if they made it back, and if not, start searching for them."

"What about Oakley?" Cane asked.

"Oakley is gone. Ness has her, and you'll never find her." She didn't know her sister's fate for sure, but hopefully, this would get them moving.

Both men scowled at her.

Man, what kind of hold did her sister have on these two? "She'd want you to take care of her brother before worrying about her."

That seemed to cut through their concern. Raptor gave a slow nod. Cane blew out a frustrated breath but didn't argue.

She darkened the screen and stuck the phone in her pocket again. She twisted the key in the lock, let them out, then left the open lock on the ground next to a sharp rock. Hopefully, Dad would think someone came to break them out using the rock.

After Cane squeezed her arm in thanks, he and Raptor took off into the shadows.

Who was she kidding? Dad would be suspicious of her as soon as he learned of the escape. He was suspicious of everyone.

———

THE THREE OF them were silent during the slow trip back to the bunker. Though Agent Brooks tried, he couldn't keep a normal pace, causing them to arrive well after dark. When they entered, the place was silent. A blue glow came from an emergency light in the corner of the main hallway.

Panic overtook her. She yelled, "Dad! Eric!"

Taye's whisper came from the corner. "Shh. Your brother is sleeping at the end of the hall."

She took in a deep breath. Eric was here and safe. After giving Taye a grateful smile, she walked down the hall and peeked into the room. His blond hair, so much like Felice, was pushed back from his forehead. Perhaps her father had been stroking his forehead to get him to sleep.

Dad stood from a chair by the bed. He ushered her out before speaking. "I can't believe you're here. I thought the Australian guy took you."

"He tried." And so did Glaser, but no reason to mention it.

Dad's eyes went wide. "Did you kill him?"

Of course, he'd go straight to her killing someone to escape. It didn't seem likely he knew the extent of what she could do, but he'd seen the results of her power on Mom.

"If you did, I'm not upset. I mean, I'd be proud of you. I put you in that situation."

His faltering recovery didn't make her feel better. He would always see her as a killer. No different from the way Lumas saw her. Dad didn't want to exploit her for it, but he couldn't seem to see past it either.

What did he mean, he put her in that situation? He certainly wouldn't have let Adler kidnap Eric. Maybe he thought he should have kept a closer eye on his son.

"We have to get both of you out of here," she said.

Agent Brooks sat gingerly in a chair and put his hands on each side of his thigh as if holding it together. "Not sure how you arrived"—he gave a side-eyed glance to Dad—"but I can call a civilian boat. It will take several days to get here. Or come to think of it, I saw some keys in the secure area. Oakley, can you grab those."

He handed her a piece of paper with the code. Probably Auburn had given it to him. She opened the secure door, rummaged around, and found a set of keys with a nautical keychain lying in a desk drawer. As she grabbed the chain, a strange pounding noise caught her attention. It came from the wall on the southern side of the bunker. She quietly walked toward it.

Muffled voices muttered from the other side. Her heart raced. It couldn't be Lumas. He would have easily opened whatever mechanism was necessary. Peering closely, she identified the seams of a hidden door. She ran her fingers along the top and sides. It was flush with the wall. No gaps at all.

She dropped to her knees. The door butted up to the floor with an inch high baseboard. She felt along the bottom. The baseboard shifted slightly.

She pushed harder, and it shifted up on the right side by three inches.

An indentation along the bottom was just big enough for her fingers. She inserted them and pulled.

A click sounded, and the door swung toward her. She jumped out of the way in time to keep from being struck.

Cane and Raptor stumbled into the room. They both gaped at her and then grabbed her in a huge sandwich hug.

"Uh, I'm glad to see you too, but are you guys okay?"

"Auburn told us Ness took you," Raptor said.

"That's impossible. He's dead." She related the events of the attack.

When she finished, Cane hitched his thumb toward the door. "Thanks. There was a keypad on the other side, but we couldn't remember the longer code that Auburn used."

"How did you get here?" she asked.

"Auburn helped us escape," Raptor said.

"Why?"

"She must have decided I wasn't a threat to Lumas," Cane answered.

That probably also meant Auburn was having doubts about following Lumas's orders. Maybe her sister wasn't as far gone as she had thought.

She led the men into the main room. Brooks was working

on a laptop, and Dad hovered at the doorway to the room where Eric slept.

Dad blinked in surprise at Cane and Raptor. "About time you two showed up again. Where did you come from?"

"A tunnel," Raptor said.

Without looking up, Brooks tapped on the screen. "Interesting. Lumas's computer has an app called Extinction Island Underground on it. Let's find out what it is."

While he worked, she took the opportunity to bring Taye up to speed on all that had happened at the sanatorium. In his usual manner, he took it in with barely a furrowed brow.

A few minutes later, Brooks motioned for them to join him. "It's a map of tunnels across the island. You can tell because some of them have heights listed to plan for moving equipment into the bunker."

"Just like what Auburn showed us," Cane said.

Brooks swiped a finger to the east. "This one leads straight to the ocean."

Dad looked at him blankly, but she got it. Lumas had arrived here by boat. She held the keys out to Dad.

"As a government agent, I'm not endorsing theft." He cleared his throat. "However, if you were to take Lumas's ride, I doubt he'd report it stolen."

She was beginning to like this FBI agent.

Dad clenched the keys like a lifeline. "We'll leave in the morning."

"In the meantime, somebody should bar that door in case Lumas figures out what happened to his captives."

Raptor went to do just that. Agent Brooks adjusted his position on the chair and winced.

"You need Dr. Anderson," Oakley said. "I'll go get her."

"Wait for morning," he replied.

She looked at Taye. He nodded his acquiescence. They were probably right. Mutant Mantis was searching her out even more often than the other predators around here. Traveling at night wasn't the best idea if she wanted to keep her own head.

"I've got enough stuff on this laptop to keep me busy all night. I probably won't feel the pain."

She dug up some pain relievers from a first aid kit anyway. The tough guy routine was probably an act. At least his leg seemed to have stopped bleeding.

As she turned away from Brooks, she almost ran into Hudson. He'd been her shadow all day.

"Can we talk?" he asked.

She came close to throwing out a harsh comment, but the vulnerability on his face kept her words inside. He'd been through his first tooth-and-claw ordeal today. That usually made people want to talk. She followed him to a pair of chairs in the corner.

"I want you to know that I'm not just some convict fame junkie," he said.

She raised her brows.

"Okay, it might have started that way. But I came here to help you. I believe you were framed, and I can't let you die because of it."

While she appreciated the vote of confidence, he had no way to know if she was innocent because he didn't truly know her. "Hud—"

"You're going to say I don't even know you, and you're wrong. I was on the boat. I saw what you did."

"What boat?"

"At the swamp tour. I watched you jump into the water with an alligator to save a little boy. A killer doesn't do that."

She rubbed the stubs of her missing two fingers as the memory pinched her heart. Now it made sense, why he seemed fixated on her. But the big issue wasn't her innocence, it was him, specifically his *lack* of innocence. "Actually, I'm going to say I want you to stop using me as the reason for why you killed those women."

He looked down and appeared humbled by her words. His voice came out in a raspy whisper. "Sometimes, true justice requires sacrifices."

Unbelievable. The man could justify anything to achieve his ends. She shook her head. "I wouldn't have wanted you to pass judgment on them or sacrifice them for me. Until you figure out why, we have nothing more to talk about."

She stood and dismissed him with a wave of her hand. He continued to sit in the chair while she checked on her dad who'd fallen asleep in a neighboring room. Eventually, Hudson went into the secure part of the bunker, presumably to find a bed.

She couldn't leave Eric just yet. She was small enough to curl up on the bed behind him. His soft breaths filled her with contentment. She drifted off with her arms wrapped securely around him.

Chapter Fourteen

AT SUNRISE, the men moved the desk that was barring the hidden door, and Oakley said a tearful goodbye to her father and brother. Eric didn't understand why she couldn't come with him. Even though she no longer had a tracker, trying to leave the island in sight of an FBI agent would have caused her death sentence to be carried out immediately. Agent Brooks would have been forced to shoot her rather than let her leave.

She and Taye headed to the door right after Dad and Eric disappeared into the tunnel. Hudson had agreed to wait here for her return. Taye told her he suspected Hudson didn't want to cross paths with Kaleo again.

Before they left, Agent Brooks held up his hand to stop them. "Raptor ..."

Raptor came into the room.

For several seconds, Agent Brooks looked from Raptor to Oakley, then back again. Finally, he crossed his arms over his chest and said, "Never mind."

Her eyebrows rose. Had the agent been about to order Raptor to keep an eye on her? If so, he'd quickly changed his mind. He was trusting her to come back on her own.

As she walked out the door, Raptor gave her a small smile, which she returned.

The trip to the shack passed with only the sighting of a herd of *Parasaurolophus*, her favorite dinosaur. The long, sweeping tube on their heads created a symphony of rich, fluid notes. A wilderness serenade was just what she needed.

At the shack, Taye gave the appropriate knock on the door, and Kaleo opened it. She nearly jumped into his arms, restraining herself to make sure she didn't throw her full weight at him.

His strong arms enveloped her, and the walls she'd put up to get through the last two days crumbled. Her eyes misted with tears. If only they were alone so she could tell him all that weighed on her heart. *I barely escaped being trafficked. My sister hates me. My dad thinks I'm a killer, and he's not wrong. A man was beheaded right in front of me.*

But they weren't alone. She swallowed the trauma through a raw throat. At least her brother was safe. And so were Penna and Teagan, who both gave her smiles from the corner.

Taye went immediately to Neve's side. She was awake, and the sight of her open eyes must have given him such joy because he planted an impulsive kiss on her cheek. So not like him. Neve blushed, but her smile grew.

Oakley buried her face in Kaleo's chest and breathed in his scent of coconut and hibiscus. When she pulled back, she looked up into his warm brown eyes. He placed a hand on her cheek and leaned in for a soft kiss. He was being polite in their mixed company. It took all her self-control not to grab his shirt and kiss him hard enough for his dark Hawaiian skin to flush scarlet.

"How are you?" she asked.

"Sore, but only in the back half. I owe Red Grizzly some slashes."

That was her Kaleo—the toughest man she knew. She

planted another chaste kiss on his lips, then pulled away. She had someone else to talk to.

She kneeled at Neve's other side and squeezed her hand. "Good to see you awake." She hesitated to ask the next question. But she had to know. "Why did you do it? Why did you take the tracker for me?"

"Because you didn't deserve this tracker," she answered. "Your innocence matters."

The response made Oakley tear up again. She might have been innocent when she'd arrived, but no more. She'd wielded death as the most gruesome of weapons. And Neve, for one, was completely innocent. The most she'd ever killed was a *Hadrosaur* for food.

"I'm sorry you were hurt because of me."

Neve pursed her lips. "This wasn't you. The person who pulled the trigger is responsible."

"He's still out there. I'm sorry."

"So much apologizing." Her voice had started to fade. "It's the war inside, Oakley."

She furrowed her brow.

"All people have a friend and an enemy within themselves. They are constantly at war." Neve closed her eyes like she was praying for her, or maybe Glaser, right then.

This woman didn't make sense. But she had more peace inside her than Oakley had ever possessed.

There was only one more thing she could say, again. "Thank you."

Neve patted Oakley's hand and closed her eyes once more.

Oakley placed Neve's hand in Taye's and stood to relate the recent events to the whole group. She ended with Cane and Raptor coming to the bunker. Wells, in particular, let out a sigh after she heard Cane was safe.

Oakley met her gaze. "Is Neve well enough for you to come with me? Agent Brooks's leg, uh, it might be a little caved in."

Wells looked at Neve uncertainly.

"I'll stay by her side," Taye volunteered. "If she has any problems, I'll come get you."

"My back is sore, but I'm fine," Neve said without opening her eyes.

"Okay," Wells agreed. "Any signs of shock for Agent Brooks? You know, confusion, clammy skin, rapid breathing?"

She shook her head. "Not so far."

"Good. Let me gather a few things."

"I'm coming too," Kaleo said.

Wells narrowed her eyes at him.

"Just wrap my legs up tight."

She didn't argue, merely handed Oakley a pair of scissors and a bedsheet to cut for bandages. Then, she rummaged around in her first aid pack to gather supplies.

While Wells wrapped Kaleo's legs, Oakley wandered over to Penna. Teagan huddled a few feet away in a corner by herself. What would it be like to always be the youngest one in the room? And the most perceptive?

With a nod toward Teagan, Oakley asked, "Is she okay?"

"Yeah," Penna said. "Being indoors with so many people overwhelms her senses."

There were half a dozen other cave dwellers in addition to the patients. "Oh. I hadn't thought of that. She could come with me back to the bunker. There are a few less people there."

"Yes. I think she'd rather be with you and Cane. It's easier for her with you two." Penna paused for a minute before explaining her statement. "The pheromones help her understand what you're feeling, so she doesn't have to do as much interpretation of your biological signals."

"Speaking of pheromones, this Mutant Mantis creature is almost worse than Red Grizzly and Fangtooth. It seems to find me everywhere. I need to get better at turning off these pheromones. I can do it, but it takes a lot of effort."

Penna tapped one finger on her knee. "It may not solely be the pheromones."

"What do you mean?" The mysterious hormones emanating from her had always been the draw for the genetically modified dinosaurs.

"Well, if Auburn used my research, then the DNA modified to generate this creature would have come from the mantis shrimp. They are quite adept at seeing polarized light."

Penna blinked at her as if this made perfect sense.

Oakley ground her teeth before asking, "And that's a problem why?"

"Light waves are merely electromagnetic particles moving in a wave." At Oakley's frustrated look, she quickly continued, "You know, electrons moving in a wave. Polarization is when those waves move in the same orientation, that is, the same direction. Creatures who can detect polarization are detecting the electrical vector of those light waves, even in the nonvisible spectrum."

Ugh. That horrible explanation made sense. Her core of electricity was pulsing out invisible electrical waves that the Mutant Mantis could somehow see. If that was the case, she'd never be able to hide from it.

———

THE ROOMS in the secure part of the bunker were well insulated. Cane had slept through the departures of Marcel and Eric to the boat and Oakley and Taye to the shack. After he woke and Raptor told him they had all left, he crawled back into the bed he'd slept in last night. But he couldn't return to sleep. This morning, his spirit was more tired than his body.

Auburn's words rolled around in his head like spiked balls, pricking his conscience with every turn. *If you were to get out of here, would you kill my father?*

Her father. Not his, even though he was biologically related to Lumas and she wasn't. And since when had he become the kind of person who needed to be asked if he would kill someone?

Lord, how have I fallen so far?

He didn't need the Lord to answer. This mess came from a whole combination of things. Hatred of Adler for killing his mother. Fear of what Lumas would do to all of them. Desiring a relationship with a woman when their only connection came through pheromones. At the time, he hadn't even asked God if Oakley was the woman for him. It might have saved him some pain if he had.

Time to rectify that part at least.

Lord, you know I have developed feelings for the lovely doctor. These are deeper than the attraction I felt for Oakley, but is it too soon after Oakley's rejection for me to decide on this? I don't want Wells to be a rebound relationship.

He took in a slow, deep breath while waiting for an answer. Nothing came. He would continue to wait, then.

An image arose in his mind of her pixie-like face framed by short golden curls. When she looked at him, her brown eyes simmered like steaming hot chocolate. She was direct and intelligent, and her gentle bedside manner touched him. Though she had no pheromones to attract him, he couldn't be more drawn to her. But did she feel the same? Was she interested in finding out who he was deep down? Or did the pheromones alone attract her?

He rolled out of bed again. Wells would be here soon to examine Agent Brooks, and there was a shower off this room. Might as well be presentable when she arrived.

A half hour later, he walked into the main area in time to see Penna and Teagan enter. Kaleo came in behind them, a slight limp to his gait. Finally, Wells entered with her blond curls bouncing.

Her gaze met his, and she gave him a beaming smile. His

heart stutter-stepped for a few beats, then raced when she looked him over from head to toe. A slow grin spread across his face.

"You're okay?"

Of course, she was only checking for injuries. His smile faltered. "Fine."

She turned her attention to the actual patient, who had begun gingerly rolling up his pant leg. Cane winced at the sight of the baseball-sized depression in the man's thigh.

"A dinosaur did this?" Wells pressed her fingers to the side of the wound. "It looks like part of the bone is pulverized."

Brooks gritted his teeth and ground out, "Feels like it too."

"Sorry. If we can find something strong to splint your whole leg, I can temporarily help you by stabilizing the limb. Then, I'll give you a shot of antibiotics to head off infection. But you will need to get back to the mainland as soon as possible for surgery."

Brooks narrowed his eyes in suspicion. Did he know of Wells's ties to CADRE, Citizens Against Death Row and Execution? The group was known for radical stunts to draw attention to the plight of Extinction Island prisoners. If so, he might suspect she was trying to get him off the island. But not for long. One more small probe of her fingers made him groan. "You might be right."

Raptor brought in two strips of metal that looked like they had belonged to one of the cots.

Cane turned his attention to Kaleo while Wells splinted Agent Brooks. "How are you?"

"Better now that she wrapped me up tight." Kaleo leaned close. "What are we going to do about Lumas?"

"No more killing."

"Agreed. Unless it must come to that."

It was good enough for Cane. Kaleo had his own reasons for seeking the path of peace. If only they could convince Oakley.

"Okay, that just leaves Glaser. I still don't want any more death."

Kaleo frowned before blowing out a resigned breath. "Neve keeps saying the same thing."

"You two are being secretive over here," Oakley said from behind them.

Kaleo gave her a much-too-wide smile. Cane almost groaned at his inability to look innocent.

Oakley apparently decided to let the inquiry go. "I'm concerned. I swear I caught a glimpse of Fangtooth on the way back to the bunker while searching for my metal pole." Obviously, she'd found it since it rested against the far wall. "Fangtooth's flank was just visible through the trees as it turned away from me. I talked to Teagan, and she confirmed that she sensed something out there too."

"Close to the bunker?" Cane asked.

She nodded. "Twenty feet out. Why didn't it attack?"

"Maybe it didn't have Red Grizzly with it. One on one, your power would be a threat to Fangtooth. And I'm sure Teagan's presence has to be throwing it off."

Cane listened as Oakley explained Penna's theory about how Mutant Mantis was attracted to her electricity. They just couldn't catch a break.

Worry lines were etched on her face when she continued. "What if there's something else going on with Fangtooth too? Could it be as drawn to Teagan as Mutant Mantis is to me?"

Cane didn't point out the obvious—Mutant Mantis's *curiosity* seemed deadlier. But then again, Fangtooth's intelligence made capturing its attention extremely dangerous. "That's a question for Penna." He glanced over at the woman who always hovered close to her daughter. None of them would ask her for fear of arousing her own concerns for Teagan.

"So what's our next move?" Oakley asked.

He shrugged. "Lay low. I don't think Lumas will come

back here since he held a gun on Agent Brooks. That makes him a fugitive, same as us. Or we could retreat to the shack since Lumas doesn't know about that place."

Her posture stiffened. "You're underestimating him. He wants you, Teagan, and Penna for his research. And now that Ness is gone, he won't just leave me alone. He'll want to sell me again or eliminate me as a liability. This isn't over."

Cane's stomach clenched. She was right about all of it, especially her fate. Lumas couldn't control Oakley, and that infuriated him. But Cane only shook his head. He couldn't do anything to hurt Lumas. He'd promised Auburn.

AFTER WELLS HAD FINISHED splinting Agent Brooks's leg, Oakley approached and kneeled in front of him. It was time to state her commitment. "I had Wells bring the extra tracker with her. As soon as I finish this with Lumas, I'll undergo the surgery to put it in."

He gave her that strange look again, like he was trying to dissect her motives. After several seconds, he said, "I need some time here to go through this laptop anyway."

"First, you need to radio in for a transport helicopter."

He shrugged. "Later." With a wave, he called Raptor over. "You need to hear this too, Mr. Greene." In one hand, Brooks held up his phone. "I think I know how Glaser keeps finding you."

"How?" Raptor asked.

"For ops where surveillance is difficult, agents will often use microcomputers on clothing or bags to track suspects. They look like little filaments or stray hairs, and they stick to everything."

She began patting down her jeans.

"Don't bother. You wouldn't find them anyway." He tapped the screen on his phone. "I can see which apps have been active on Glaser's phone during the short time he uses it. In the last twenty-four hours, he's accessed the tracking app three times."

She snapped her fingers. "If he's using his phone, you can track his location."

"No. He's smarter than that. He keeps it on for a few minutes, then goes dark, so I can only see where he's been. I'm sure he moves quickly afterward. However, I can set an alert to notify me the next time he turns on his phone. If we're close enough, we could catch him."

Great. One step behind, as usual.

But Brooks would no longer be the one to contend with Glaser. He must have realized it because he said, "You have to assume he can find you anywhere."

She let out a long sigh. Just like every other predator here on the island.

Agent Brooks glanced at Raptor briefly. They exchanged a cryptic look, then Brooks gave her a side-eyed glance. "Do you think there's a chance to clear your name?"

So that was what his scrutiny was about. He was entertaining the idea she might be innocent. Hope flared inside her, but a response didn't come. No one in law enforcement had believed her the first time around, and now one of them was even hunting her. In a heartbeat, her hopes crashed. Adler—the person responsible for Monica's death—was dead. Who would listen to her pleas of innocence without a confession from him?

Brooks seemed to understand her silence. "Bringing Lumas into custody would be good for your case." He pointed to a duffel bag in the corner. "In that bag are zip ties and two tranquilizer guns with darts. Raptor will go with you. And I'd consider it a personal favor if you brought in Glaser as well."

She smiled at him even as her insides hardened into a determined knot. "Will do."

After scooping up the weapons and zip ties, she and Raptor rejoined the others.

Kaleo brushed her shoulder. "You sure you want to do this?"

"Not you too?" If both Cane and Kaleo disagreed with taking action, maybe she should listen.

"I'm not saying we shouldn't go after him. In fact, I have some ideas to help, but this is taking a toll on you. You're not responsible for all of this."

He was wrong. Many of these people depended on her to fight, especially since Cane wouldn't. Penna, even with all her brains, was no match for Lumas's ruthlessness. Teagan was just a teenager. And she had to protect Hudson for the simple fact that he wouldn't leave her alone.

Cane kept saying God had allowed her to be created this way. It was about time she embraced it.

"My bet is that Lumas is still back at the sanatorium, hoping we'll come for him there," she said as she picked up her metal pole.

The men agreed, and they made plans to draw Lumas out. While Cane helped with the planning, he refused to come along. She respected his decision, considering she had some of the same struggles regarding violence. Besides, she had Kaleo and Raptor to watch her back this time.

Before they left, she gestured for Raptor to follow her into the hallway. She had a question she didn't want the others to overhear.

"So much has happened that I'm just now getting around to asking you about events at the sanatorium. How did Ness know exactly where to look for me outside?"

A shadow crossed his face. He clenched his jaw but didn't say anything.

"Tell me the truth."

"Your dad felt you could take care of yourself, and he needed to protect Eric at all costs."

She bit her lower lip. It made sense. She would have sacrificed herself to save Eric. He was innocent and vulnerable. More than that, he was pure. His DNA—no, his very essence, wasn't tainted by evil. Not like hers. So why did her dad's actions burn like acid in her heart? Why did it feel like a betrayal?

"I appreciate your honesty." She handed him one of the tranquilizer guns. "Let's go after Lumas and Glaser."

He grinned at her, and she returned the grin, though it seemed to harden on her face. This was something she could do. Something she was good at, even. Lumas had bred her for this. He would come to regret it.

Chapter Fifteen

AFTER THE OTHERS LEFT, Cane fidgeted while Wells continued to hover over Agent Brooks, offering him pain medication and bringing him the instant ice packs they had found in a closet. Finally, he helped her get Brooks situated in a cot in Raptor's room with the laptop on his lap.

Wells smoothed the blanket and felt the agent's forehead again. Cane awkwardly stood in the doorway. Brooks grasped her wrist and tugged her to sit beside him.

A sharp pain squeezed Cane's chest. Was he jealous? There was nothing forward in Brooks's intentions. He merely asked Wells for more details about what happened when she arrived on the island. Checking the story once more. The man clearly had doubts. But was it about Oakley's guilt or her innocence?

And why did the agent have to keep hold of Wells's hand? He swallowed down his irritation. This had nothing to do with Brooks and everything to do with how quickly his feelings had grown for her. Was this connection real? Or was he simply rebounding from the rejection Oakley had dealt him?

Better to keep himself busy. He went to the secure part of the bunker and gathered up a small meal for the three of them—strips of beef jerky and granola bars. He laid two portions on a table, then brought one portion to Agent Brooks, along with a glass of water.

"Thanks," he said.

Cane nodded, then turned to Wells. "I've got some for you out here."

She smiled and followed him to the table. They sat across from each other, eating in silence.

He looked up at her every few seconds because he felt her gaze on him. But as soon as his eyes lifted, hers darted away.

He grasped her hand. "What are you thinking?"

Her eyes went as wide as a deer caught in headlights. "Uh, I wish I could stay here … you know, to keep an eye on Agent Brooks, but I should get back to check on Neve."

She likely had been thinking of Neve at some point, but that wasn't what he'd meant and she had to know it. Still, he couldn't expect her to confess emotions when he wasn't willing to do so yet.

"I'll walk you back. Then I'll return here to stay with him."

She opened her mouth like she would say more. Nothing came out. With a snap, she closed it and gave him a dazzling smile. He basked in the warm glow of her gaze for a few minutes until her smile flipped down into a frown.

"Cane?"

"Yes?"

"You weren't listening, were you?"

Uh-oh. "Sorry. What did you say?"

"Agent Brooks will be taking me to the mainland when the helicopter comes for him."

A jolt hit his heart. "What? I mean, why?"

"I'm not military. I'm just a citizen who was given a temporary leave to come here. It's illegal for me to stay beyond the time the FBI allows."

Oh, man. She was right. Of course, he'd come here using the religious exemption and his rights as a pastor.

"I love feeling like I'm making a difference here. I think it's inhumane to send people here in these conditions. No basic supplies or medical care. It's barbaric."

"I agree. You've saved so many people since you've arrived. Kaleo. Neve." He blew out a breath. "Me." He reached up to toy with one of her curls. "Join my congregation. As a member, you can stay indefinitely to give peace and comfort and medical care to the inmates."

The words had flown out of his mouth without much thought. She probably had a life on the mainland. Was it fair to ask her to give it up?

She pursed her lips. No telling if it was a good or bad sign.

"Boy, God throws some crazy curve balls at us sometimes." She rolled her shoulders as if working out the tension or maybe working out the problem. "I have some supporters on the mainland who are willing to smuggle supplies in if I distribute them to the prisoners and give medical care. I'd be willing to stay, but I need to know one thing."

"What's that?"

"Do *you* want me to stay?"

It was his turn for a gaping mouth with no words coming forth. His whole body screamed yes, but his heart climbed into a cocoon of fear.

A shaky breath. His fear was not from God. Although God had no obligation to provide him with a woman to share his life with, what if He had done just that? He'd never know if he let her go.

She moved to stand, but he captured her hand. "I can't make promises, but *I* want you to stay for my own selfish reasons. At least for a while."

A slight smile tugged at the corners of her lips. She nodded. "For a while."

A simple nod had never held such meaning for him. His heart felt three times lighter.

After he walked her back to the shack, he returned to the bunker to find Agent Brooks asleep. A nap sounded good. Cane made himself comfortable on the bed he'd slept on last night. He closed the door, lay down, and drifted off to sleep with a smile on his face.

⊏⊐

A FUZZY HAZE surrounded Cane's vision, as happened in most of his dreams. He was in a coffee shop on the mainland —a place he hadn't been for at least four years—seated across from Wells. She chatted about how Neve was the best patient she'd ever had and how the steamy jungle made her hair curl even more. Why were they talking about Extinction Island? He had so much more to say to her. But his dream self couldn't form the words. Instead, he soaked in her mannerisms—the way she flicked her hand for emphasis and how she twisted her mouth to the side while she thought of her next topic.

Suddenly, she asked him, "Can I get to know the other person inside you?"

His skin broke out in a clammy sweat. She didn't know he was genetically modified, much less that he'd had a twin. Then she touched his arm, surprising him with how it calmed him and ignited a slow burn inside his heart.

Her image disappeared in a blink as a faint creaking noise woke him. Probably just Agent Brooks trying to use the bathroom. He must have woken from his nap. Cane ignored the noise and closed his eyes. Maybe the dream Wells would come back. Then again, maybe Agent Brooks needed help.

He forced his eyelids open and drew up to his elbows. He gasped at the outline of a figure leaning against the closed doorway of the small room. Her shape was familiar.

"Oakley?"

"No."

He recognized the voice, a slightly different timbre than Oakley's. "Auburn, how did you get here?"

"Same way you did."

Of course, they hadn't blocked the tunnel again after Marcel and Eric left. "Is Lumas here?"

"Don't ask me questions I can't answer."

Did she mean Lumas was here? Or that she didn't know where he was?

"I came for this." She lifted a square object off her chest.

In the semi darkness, he identified it as a laptop. "Did you take that from Agent Brooks?"

"No, it's mine."

Where had she retrieved it from? Brooks had searched the entire bunker for electronic equipment. "I'm sure the agent would like to see that one also."

"Too bad." She clutched the laptop to her chest again, lifting to her tiptoes like a butterfly about to alight.

This was as good a time as any to ask her the question burning a hole in his mind. "Since you're here, I'd like clarification on something you said earlier. What kind of ability did my twin have that my body …?" He couldn't seem to accept that he'd absorbed tissue from his twin. It was surreal.

She didn't answer for a second, then she gave him two sentences spoken with a finality that said she wouldn't give any more. "The ability is based on the gecko and the axolotl. Pray you never need it."

He squinted as he fully sat up. "A gecko? You mean I can walk up walls? I guess I've never tried."

She coughed out a laugh, and it sounded almost painful. She obviously wasn't hanging out here to chat. She cleared her throat. "I have a message for Oakley. She needs to stay away from my dad, or I'll be forced to stop her."

The words *stop her* were delivered in a low, ominous tone.

"What do you mean?"

Auburn tugged a cell phone from her back pocket, checked it, then spun around to leave.

He climbed out of bed. "Auburn, what do you mean?"

She stepped to the door, then turned back to him. "When you were both at the lab, I implanted a microdevice in your bloodstream. Unless I activate it, there's no impact on your body. It floats harmlessly around."

"And if you do activate it?"

Auburn put a hand on the doorknob. "Then the device will find its way to the heart, burrow inside, and grind through the tissue until it destroys the organ completely."

His mouth went dry. She had the capability to create something like that, but the fact that she had …

Auburn cracked the door a few inches and then slipped silently through.

A deep voice sounded just before she closed the door—Lumas. "Anyone in there?"

He didn't hear her reply, but since Lumas didn't enter, she must have lied. Such a confusing woman to protect both him and her father at the same time. She was balancing on a tightrope. One that was sure to break.

His bow and arrow set rested by the front door of the bunker, not that it would do much good against the gun Lumas likely carried. Cane waited several minutes to be sure they had left before he peeked out the door.

No sound. No movement.

He crept down the hall to the main portion of the bunker. Agent Brooks was in Raptor's room where Cane had left him to nap. He lay on the cot with his eyes open and a peaceful expression on his face. His chest didn't expand or contract. He'd been killed instantly as he woke. No chance to even use the tranquilizer gun lying near his right hand.

A three-inch quill stuck out from his neck.

Chapter Sixteen

OAKLEY AND KALEO had just finished laying the wire for their plan—confiscated from a trap at a location Kaleo had memorized—when Cane arrived. He hadn't wanted any part of this. What had made him leave the bunker? His pheromones indicated something serious was going on.

She led him away from the group, who was gathered out of sight of the sanatorium, while motioning for Kaleo and Raptor to follow. Hudson had become too clingy since Kaleo had joined them, and there was no sense worrying Penna and Teagan unless it became necessary.

Cane's account of what happened at the bunker came as a shock.

"Auburn killed Agent Brooks?" Oakley asked.

Cane shook his head. "I don't think so. Lumas was there too. I have a hunch he did it with Auburn's quill."

Fury boiled Oakley's blood, bringing her electrocytes to quivering capacity. Oh, she ached to kill him. She sucked in several deep breaths. As her body adjusted to the anger, despair crept in as well. Agent Brooks seemed like he'd been coming around. Like he might have believed in her innocence. And now, he was gone. A loss not only for the law enforcement community but also for her own chances of clearing her name. No other authority had believed her about Lumas and Adler.

Brooks's execution meant she'd never leave Extinction Island. Might as well just rename it Execution Island because she would die here as well. Lumas had gone too far. There would be no bringing him to the authorities. She'd exact justice in executing *him*.

Except the others wouldn't consent to that. Penna and Teagan had only agreed to help capture him. Cane certainly didn't want more violence. In fact, his muscles shook with tension.

He rubbed a hand down his face before meeting her gaze. "Walk away, Oakley. Don't make Auburn choose between you and her father."

"He's not her father," she growled.

Kaleo came over and put a hand on her shoulder. She took strength from his touch.

"She'll kill you," Cane said.

"I'd like to see her try," Kaleo replied.

His vote of confidence caused her heart to swell. They could do this. Not just for her but for Cane and Teagan, and even Auburn herself. Her sister didn't know what it was like to live free.

Cane went on to explain another reason he'd come out here, to warn them of the real danger. As he recounted her sister's threat, the words drifted in the air between them like confetti refusing to land. He couldn't be serious.

She ground out her response. "My own sister implanted a kill switch inside both of us."

Cane let out a long sigh. "At the time, I think she wanted insurance to keep us under control. Now she wants revenge. And so do you. It's making you both blind."

He wasn't wrong exactly. Yes, killing Lumas would protect the people she cared about. But another part of her *wanted* to kill Lumas for what he'd done—creating assassins for hire, sending her here, and kidnapping Eric. He deserved to die. But just like with Adler, a portion of her humanity would die along with him. Was it worth it? To give up these little pieces of her soul? And if she kept letting that deadly part of herself loose, would she eventually lose control?

She ripped out her ponytail holder, swept her hair back up, and refastened it. "I'm getting really sick of everyone trying to kill me."

"Then maybe you should stop trying to kill them." Cane's soft tone held no condemnation, but the words stabbed her heart just the same. The right thing to do had gotten so complicated. Could she even sort out what parts of this saga were her fault?

Raptor spoke up from behind her. "Killing Agent Brooks wasn't just a way for Lumas to keep himself from going to jail. It's a message to you."

"What do you mean?" she asked.

"He used Auburn to kill Brooks in the exact manner he wants to use you, to commit undetectable murder. If we turn in the quill to prove Lumas killed him, then we expose the program he created, not just Auburn"—he swept his hand to encompass her and Cane—"but all of you. And if we take Agent Brooks back to the mainland, the autopsy will conclude he died of a heart attack. They wouldn't look for tetrodotoxin unless someone asked them to, and that would be too suspicious. In essence, he's showing you what you're made for."

Cane stomped his foot in an uncharacteristic display of anger. "Lumas doesn't get to decide what you're made for. You do."

Oakley gnawed on her lower lip. How she felt about Lumas's message didn't matter. There were no good choices here. If Lumas died, whether she meant for it to happen or not, Auburn could kill her with a simple computer command.

But going through with the plan was worth the risk to give Penna and Teagan the chance to live free.

Above all, Cane was frustratingly right. She must decide how to use her power, and she shouldn't start out with the intent to kill someone … even Lumas. "We stick to the plan. Capture only. Raptor can take him back to the mainland for the FBI to prosecute him for kidnapping Eric."

"You need to stay out of it," Cane said. "If Auburn sees you, she's likely to kill you."

She gave him a thumbs-up. "Not a problem. Teagan is the bait for this particular trap. Do you think she can track us with that device in our blood?"

"I don't think so. Otherwise, they wouldn't have needed to draw you out the first time we were here."

"Good point." She moved away from the men to question Penna and Teagan. "Ready?"

At their nods, Oakley moved into the bushes as far as the wire would reach. Then, she moved even farther, to the length of her metal pole. She let out a short whistle to let the others know she was in place. She could see most of the clearing in front of the sanatorium door, but they couldn't see her through the surrounding foliage. Hopefully, she was far enough away that Auburn couldn't distinguish her pheromones from Teagan's and Cane's.

Teagan stepped into the open, stopping short of the wire, followed by Penna, who stood just behind her. Cane, Kaleo, and Raptor were at the far edge of the clearing, just visible at the tree line, providing backup. Cane was now armed with Agent Brooks's tranquilizer gun, but he wasn't the only one. Kaleo had his whip. Raptor had another tranquilizer gun and his emergency rifle strapped around his chest.

In a surprisingly loud voice, Teagan called out, "Father."

Penna flinched. It had to be hard knowing a man like Lumas would always be the father of your child. Much the same as how hard it must be for Cane to deal with Lumas as his father. Did Teagan have the same conflicting emotions? Except she would be able to discern his true motives and desires.

Teagan called out two more times before the door cracked open.

When Lumas emerged, he stepped down to the grass and stared. He was flanked on one side by Erman, who held a gun, and the other by Auburn, who held a laptop.

A shiver ran down Oakley's spine. For her and Cane, that laptop was more deadly than the gun. Auburn's threats had been directed toward Oakley, but would she harm Cane because he'd come here too?

"My dear," Lumas said in a saccharine sweet voice. "It's nice to finally speak to you."

"Is it?"

"We should have never been kept apart."

Teagan folded her hands in front. "I'll be the judge of that."

"Your mother has probably told you many incorrect things about my work."

"You mean, her work."

"Excuse me?"

Teagan shifted on her feet. "It was her work that you used for yourself."

Lumas gave a scratchy cough.

She peered at him and placed both her hands to her temples. Was she getting a migraine? Maybe this was too hard for her.

Oakley opened her mouth to speak but didn't want Auburn to know she was there. Wait, she didn't have to speak out loud. She closed her eyes and pushed both her thoughts and pheromones toward Teagan. *Don't be fooled. He wants to use you to hurt people.*

No words came back. Instead, a clear image popped into her head of Teagan watching from behind as a man stepped off a high balcony. It was a suicide, but one influenced by her. Completely undetectable murder. Except Teagan had never been off the island, much less in a fancy high-rise building.

Of course! Teagan was transferring to her the intent she saw in Lumas's mind.

Why does he want this?

Another image came. This one of Lumas seated in the lap of a giant President Lincoln inside the Lincoln Memorial. *Power.* And all this time, she'd assumed Lumas had done it for the money people would pay to get away with murder. Instead, he wanted the power to take out any person who stood in the way of his ambitions. But what were his final goals?

The last image just about made Oakley gag. Penna stood in a short skirt and high heels attached to Lumas by a four-foot-long metal chain. He tugged her this way and that like she was a pet on a leash. He was obsessed with possessing her. His version of love meant domination.

At least Teagan was one person he couldn't fool. The ultimate lie detector. He might have plans for her, but she was also the one person he couldn't influence by force. Unless …

At a nod from Lumas, Erman pointed his weapon at Penna.

Oakley's heart rate soared.

But Teagan actually laughed. She narrowed her gaze on Erman. A second later, he pushed the button to strip the magazine from his pistol and then pulled the slide to eject the cartridge from inside. Finally, he threw the magazine and stray bullet into the bushes.

Lumas shook his head. "Hard to find good help."

He tugged out his phone and pushed several buttons. What was he doing?

His face flushed, and his breathing grew rapid in short, shallow bursts. Had he triggered something inside his body with his phone?

Oakley flipped her gaze to Teagan. Her eyebrows shot up, forming an upside-down *V* on her forehead. Her mouth hung open. She looked bewildered.

Lumas tugged a gun from behind his back and held it on Penna as he came toward Teagan. Just a few more steps, and he'd be at the wire.

But Oakley had enough experience with electrocution by this point. If she shocked him, his trigger finger would seize up and the gun would likely go off, shooting Penna.

Teagan stepped forward, putting her left foot right on the wire. No way was that an accident. Suddenly, she shifted to her right, taking her attention off Lumas. Her hand swept in that direction, and a loud growl sounded.

Oh, crap. They weren't alone. Chances were it was one of the raptors. Mutant Mantis would have come in swinging already.

Cane trained the tranquilizer gun on the bushes. Raptor dropped his tranquilizer gun and brandished the rifle. However, his government mandate would restrict him from firing unless human lives were at risk. Fangtooth jumped from behind a short bush, then stood bobbing on nimble feet, alternating between staring at Teagan and Lumas. It paid no heed to the other men.

Lumas took a step back.

Fangtooth didn't advance. Oakley had seen this maneuver before.

This is just a diversion. Search for Red Grizzly.

Had Teagan heard her unspoken words? For several seconds, nothing happened.

Then, a large streak flew through the jungle between Oakley and the clearing. Red Grizzly blazed a trail, heading straight for Teagan.

Step back! Oakley yelled inside her head.

Teagan obeyed, taking her foot off the wire.

Run! Oakley mentally yelled again.

As Red Grizzly broke free from the jungle, the men let loose. Kaleo missed with his whip as did Cane with his shot. RG was moving too fast. Raptor landed a bullet in its flank, which barely slowed it down. Teagan's and Penna's bodies blocked any other shot he might have taken.

Teagan moved to run, but Fangtooth nipped in their direction. Penna wrapped her arms around Teagan as Red Grizzly barreled down on them. The *Utahraptor* let out an awful screech.

Oakley held her breath. *Please let it cross the wire. Come on. Please let it cross the wire.*

With the metal pole touching the end of the wire, she kept her gaze focused on its pounding feet. It was like trying to watch the spinning feet of the cartoon Roadrunner.

Finally, Penna and Teagan arced around and ran toward the jungle. Fangtooth pursued them, but so did Cane.

Apparently deciding to leave the women for Fangtooth, Red Grizzly pivoted and set its sights on the next closest person—Auburn. She snapped her laptop shut but froze in place.

Fear churned in Oakley's belly, spreading to her chest, and into her hands. Auburn might want her dead, but the feeling wasn't mutual. She had no other options. She had to electrify the wire and hope it caught the charging dinosaur.

She pushed her spark through the metal in a mammoth pulse just as Red Grizzly flew over the wire. It registered the pain with a sharp yelp.

But the dinosaur kept going. It was too close, only one stride away from Auburn.

It leaped into the air, slashing its claws at her as she turned away. She screamed in pain and fell out of Oakley's line of sight.

Then, Red Grizzly's body jerked backward.

Kaleo had circled behind and gotten his whip wrapped

around RG's neck. Raptor joined in to pull the creature stumbling to the ground, right on top of the wire.

Oakley pushed a pulse into the wire with all the strength she could summon. How dare this animal threaten her friends or her sister.

RG's ear-piercing screech sent panicked birds flapping out of the trees. Its body thrashed and writhed with the intensity of the megawatts Oakley pumped through it. But she didn't let up for even a second.

This creature had hunted her since the moment she'd arrived. It had hurt Kaleo and now Auburn. She wouldn't let it do any more damage.

A circle of smoke rose from around the dinosaur's rib cage. Its small arms clawed at the air in jerky motions, the muscles half frozen from the current.

The dinosaur rolled to its side and got one leg under its body. It pushed off the wire, breaking the connection. A line of red blisters crossed its back where the wire had burned.

RG let out a low menacing growl. It stepped toward Kaleo but hesitated before crossing the wire.

Kaleo struck out with his whip again, but the dinosaur ducked to avoid it.

Finally, Auburn seemed to wake up. She crawled to her feet and picked up a thick tree branch. Holding it out in front like a javelin, she charged the creature, matching its growl with her own.

Red Grizzly took a step, but a halting one, as if it didn't trust its muscles.

Auburn sped up and slammed the branch into its spine. The blow knocked the dinosaur forward but wasn't enough to cause it to fall.

She, however, fell to the ground, along with the branch.

RG lifted its leg to lash out backward at Auburn.

Before it could, Kaleo had coiled the whip around its neck.

Together, he and Raptor yanked Red Grizzly down onto the wire once again.

Oakley had to finish it this time. Rage and fear and pure wrath pulsed from her fingertips. She poured out every last spark of energy from every last cell in her body. No pity. No mercy.

A full minute of death throes pulsed through the animal's body. The acrid smell of burning skin turned her stomach. Eventually, the thrashing slowed to shuddering. Random muscle twitches caused its limbs, its chest, and its neck to jerk haphazardly.

At last, Red Grizzly stopped moving. Its head flopped to the side, and its tongue slumped out of its mouth.

She took a deep breath, released the pole, and shook her hands out. The clearing was dinosaur-free. Lumas and Erman had also retreated, either because of the dinosaurs or because the people they wanted—Penna and Teagan and Cane—had gone. But where were they now?

━━━

CANE CAUTIOUSLY RAN BEHIND FANGTOOTH, staying in its blind spot. If the dinosaur turned around, it would take him out before he had a chance to fire a tranquilizer dart, since he'd placed the gun in his waistband in order to run.

Fangtooth was gaining on Penna and Teagan. He couldn't wait much longer to make a move.

Suddenly, the animal dipped its head, opened its mouth, and ran straight at Penna's legs. She screamed as its teeth nipped the flesh of her calf.

She went down.

Cane whipped out the tranquilizer gun.

Rather than stop and finish the kill, Fangtooth continued after Teagan.

Cane planted his feet and took aim. The gun only had one

dart, so he had to make it count. Teagan flipped around and quickly jumped to the side to avoid an attack.

Fangtooth spun and came at her again.

Cane fired the dart.

This time Teagan danced out of the way, and the dinosaur tripped on its own fast-moving feet. It pitched forward, causing Cane's dart to sail just past the trunk of its body.

Fangtooth faced Teagan again, squaring its shoulders. Its lip curled, exposing more dagger-like teeth.

For her part, she stared right back. Her expression was focused and intense, not fearful.

But this wasn't a healthy standoff. Cane circled around and crept up to her side. "We should go."

"I can't."

He understood. She wouldn't leave Penna. "It may follow you and leave her."

She put a hand out toward the creature. "It's confused."

"Does that mean it doesn't want to eat us?"

"That's why it's confused. It does want to eat us, but I'm pushing on a center in its brain that feels like it holds a pack mentality."

A pack? "So, you're making the dinosaur lonely?"

"Kind of."

Fangtooth glanced past them, maybe searching for Red Grizzly. Then, it peered back at Teagan. She pinched her eyes until they were almost closed and lines crinkled around them.

Without looking down, Teagan put a hand on his gun hand. "That won't help. Fangtooth can read your intention before you fire."

"It's empty anyway." He dropped it on the ground. Raptor had more darts in his pack, but who knew where he was?

How were they supposed to defeat a near-telepathic dinosaur? He could try to dose it with hydrogen cyanide, but that probably wouldn't kill it. It was likely immune to the poison in the same way that all the people Penna created were immune. Maybe his poison could knock the creature out? But it also might affect Penna.

Fangtooth broke eye contact and bobbed in a nervous circle.

"No, you don't." Teagan took a step toward the creature.

"What are you doing?"

"Making sure it can't ignore me." She brushed stray hairs from her forehead. "I can get inside its head. I know I can."

Several tense seconds ticked by. Teagan furrowed her brow and arched her back. Fangtooth mashed leaves beneath its clawed feet. Cane forced himself to take slow even breaths.

"Ow." Teagan grunted and put a finger to her temple.

She backpedaled at the same time Fangtooth advanced. It was definitely time to get out of here. They had to lead it away from Penna.

He grabbed Teagan's arm and pulled her sideways just as Fangtooth lunged at her. You didn't have to be a mind reader to read dinosaur body language.

Fangtooth slammed headfirst into a thick tree trunk. Enough to stun it, but not enough to put it out of commission.

They ran, forcing their way through vines and branches. The forest quieted, almost in reverence of their flight for survival. Cane's feet moved in automatic, experience-driven panic. Through a dry streambed. Up a steep incline. Kicking through a pile of brush.

Scraping and clawing, Fangtooth climbed up the incline behind them. It was gaining.

At the top of the hill, Teagan grabbed a huge handful of leaves and threw them into the air. Before he could ask what she was doing, she'd hauled him behind a nearby vine curtain, tripped him to get him on the ground, and surrounded him with her lanky arms.

He barely heard her whisper in his ear, "Shh."

He held his breath while she concentrated harder than

ever, if her trembling arms were any indication. Veins pulsed in her temples. Her nostrils flared.

Stomping feet stormed in a wide area beyond the curtain, which draped partly on top of the hill and partly down the slope. But nothing came through.

They stayed huddled together, unmoving.

After several minutes, he dared to take a long, slow breath.

An enraged howl sounded about ten feet away. Teagan's arms tightened around him. The silence was punctuated by the sound of huffing breaths. Fangtooth was sniffing around for them like a bloodhound.

Cane did what he could to turn off his pheromones, the way Adler had done, though he wouldn't be able to tell if his efforts had worked. Hopefully, Teagan had thought of that as well.

Finally, the sniffing sounds moved farther from them. Several low growls resonated from about thirty feet away.

They didn't move from their position for twenty more minutes. Cane's back and thighs had started to cramp. As soon as the thought passed through his mind, the pain disappeared.

He lurched out of Teagan's embrace. "Don't do that."

"Sorry. Habit. My mom likes me to help with her aches and pains." Her gaze dropped at the mention of her mom. Fangtooth had gone in the other direction. Hopefully, it hadn't circled back to Penna.

He gestured in the direction that it went. "How did you …"

"I made us invisible. I've done it lots of times in the jungle with just myself. It's like putting a Road Closed sign in front of the dinosaur." She wiped a line of sweat off her brow. "It's a lot harder with two people."

"Well, thanks."

She gave him an innocent grin that reminded him she was

only fifteen. But then her countenance darkened. No doubt thinking about her mom.

"Let's go find her," he said.

━━

AFTER RED GRIZZLY had stopped breathing, Oakley watched Raptor dart toward Auburn. But Kaleo made his way in their direction.

"I knew there was something special about you," Hudson said in a voice tinged with worship.

"Not now. We need to go help too," she said.

A loud, deep roar sounded from over her shoulder. Birds stopped chirping. The whole forest went quiet.

Her blood froze in her veins. That was no raptor. It was much bigger. Something like a *T. rex*.

Had the smell of barbecued raptor brought predators out already? But the adult *Tyrannosaurus rex* was an ambush predator, contrary to the stomping monster the movies portrayed, which meant she'd never hear it before it killed her.

So why had it announced itself? Maybe this was something else.

She spun around and backed away from the crowding jungle. Even though she hadn't seen it yet, the animal surely knew they were there. Kaleo had told her some dinosaur predators could smell a drop of blood in a square mile of jungle. Apparently, that applied to charred dinosaur as well.

Hopefully, Kaleo wasn't still coming their way.

A higher pitched roar came from the same area. A juvenile?

She'd been so focused on the dinosaurs that seemed to constantly hunt her down she hadn't given much thought to the ones that might accidentally stumble across her.

Time to go. She motioned with her thumb for Hudson to follow her backward and then turned her palm down to tell him to go slowly. He nodded, and they stepped several feet back.

The leaves shook in front of them, as if waving them away from the danger. But the warning was too late.

A juvenile *T. rex* parted the foliage, bared its teeth, and lunged toward her midsection. She shifted her hips in a belly dancer's sway, and its teeth tore through her shirt.

They were in trouble. A juvie *T. rex* was more dangerous to humans than an adult. Faster. More agile. With the bite strength of a crocodile, it only had to get one nip in to make a kill. Thankfully, this one had merely scratched her. But it wasn't done with her yet.

As the juvenile righted itself, the tip of Kaleo's whip shot out and cracked across its snout. The animal cried and snorted in pain.

The deeper roar came again. Louder. Angrier.

She didn't need to yell for them to run. Without prompting, they all sprang into action.

Kaleo took off in an easterly direction. Hudson went to follow, but the juvenile *T. rex* barreled between them. It had learned its hunting lessons well. Separate the prey. Trap them between two predators.

The adult *T. rex* roared from their right. The juvenile snapped at Hudson's heels on the left.

Oakley twirled her metal pole from her right hand to her left, then swiped it at the juvenile's stomach. A residual charge came from her hands; most of her energy had either been drained on zapping Red Grizzly or was invested in controlling her panic.

It was enough to make the animal yelp.

She followed up the shock by tripping it with the pole. A quick jab and a faster pull back so she wouldn't lose her weapon.

The animal went down, rolled in the leaves, then leaped quickly back to its feet. Not really helpful.

A sharp whistle sounded ahead of them. Definitely human. Probably Kaleo. He had memorized the location of all the traps on the island. She had tried to do the same but succeeded only in memorizing traps near the compound and the cave. Was he trying to get her to lead the *rexes* into a trap?

The ground thumped next to them as the adult *T. rex* gave up any attempt at stealth. It parted the leaves and swung its gigantic snout toward her, trying to push her toward its offspring. She jumped over a log in a full crouch to keep her profile small.

It almost worked. The snout would have sailed over her, but the adult readjusted at the last second. The snout hit her on the side of her face. Rough, porous skin scraped her cheek. The force sent her flying to the side.

She bounced into the juvenile and slammed to the ground. Her pole pinged off the log, then rolled into the underbrush.

The juvenile pivoted, ready to run at her.

She scrambled for a place to hide or escape. The backside of the log didn't offer any protection. She couldn't get to a bush in time. There was nothing.

The juvenile screeched and lunged at her again.

"No!" Hudson leaped into the air and tackled the juvie like a star defensive end.

Their momentum took them several feet through the air before they crashed down in a heap on a pile of sticks. The juvenile thrashed out with its surprisingly strong arms and snapped at Hudson with its mouth. Blood darkened his T-shirt as the serrated teeth cut through his torso.

Hudson tried to shove himself up. He fell to one knee, leaning his shoulder on the animal.

The juvenile brought both legs back. The sharp claws dug into Hudson's chest. It kicked him a few feet backward. His body slid without resistance.

A twinge constricted her chest. He had saved her from a

full frontal assault. Why had he jumped in front of her like that?

The juvenile got to its feet and glared at both of them. Hudson wasn't moving, so she became its primary focus. As if she might forget it was there, the adult rumbled just behind the juvenile.

In the distance, the whistle came again, more insistent. A trap was the only way out of this. She whistled back and took off, darting through the small gap between adult and child.

Chapter Seventeen

KALEO HAD CURLED the end of his whip around a tree first, then he'd wrapped the fabric around his fist. As the moments passed, he'd started to regret not staying back there. But finally, he'd heard Oakley's answering whistle.

Now that she was on the way, he steeled his arms. With such a big dinosaur, the only way this kind of trap worked would be to use a massive trip wire. His biceps would have to take the brunt of the force because his legs weren't up to it.

The deep pit yawned next to him, yearning for a victim. Would he be able to get both dinosaurs in there?

At the sound of thrashing in the underbrush, he gave one more short whistle, lower this time. Hopefully, it would clue her in to where he was waiting. There was no clearing here, so she wouldn't have much time to adjust her trajectory. But this was Oakley. Even at high speed, she wasn't likely to stumble into a trap, especially one that wasn't concealed.

The foliage bounced to his right just before she appeared. She ran over the top of the whip, which was lying on the ground. At the last second, she recognized the danger and darted in his direction.

He waited until he saw the dark holes of the adult *T. rex's* nostrils to pull the whip out of the dirt. It stretched taut.

The whip caught the *T. rex* around the knees. This dinosaur was immense. Probably a female from the size. The pressure on the whip almost yanked it free from his hands. But at least he had leverage from the tree anchor.

The adult let out a strangled cry as it pitched forward. It struggled to get one foot under itself, and the whip jerked out of Kaleo's hands.

Oakley grabbed it before it flew out of range. He wrapped his arms around her, and they held it together. One of the animal's legs had gotten free, but the other was still hung up on the vinyl whip. The *T. rex* was essentially doing the splits. It yanked at its trapped back leg.

They had to hang on. If they let the adult get back on its feet, they would have no chance for escape.

The juvenile came sprinting out of the forest. Kaleo couldn't have planned the next events better if he'd obedience-trained the juvenile. It saw the whip stretched about three feet off the ground and jumped to avoid it.

The juvenile landed on its mom's hip, throwing their position to the far side. The adult overadjusted to the opposite side, and their downward momentum carried them to the edge of the hole.

As it fell, the adult must have anticipated the danger. It tried to twist away from the open pit but too late.

The twisting motion threw the juvenile into the trap first.

A yowl pierced the air as the juvenile hit twenty spikes that were fixed to the bottom.

The scream was short-lived.

The adult fell on top of its offspring. With a sickening sluicing sound, it pushed the juvenile deeper onto the spikes as it, too, was impaled.

The adult merely let out a gurgling gasp as its lungs filled with blood.

Kaleo slumped to the ground, still cradling Oakley in his arms. If only they could stay this way, basking in the joy of just surviving, just being alive … together.

He pulled her close and lowered his cheek to rest on hers. "Good job, Hook."

She placed a hand on his stubble and gave him a gentle kiss. "We have to go back for Hudson. He's hurt."

Of course. Somebody was always hurt. His own stitches burned on the back of his legs from the exertion of the fight. But if they stayed here and left Hudson to die, they'd be animals, no better than the dinosaurs they'd just killed.

———

RAPTOR HAD LAID his rifle to the side and approached Auburn to find out if she was okay. But she'd shot upright and brandished some sort of porcupine quill.

He'd put his hands in the air as if she held a gun. Cane had told them all about what her poison could do—had done to Agent Brooks. The agent hadn't deserved that, but it probably wasn't her fault. Lumas was using her, just as he did everyone else.

After reassuring her that he only wanted to help in his "soothe the wild animal" voice, she stuck the quill into the dirt.

While he swiped his backpack off his shoulders, she stared sideways at the door to the sanatorium. In the chaos of the attack, Lumas had yelled her name once before he'd allowed Erman to drag him back inside. Not even willing to spend some ammunition to save his "daughter." For her, that had to be worse pain than the raptor attack.

Before she could protest, Raptor made a quick switch—swapping a first-aid kit for her laptop. He tucked the laptop in his pack, under her protests.

"I'm keeping it. Too many have died because of your

science experiments." He wagged the kit at her. "Do you want help or not?"

She looked down at the blood dripping from her arm as if she just realized she needed help. Fortunately, she didn't pull out another quill and demand the laptop. She merely clenched her jaw and nodded.

He proceeded to rip open packets of gauze pads to staunch the bleeding, then wrapped long gauze around it as a bandage. "The cuts are mostly superficial. I don't think you need stitches, but keep an eye on them to make sure they don't get infected. Raptor claws are nasty."

"They won't get infected."

Obviously, she had some anomaly to assist in that too. He shrugged. He'd barely come to terms with genetic engineering in general. Bringing the dinosaurs back was fine with him. But changing genes, manipulating embryos of people … it was just wrong. It involved too much trial and error. How much of that genetic material could have survived if they hadn't messed with it? How many people would have been alive if not for failed attempts at manipulation?

And yet, if they had succeeded right away, there would have been no need for further embryos and Oakley might not be here. His head began to pound with the complexity of it all.

When he was finished wrapping her arm, he stood and offered a hand to help her up. She took it, but once she faced him, she crossed her arms over her chest and glared at him. "I've got the same programs on my backup laptop at the lab."

He smirked. That floating lab was a thousand miles away. "So run along and grab it."

Not only would taking the laptop protect Oakley and Cane here and now, but it would likely generate more information to use against Lumas. With any luck, the lab would be shut down before Auburn returned. *If* Raptor could get anyone in the higher ranks to listen to him now that Brooks was dead.

Raptor bent to pick up his backpack.

A metallic click came from just over his shoulder. No mistaking the cocking of a weapon.

He turned his head, but the weapon wasn't pointed at him. It was aimed at Auburn.

Agent Glaser stood ten feet to the side with hatred displayed on his face. His normal gun hand was wrapped in some sort of makeshift splint, so he held the gun in his nondominant hand.

"That's not her!" Raptor yelled.

Glaser's finger trembled on the trigger. After several seconds of peering at Auburn, he shifted the gun to point at Raptor's chest. "I'm not going to shoot the wrong girl twice. I don't care who this lookalike is. Where is Oakley?"

If Glaser was tracking them like Brooks had said—which was the only way to explain his sudden appearance—why didn't he already know where Oakley was?

Then understanding filtered through him. Even though Oakley was the quarry, Glaser had planted the trackers on Raptor, not her.

He met the man's hardened gaze with a steely one of his own. Despite what Glaser thought, Oakley hadn't truly done anything wrong, considering she was innocent and shouldn't have been sentenced here in the first place. "If you're looking for the person responsible for your partner's death, you've found him. You don't need Oakley."

"Explain."

"When she discovered her tracker was inactive, she left the island to investigate her background. Then your partner and Dr. Wells arrived to replace it. I had to distract them until Oakley returned. I asked some inmates to take them some-place safe. But they were attacked on the way. Agent Jack

Fischer's blood is on my hands. Oakley wasn't even on the island at the time."

The revelation swept over Glaser's body like a wave of acid rain. He shook all over for a few seconds. His scowl faltered before reappearing in full force.

"All you've done is implicate both of you." His tone took on a mocking air. "As an officer of the United States government, I'm obliged to carry out her death sentence immediately for the crime of vacating Extinction Island without permission." Glaser stepped closer. "Take me to her, or you will face the same penalty."

So much for the truth setting him free. "Fine. This way."

He began to walk, but Glaser didn't follow. "Your other friends ran that way, followed by a *Velociraptor*. Do you think I'm stupid?"

Raptor quirked an eyebrow to say that was a distinct possibility and waited the man out for a few seconds. When he spoke, he kept his words flat. "All I can tell you is she was over here watching."

His lie wasn't enough to fool the experienced agent. "I think you would lead me in the exact opposite direction of where she is. So, let's go this way." He pointed with the weapon in the direction of where Oakley had actually been watching.

With a sigh, Raptor began walking again. Hopefully, she wasn't still in the area.

IT TOOK them several minutes of searching for them to retrace Oakley's crazed flight from the *T. rexes*. When they reached the area where she'd left Hudson, she had to hold in a gasp. He lay face up with his eyes closed and blood pooling around his mutilated stomach. How much blood could someone lose and still survive? Perhaps he was already dead.

But no, one corner of his mouth grimaced as she approached. He tried to sit up, only lifting his head an inch before it flopped back down. The movement caused a pulse of blood to dribble from his stomach wound.

"Please don't move," she said.

He didn't respond; probably couldn't do much more to move anyway. His eyes closed again.

She kneeled at his unbloodied side, placing her hands on her knees. "You saved me."

His eyes flew open. His gaze roamed around a bit before settling on her. "You're … okay." His words came in fits and gasps. "Thought … not real … dreaming."

He'd thought she was a hallucination. Not a good sign. She looked back at Kaleo with raised eyebrows to say, *Can we get him help?* Kaleo gave a barely perceptible shake of the head.

Her emotions flooded over her in confused waves. This man had killed innocent women in her name. One noble act didn't erase that horror. And yet, he'd saved her, given his life for hers. Would he soon face some sort of judgment for what he'd done? Would the end of his life make a difference?

She had no answers. Only questions. And no means to repay him for what he'd done. She could help him in only one way—to end his suffering.

"Hudson, you've always wanted to know what it's like to be near me. Would you like to feel my power?"

One eye closed, but the other stayed fixed on her. "Yes … please."

"It will take away your pain."

He grabbed her hand and squeezed.

She held on to his hand and placed her other one on his chest, directly over his heart. The current would act like the defibrillator machines they used in the hospital. Except, she'd never killed anyone this way before.

A quick glance back at Kaleo centered her. Right or

wrong, this was how she was made. This was her power lived out as she saw fit.

A deep breath. Her power fluttered and quivered inside her. She let out a small, intense pulse of electricity to disrupt the rhythm of Hudson's heart.

His forehead broke out in a sweat, and his body shook for a few seconds. Then, he went still. The man who had killed and rescued would do neither ever again.

Chapter Eighteen

"I CAN FEEL HER. She's alive," Teagan said.

Cane gave her a thumbs-up as he led the way to the place where they had separated from Penna. Her injuries hadn't seemed life threatening, but there had been a chance Fangtooth had circled back this way to finish the attack. All the more reason to get her out of here.

They found her lying in a *Heliconia* bush. The spiky, bright red and orange flowers surrounded her like a cloak of jewels or maybe a punk rocker's pointed hairdo.

Teagan touched her foot, and Penna let out a small moan. "Mom, are you okay?"

"I'm fine." She slid out of the bush to land hard on her backside.

What had looked like another branch of *Heliconia* flower followed her out. It was her bloody calf.

"Let me take a look," Cane said.

He gently rolled up the shredded material of her pants. The bite wept blood. At least Fangtooth hadn't cut much into the muscle. But it would need stitches. And it wasn't enough to just stop the bleeding. Bite marks could kill slowly, painfully, days or weeks later through infection.

He scooped some leaves off the nearest tree and handed them to Teagan. "Put some pressure on the wound. I'll be right back."

Teagan did as he instructed while he searched the area in a wide circle. Finally, he found what he was looking for—the pink trumpet tree. It would have been easier to find if the vibrant pink flower had been blooming, but that only happened during the dry season, which was still a few weeks away. Instead, he'd had to find the tree by the gray bark and the leaves in clumps of five, like fingers.

He pulled his pocketknife from his front pocket and cut off as big a branch as the small blade would allow. He returned to the women but didn't stop. He'd heard a stream only a few feet beyond. On the way by, he picked a large lily to use as a container. No need to explain his plan to Teagan; she would know already.

At the stream, he laid the lily aside and stripped the bark from the branch. Then he cut deep into the meaty part of the wood. When he had several strips cut, he soaked them in the water one at a time, in turn holding them over the lily so that the liquid dripped off.

When he had several teaspoons of liquid in the lily, he abandoned the branch and headed back.

For Penna's benefit, he said, "This tree has antibacterial properties—"

"Pink trumpet tree?" she asked.

He chuckled. Of course, she likely knew more about the plants on this island than he did.

When he pulled the leaves off the wound, much of the bleeding had stopped. "Sorry, I've got to open it up to get this in there."

"Just do it fast."

He used one hand to split the skin a fraction and the other to pour the liquid in. Penna gritted her teeth but didn't make a sound.

Footsteps distracted him. He'd thrown the tranquilizer gun down after he missed Fangtooth. It lay about ten feet away, but since it was empty, it wouldn't do much good now, except for bluffing.

The leaves parted, and Auburn broke through the foliage, holding her blood-soaked arm. Someone had wrapped it with gauze.

She spoke in a rush. "Some guy named Glaser took Raptor, and he's going after Oakley with a gun."

Her pheromones confirmed her story, but he was still skeptical. Why had she come to find him? "What's it to you if he kills her?"

A dark shadow passed over her face, followed by a flush of either embarrassment or anger. Her pheromones had suddenly become jumbled, like tangled vines.

He narrowed his eyes. "Oh, I see. Only you get to decide if she lives or dies. I should start calling you Lumas 2.0."

Auburn's gaze fell to the jungle floor. "Are you going to help them or not?"

It could be a ruse to divert him from protecting Penna and Teagan. Maybe Lumas was waiting nearby to kidnap them. Of course, hiding really wasn't Lumas's style.

Teagan put a hand on his arm. "It's okay. Go."

Her, he believed. He took off, scooping up the tranquilizer gun on the way, just in case, and holstering it in his jeans.

<hr/>

AFTER CANE'S DEPARTURE, Auburn stood awkwardly with her hands by her sides. Should she leave Penna and Teagan alone? Probably. But this was Penna—the woman she called mom until she was nine years old. The only woman she'd ever called mom.

And the woman who'd left her, discarded her like a used tissue.

When Auburn first saw Mom's face in the old botanical gardens, she was shocked at how she had aged. Penna had tanned skin and deep furrows around her eyes. But she was still a beautiful woman, with thick reddish-brown hair and high cheekbones. In the botanical center, the words hadn't come. This time would be different.

Keeping her tone even, she said, "You took me from my birth mom with a promise to raise me. Then you left."

"Yes. I failed you. It was unavoidable." Penna's short words didn't match the compassion in her tone. She reached a hand out as if to touch Auburn.

Auburn flinched away. "Unavoidable," she echoed.

"I was going to fail on some level. The situation dictated it." Penna sucked in a pained breath. "If I stayed, Lumas would make more people who were bred to kill."

"So you chose to protect those future people"—she looked pointedly at Teagan, who crouched while pressing leaves to the wound—"rather than me?"

Why had she said that? Her father hadn't abused her. He'd been good to her as she grew up: letting her play with all the research animals, funding her investigations into any area she wished, even tolerating her relationship with Adler.

He'd kept secrets, though. Big ones. And it was becoming harder and harder to believe he'd done it to safeguard his grand idea of a peacekeeping force.

Penna covered her eyes with her hand, a crestfallen gesture. "I wish I could have taken you with me. I could only escape alone."

The admission did little to fill the hole in Auburn's heart. Maybe more answers would give her something to explain it. "When this project started, what was it about?" It was probably a pointless question since she likely wouldn't believe Penna's answer. But she couldn't believe her father either.

"My firstborn son was autistic. He was locked away inside himself." Penna sighed. "I wanted to create someone who could interact with him, someone he could talk to without words. I realized too late that Lumas's goal was to control people."

Her father had a god complex. Not such a surprise. But didn't a lot of men? They all wanted to be in control.

Maybe not all of them. An image of Marcel jumped into her mind. He was the weakest man she knew. His pathetic attempts to connect with her over the years had been easily squashed by Lumas. And she'd been grateful. Why would she choose to spend time with Marcel—who had no agenda and no plans—over time with a visionary like her father? But Dad's results-driven plans were all consuming. They had overrun her.

Teagan spoke up. "He has land purchased near Paraguay."

He'd never mentioned this to Auburn, but she'd seen a few documents from that country. She'd passed them off as plans for a new research facility. "What for?"

"A new society and a new country," Teagan said. "One he can control completely."

If that was true, why wouldn't he tell her about it? Why keep her in the dark? Maybe she was just another chess piece in his game. To the point where he would leave her outside with the raptors to die. If Penna was his end goal, what did it matter to him if a dinosaur took out a pawn as long as the queen was still available for capture?

"He needs you," Auburn told Penna. "I copied your designs, but I could never create like you did."

"Even if he had me," Penna responded, "it would take twenty years to raise another generation of his assassins."

Auburn winced at the word. Was that how Penna saw her? A moment later, she shook her head. "Unfortunately not. For the last several years, he's been pouring money into my research on somatic gene editing."

Penna's mouth fell open.

A few seconds later, Teagan's did too. She whispered the words, "He is searching for ways to modify the genes of already established human beings."

To hear it spoken out loud by such an innocent girl brought a flood of shame. Auburn had drifted into the subject by accident because it was so fascinating. No, not by accident. An article had been left on the corner of her desk. Her father had denied knowing anything about it, so she'd assumed one of the other scientists had left it.

A week later, when she'd asked her father for a budget to look into it, he'd already created the account. Why hadn't she seen the threads of his manipulation earlier? But did it matter if he'd wanted the research to be her idea? That didn't mean he had dark intentions. Although it did explain why he'd always taken such chances with Oakley's and Cane's lives to get to Penna. *He can make more Oakleys and Canes if Penna or I can create them from anyone.*

OAKLEY STARED NUMBLY at Hudson's immobile body. So much blood.

Kaleo put a hand on her shoulder. "We have to go."

No, they should bury him, not just leave him for the scavengers. But this location was too close to the sanatorium. Their scent—Cane's, Teagan's, Auburn's, and hers—was all over this area. Another dinosaur couldn't be far away.

With his injured legs, Kaleo didn't have the strength to carry Hudson's body out. They'd have to leave him.

She gathered some leaves and covered him as much as possible.

They hadn't made it more than five yards before Kaleo grabbed her by the waist and spun her behind a tree. She held her breath and peeked out to spy what he'd heard.

Raptor's messy hair appeared. She almost went out to greet him, but Kaleo kept her pinned.

Then, Glaser walked out of the forest with a gun trained on Raptor's back. They both stopped beside Hudson's body.

Glaser examined the fallen man. "She was here. I guess Oakley Laveau has claimed another victim."

On that account, he wasn't wrong. Hudson's death was, in a certain way, her fault.

Kaleo motioned for her to stay put. She frowned but didn't see the sense in both of them moving together. It would just make more noise. He disappeared into the greenery with the stalking silence of a jungle cat. Even weighing seventy pounds more than her and with his injured legs, he mastered a lightness of step that she couldn't.

"I won't track her for you," Raptor said.

"You don't have to." Glaser touched a broken twig on a bush.

Shoot. They hadn't been worried about not leaving a trail.

He moved on to a disturbed patch of leaves. Now only half a dozen feet away, he lifted his head to scan the trees. She ducked behind the trunk again.

A few seconds later, a heavy grunt sounded.

She slowly peered out from her hiding place. Kaleo and Glaser rolled on the ground, grappling with each other. Raptor bent over the pair, like he wanted to enter the fray but wasn't sure how.

Kaleo grunted in pain. Glaser's blows had found his injuries. Glaser's own injured hand seemed to be wrapped up tight enough for him to use his arm as a club. They kept thrashing, each trying to gain advantage over the other.

A dark object went flying out from the tumbling mass of limbs. *The gun.*

She crept toward it.

Raptor finally grabbed Glaser by the back of the collar and yanked him off Kaleo.

Her hand closed around the gun. She lifted it and pointed it at Glaser's chest.

Anger burned inside her, sparking her electricity. Her current spiked as it hit the metal and sizzled as it went back into her skin in a continuous loop. The gun felt like an extension of her, another instrument of death.

She could kill him.

This was the man who'd shot Neve. The man who'd tried to kill her several times over because of a random dinosaur attack. She'd never meant for his partner to die.

"Why can't you leave me alone?" Her voice shook along with her trigger finger.

His eyes burned with rage as strong as hers. "He was a good man. You might not have been here, but he died so you wouldn't have to be tracked. You left the island, and you'll do it again. I won't let you get away with it." He sucked in a ragged breath. "You belong here, and you will die here."

She scoffed. "Soon, if you have anything to say about it."

He gave a wicked smile.

"Why shouldn't I kill you?"

Cane arrived then, stopping short as he took in the scene. His gaze turned to her, a plea in his eyes. She flicked a glance at Kaleo. No censure in his gaze, just concern. Raptor stood behind Glaser, his expression an impassive mask.

"Do it," Glaser said. "It's who you are."

That thought had been echoing in her head since she'd come to Extinction Island. But to hear it from a man who didn't even know about her deadly ability hit her like a sucker punch to the throat. She could blame it on the circumstances, blame it on the location, blame it on defending herself or others—but it all came down to this: killing was a part of her now. No way to go back to a time when she was innocent. Death clung to her soul like soot in a chimney and always would.

A soft chirping sound came from behind Raptor, and a

Coelophysis wandered through the foliage near Kaleo. It wasn't Cody, but it made her thoughts turn to her pet. How his big brown eyes would stare at her with easy trust. He saw the best in her. The same way Cane, Kaleo, and Raptor did. She couldn't live up to their unconditional acceptance, but maybe she should at least try.

Almost involuntarily, her finger slid off the trigger. She forced it back into position. She should kill him for what he did to Neve, what he wanted to do to her. She imagined putting a bullet in his brain. Blood would splatter on Raptor, who stood behind, and Kaleo, who stood to the right of him. The image cracked her resolve in half. Her finger slipped from the trigger a second time.

Movement drew her gaze to over Raptor's shoulder. A mottled scaly head with yellow crests poked out of the greenery. *Mutant Mantis.*

Had it been drawn by the blood or by her?

The creature didn't look at Hudson's body or make a move toward any of the men. It searched the area until it found her, then its gaze locked on, penetrating and immobile.

It could sense her. Or *see* her electricity.

For a brief second, nothing in their area moved. The humans stood frozen, barely daring to breathe.

Mutant Mantis flared its nostrils.

In slow increments, she arced the gun toward the creature. But as soon as the aim of the gun left his chest, Glaser rushed at her, shoving the weapon more toward the dinosaur.

A blast kicked the gun out of her hand and sent it flying into the bushes.

Mutant Mantis roared.

As Glaser took her to the ground, she chanced a quick glance at the dinosaur. She'd missed. Its only injury was the dried-up hole in its shoulder from Glaser's previous shot.

Her back hit the dirt, the shock expelling both air from her lungs and electricity from her body.

Glaser yelped in surprise and quickly rolled off her.

Mutant Mantis charged.

The agent jumped to get out of the way but didn't quite make it. The dinosaur hit his side with a glancing blow. He grunted in pain.

She jumped around the backside of a nearby tree just as the animal sent one of its deadly legs crashing into the front. Bits of bark and chunks of wood flew past her on either side.

A loud crack rang out. A whip?

"I can't hold it!" Kaleo yelled. "Run!"

She darted from her cover and ran at an angle. She glanced back to see Kaleo's whip wrapped around one long appendage. He had tripped the monster, but while on its back, it flailed its other leg dangerously.

He ducked, narrowly avoiding a swipe to the head.

Mutant Mantis spied her. It rolled to its side and swiped the whip off with its other leg, knocking Kaleo and Raptor down in the process.

She tore through the trees. No destination. No weapons. If only she still had her metal pole.

The bushes behind her thrashed with the dinosaur's pursuit. Its shriek pierced her eardrums. No time to slow down to cover her ears.

She couldn't hide either. The electricity in her core would make her stand out like a beacon to this creature.

Unless she found a way to hide her electricity. An idea blasted through her fear. What if she hid herself in something that would disperse her current?

Like water.

But she'd already turned away from the stream.

With each lunging step, Mutant Mantis thudded against the ground with its front appendages. Too close.

She kept pushing her legs, running with all her strength.

A black iron structure came up on her right, covered in vines and branches. The remains of a gate.

Hope flashed in her heart. If this was a gated community, it would have had at least one large pool, right?

On her next step, she pivoted to face the open mouth of the gate. She ran through as Mutant Mantis struggled to make the sharp turn.

The problem with this plan became clear immediately. While looking for the pool, she was exposed in the open on what would have been a beautiful common area and gorgeous front porches. The buildings sat packed together with only half a dozen feet between them.

Mutant Mantis came screaming at her.

She dashed behind the nearest building. Nothing back here except cracked patios and decaying fences. This part of the complex backed up to the trees.

The impression of movement came from behind one of the windows. No time to worry about people. Even if someone from the gang saw her, it didn't matter at this point.

Based on the scratching sounds, the dinosaur was coming around the corner to her rear. She slunk to the front, slipped through a porch with a tattered hammock swinging in the breeze, and moved to the rear of the next building.

A carport tilted precariously on its wooden legs. Not an improvement.

She kept moving.

Mutant Mantis continued to make shuffling sounds behind her, but it seemed to have trouble navigating between the potholed concrete and the overgrown greenspace.

Finally, around the fourth building, she found water. Not a pool but a pond.

The sickly green color made her rethink her plan. Anything could be hiding in its murky moss-colored depths. But there was no getting around it. A high trellis separated this property from the next. Pretty purple flowers still dotted the iron lattice.

She turned to retreat.

Nope. Mutant Mantis blocked her escape, heaving angry breaths in and out.

It charged at her, its long limbs swinging.

She had no choice. With a huge breath of her own, she dove into the slimy water.

The lake closed over her like a grimy cocoon. She ignored the heavy feel of it, like the liquid was a little too substantial, and adopted a chest stroke under the water. She had to get as far out into the lake as possible before surfacing.

When her arm muscles ached and her lungs burned, she floated vertically for a few seconds and then let her head rise above the surface up to her eyeballs.

Mutant Mantis rutted around on the bank as if confused about where she went. She floated about fifteen yards from shore.

Ever so slowly, she lifted her mouth out of the water to take a quiet breath.

Mutant Mantis stopped and stared in her direction. *Crap.* Now she had to hope this thing couldn't swim.

It didn't enter the water. Instead, it sidled along the edge of the shore.

She swiveled her head around to judge distances. About twenty yards to the other end of the lake, and about twenty-five to the western side of the lake. The western side was farthest from Mutant Mantis and offered concealment in the form of the back side of the trellis.

Time to see how long she could hold her breath. She sucked in air until her lungs hurt, then she slipped under the water again. If she pushed hard, she could maybe make it in one breath, giving her precious seconds to escape.

Two strokes into her swim, something brushed her leg. A sodden branch? Some sort of freshwater seaweed?

Several strokes later, something more solid hit her calf. Small pinpricks of pain spread from the site. Like being bit by ten mosquitos at once. Fear trickled down her spine. Piranha? No, something bigger.

Whatever it was must not be able to see her any better than she could see it, because that was a test bite. She pushed her arms and legs harder, while shifting her gaze to keep an eye all around her. Probably only ten yards from shore now.

A thick branch darted across her distance vision.

No, not a branch. A tail with spikes on the end.

The tail whipped around out of sight, which meant the animal had turned back to come at her. She swung her arms and did a barrel roll downward.

A fifteen-foot-long creature with a crocodile's head and a dinosaur's body sailed through the water above her. Some sort of hybrid.

It angled its head down, attempting to take a bite on its way by.

She pushed a pulse of electricity at it, while still pumping her arms and legs. At least her electricity traveled farther through the water.

The creature shuddered. It had felt the pulse, but it merely tilted its head to look at her, undeterred.

She'd have to hit it harder. Internally, she amplified the charge in her cells.

The creature floated out of her line of sight. Her lungs burned for air, but she couldn't surface or she'd be easy prey for this thing. Pinpricks of light danced across her vision.

The creature hadn't come back. Was it waiting her out?

Maybe if she hovered near the surface, it would think she'd gone up, and then it would reveal itself. She swiped her arms a few times to raise her position in the water.

Just before her head would break the surface, she hovered. It took every ounce of self-control not to breach the water and take in great gulps of fresh air when it was so near. She blinked to clear the stars out of her eyes.

When she opened them, the creature was swimming for

the trunk of her body at full speed, mouth agape. She twisted to the left and directed a pulse at the creature's head.

The pulse disoriented it enough that she shoved it off to the side. Then, on the way by, she grabbed its tail and shocked it with everything she had left in her body.

The creature vibrated and shook for several seconds.

Her vision began to darken, but she held on for as long as she could. When she let go, it dropped through the water toward the bottom.

She propelled herself out of the water and sucked in a sweet lungful of air. The darkness receded as she scanned the lake.

Mutant Mantis hadn't left. However, she'd been underwater for so long that it had stopped traversing around the lake. It stood across from her on the eastern shore. And she was closer to the western bank than she'd anticipated—only a few yards away.

She began swimming again at the same time Mutant Mantis began running in her direction.

Chapter Nineteen

AFTER JUMPING out of the water, Oakley flipped her wet hair out of her eyes and checked Mutant Mantis's position. Halfway around the lake.

She slipped behind the trellis and around the front of the building. She kept to the edge of the common area until she reached the gate again. Just as the jungle closed over her, she caught a glimpse of Mutant Mantis rounding the corner of the building. She would lose it in the trees.

In a zigzag pattern, she ran roughly toward the area of the bunker and the shack, not sure which one to return to. Glaser knew the location of the bunker but probably not the shack.

Half a mile later, she heard a faint birdsong that sounded more like a whistle than a bird. Kaleo? Or Cane? She gave a soft return whistle.

Within a few minutes, Kaleo found her. She sank into his embrace, where her head fit perfectly in the hollow space between his pecs, and breathed in his scent of coconut and hibiscus. She let his strength seep into her and restore her.

When they pulled apart, he explained that Cane went to help Penna, Teagan, and Auburn get back to the shack so

Wells could check their injuries. Kaleo had told Raptor to pursue Glaser, and he hadn't run into Raptor again.

A tremor ran through her. She remembered her finger on the trigger, ready to end Glaser's life. The anger. The sense of power. And the ease with which she could end him, be done with him. That was exactly why she hadn't squeezed the trigger—ending his life was too easy an accomplishment. She would have felt relief, and somehow that was wrong.

Tears welled up in her eyes. She swiped at one as it dripped down.

"Hey, what is it?" Kaleo wiped away a tear from the other eye.

"I'm becoming someone I don't want to be." She couldn't even say the word *killer*. "But it seems inevitable." More tears flowed unchecked. "I'm so different from who I was when I came here. I'm afraid I can never get that back."

He cupped her cheek. She tried to turn her gaze down, but he tilted her head up to force her to look at him. "The scars from what we've done stick with us. They become thick spots in our souls, like ridges we have to climb on the landscape of our choices. But we have new choices every day. You can be whoever you want to be." He kissed her gently on the lips. "Your scars have made you different, yes. They've made you stronger than when you came here."

If stronger meant more hardened, more ruthless, then he was right. She pulled away and began walking.

"You know I've done some horrible things too."

At his words, she glanced back at him. His head hung low. He was referring to the incident that brought him to Extinction Island. He'd beat a man to death and accidentally thrown a girl through a glass door where she'd cut her neck and bled to death. Truly awful. But he wasn't that person anymore.

"You've changed for the better."

She hadn't reformed since coming to Extinction Island. Quite the opposite. The island had brought out the worst in her, although it didn't seem fair to blame a location for her failings.

They resumed walking. Both of them silent, lost in their own thoughts.

They were the last to arrive at the shack, well after dark. Cane and Raptor each gave her a hug as she entered.

"Did you get Glaser?" she asked Raptor.

He shook his head. Unfortunately, the FBI agent had escaped by running headlong through a pack of *Triceratops*. Raptor wasn't willing to take the risk of being trampled, so he'd let him go.

Oakley patted his arm. He'd done the best he could.

One member of the group hung back. Auburn stood off to the side, fiddling with the hair at the nape of her neck. Her right arm was wrapped in a thick bandage. Thank God she was alive. Why hadn't she tried to get back inside the sanatorium when Red Grizzly attacked?

Their eyes met, and an uneasy feeling spread through Oakley's gut. This was their last safe house. If Auburn had an eye implant or even if she just planned to report back to Lumas, this location could be compromised too. Cane must have made the decision to allow her to come here. Where would his kindness lead?

Oakley checked on Penna first, who was getting stitched up by Wells. Then, she made her way to Neve, who sat upright on a cot with Taye by her side. She gave them both a quick hug.

"I hear you found the guy who did this to me," Neve said.

She nodded. "But he got away again."

"That's okay." Neve gave her a small smile. "I don't need you to take care of him for me."

Oakley pressed her lips together firmly. Neve would say to leave the judging to God, but where was God when Glaser shot her in the back?

Despite all she'd been through, Neve looked good. And

the shooting seemed to have brought her and Taye closer. Oakley squeezed her hand one more time and left her to rest.

Wells had finished with Penna. She motioned for Kaleo to lay on a cot. Blood had begun to seep through the back of the new pants he wore. Oakley's heart stuttered. She hadn't given enough thought to his healing. He'd been pushing himself too hard.

"Nice," Wells said as she took off the bandages. "Don't let the blood fool you. These are healing well for being just a few days old. And no signs of infection."

Oakley breathed a bit easier. No harm done.

Teagan cleared her throat. "Excuse me, I need to talk to all of you."

Auburn stood, presumably to leave.

But Teagan put up a hand. "He is father to both of us. You have a say in this too."

So this was about Lumas. Should be interesting.

"Receiving thoughts from him is hard. He altered his system with something, but even aside from that, he has a strong mental wall to climb."

"What do you mean?" Oakley asked.

"I haven't been around a lot of people. But I'm discovering that some hide their thoughts. They have walls in place. They keep their brain cells from firing when it comes to certain subjects or emotions. If the cells don't fire, I can't read the signals." She looked pointedly at Auburn. "You do this, but I can read your pheromones to fill in the gaps."

Auburn's shoulders slumped a little. Shouldn't she enjoy being compared to her "father"?

"That being said," Teagan continued. "I did get some thoughts from him."

Everyone in the shack hung on her words.

She flipped her brown braid over her shoulder and drew in a deep breath. "He wants to create a closed society with enhanced humans that he alone controls. Undetectable-murder contracts would be the source of funding. We"—she gestured at Oakley, Auburn, Penna, and Cane—"would be the first people to live there."

"So, if this is a closed society, does he still want to force us to procreate?" Oakley asked. "Are we to help raise his next generation of killers?"

Auburn spoke up. "Not exactly. I helped him expand his research to include somatic gene editing. Using this method, he can alter anyone's genes at any time. No embryos necessary."

Oakley shook her head. This seemed too far-fetched. "This isn't possible. You can't inject some serum into a normal person and have them grow poisonous darts in their neck."

"You're right," Auburn said. "He can't change large morphological characteristics. But he can change the nature of the cells inside the body. For instance, he can't replicate the pathway you have from the electrical node in your brain to your hands. But he could use gene editing to change all the cells in a person's hands to electrocytes that would essentially generate a similar charge."

Oh no. They could not let Lumas continue his manipulations on more unsuspecting people.

Teagan's mouth turned down in an expression of regret. "For this reason, I believe we have to stop him at all cost." Then, her mouth firmed into a thin line. "I will *not* let him use my mom again."

———

CANE MOVED TO THE DOOR. This conversation would most likely degenerate into an argument between Oakley wanting to take Lumas out and Auburn wanting to convince Lumas to change. They would then look to him for advice. He didn't have any.

Just as he opened the door, Wells put a hand on his arm

and quirked an eyebrow. He nodded to let her know he was fine with the company. They slipped through the door and walked to the edge of the clearing.

"Are you okay?" Wells asked.

He gave her a small smile. If he only had a dollar for every time she'd said those words since she'd arrived. She thought of everyone else first. His heart ached to get closer to her, but there was something she didn't know about him. "I didn't just go along with killing Adler. I participated. Tried to kill him myself."

Her mouth dropped open in shock. This was why he hadn't told her before. Now she would look at him differently. He couldn't hide himself forever. This was his essence, his core.

"I can't describe how awful I felt when I truly wanted to kill him. Like the anger was this hard burning rock in my gut. I thought it wouldn't go away until I ended him. But he's gone, and the rock is not."

"And you think this situation is the same?"

"I don't know." He raked a hand through his hair. "I just don't want to feel this way anymore. I want to go back to when I didn't hate anyone."

"Do you hate Lumas?"

"Part of me does. For what he's done. But …" How could he make her understand? This went deeper. "I used to imagine what my father would be like. Of course, he had a special ability like me, and he'd use it to bring justice, like a comic book hero. I built him up in my mind so much I can't wrap my head around the manipulative, greedy man he turned out to be, much less get on board with eliminating him."

He stopped pacing and pointed to a log for them to sit on.

"I don't want any part of this."

Wells put her hand on his. "You can't abstain."

"Why not?"

"What he wants to do—manipulate people's DNA, control them, make them kill for his idea to lead a country—it's evil. No question."

"But what if he's not an evil person?"

She barked out a laugh. "We are all evil people in various places inside us. Even you, Pastor Cane Leblanc. What matters is whether we are fighting that evil—or feeding it—both inside and out."

He squeezed her hand as her words sunk deep into the crevices in his heart. She was right. The reason he wanted to stay out of this fight was because he didn't trust himself not to give in to the hate. *Lord, help me to follow your way of both peace and justice.*

Cane breathed a little easier. "I won't kill him."

"Sounds good to me," Auburn said from about fifteen feet away.

He hadn't heard her come out. A moment of silence passed as they assessed each other. She probably came after him because she needed him as an ally. He could oblige.

Auburn hitched a thumb toward the shack. "Now would you like to come back in and help me convince Shocker Girl?"

———

LUMAS PACED the worn wooden floors of the sanatorium. Darkness had fallen half an hour before, leaving the place in shadows except for the few flashlights he'd spaced around. Unbelievable that Penna had lived in this dusty, rundown place for fifteen years. She must have paced these floors herself as she was wont to do during her extended creation periods. Had she ever thought of him and the life she'd left?

He'd tried his best to make her happy. Indulged all her scientific whims. Spent millions on expanding her mind. Never said no to a pet project. Even the little jaunt into bat radar that left him disposing of a number of blind squirrels.

All the support she could ask for in pursuing her dreams, and still, she'd left.

Even harder to understand was why she'd left Auburn behind. Probably because she was going to start a new life with a new child. *Teagan*. His child by blood, but she didn't know him. The same as Cane. These women had no right to keep his children from him. Eloisa, Cane's mother, had already paid for her treachery with her life. But with Penna, it was different. He needed her. They could still get back the relationship they'd lost. Besides, the best punishment would be to force her to support *his* dreams for a change.

He kicked at a loose piece of flooring. What was taking Erman so long to return from his mission? He'd given an abbreviated report by text, but Lumas wanted all the details.

As if on cue, the front door rattled. Lumas crossed through the dilapidated foyer to remove the wooden beam and open it.

Erman came inside with a road weary grin. He'd made it through the jungle at night. Good thing he'd been better accustomed to tracking and avoiding predators than his former boss. They'd found the headless chewed up remains of Quincy Ness half a mile away.

Whenever they were ready to leave, Erman would have to convince the sailors on the waiting boat to say Ness had died onboard and was buried at sea. The crew would agree because they wouldn't want to pay the consequences for letting Ness illegally disembark on Extinction Island.

"They're in an old shack," Erman said. "Packed in there like sardines."

"You're sure they didn't see you following?"

"I didn't follow them. I tracked them." He snatched a water bottle and downed half of it. "At least a dozen, maybe more in there, including your girl."

His heart pounded. *Auburn was alive.* Erman hadn't mentioned her in his text message. She'd been too close to that large *Utahraptor* when it attacked. So, he had to shut the door. It couldn't be avoided. But he smiled at her resourcefulness.

"She convinced them to take her in," Lumas mumbled, mostly to himself. Perhaps she was even now working things inside the group to his advantage. Except if she wanted him to know she was there, she would have turned her phone on to signal him.

He might need her there. Or he might not. All he really needed was her laptop, and he'd recovered it an hour ago from a backpack in a nearby bush. The bag had nothing else useful, so he left it where it lay.

He made one more restless trip down the hallway. "Let's go."

"Back there?" Erman asked.

He gave the man his most confident smile. "I'm tired of waiting for them to find us. Let's stir up the fight this time."

Chapter Twenty

EVERYONE in the shack bedded down where they could. Oakley curled further into her blanket, trying to find a comfortable position on the floor. They only had so many cots in the shack, and Kaleo needed a good night's sleep. Walking all day, running from dinosaurs, and working on healing his legs had driven dark circles deep under his eyes. His normal ready-for-anything expression had been replaced by resignation.

She rolled over, and a floorboard creaked. A pair of suspicious eyes darted in her direction. Auburn lay on the floor on the other side of Kaleo's cot, her oatmeal-colored shirt made her more visible in the low light. Just what Oakley needed—an angry stare-down while she slept.

To be fair, trust wasn't forthcoming on either side of their relationship. Auburn claimed Lumas killed Agent Brooks, but she had given him the quill. Didn't that make her partly responsible? At least Auburn didn't have her laptop. Raptor said he'd confiscated it and put it in his backpack, but then after Agent Glaser led him away at gunpoint, someone must have taken it because it wasn't in his backpack when he returned. For the moment at least, Auburn had absolutely no way to kill her. Oakley gave a wink, which earned a scowl.

She'd just closed her eyes when the coded tapping began on the door of the shack. Raptor was the only person who wasn't here. He'd come to the shack briefly, then said he had something to take care of at the bunker.

She moved to the door and whispered, "Raptor?"

"It's me," he answered from the other side.

She removed the wooden board, allowed him to come in, and barred the door behind him.

"What were you up to?"

"Several things. I had two of the FBI agents help me move Agent Brooks's body, minus the poisonous quill, to their camp. The assumption is that he had a heart attack. They will call in the morning to have him picked up. I also didn't want to leave my phone in the bunker for Lumas to take if he comes back. But most of all, I needed to shower."

True, hygiene was a problem at the shack. The closest she'd gotten to a shower in days was the dunk in the lake while escaping from Mutant Mantis. But he went on to explain exactly why he'd needed to shower immediately.

"I don't know how Glaser planted those hairlike trackers on me and not you, but I scrubbed to get them all off and then I changed clothes. I left my backpack at the bunker too because if the trackers are on it, I probably can't wash it enough to remove them all from the fabric."

She motioned for him to sit against the wall, then she handed him a blanket and sat next to him.

"What's the plan?" he asked.

She shrugged. "Ideally, we kill or capture Lumas and Glaser, then definitely kill Fangtooth and Mutant Mantis."

"So, no plan yet."

"Nope, we spent pretty much the whole evening debating the kill-or-capture issue."

Thankfully, he didn't ask which side she came down on.

Though she'd argued for death, she hadn't been able to pull the trigger when it had come down to it with Glaser. And Cane's words continued to haunt her. *You are more than the sum of your choices.* If that was true for her, was it true for Lumas? Or Glaser? Was there a core of something inside them that had value just because they were human? The US government didn't agree. They sentenced people to death all the time, the instrument of death just happened to be dinosaurs.

Raptor smirked. "What did I always tell you about capturing alligators?"

"Use their strength as their weakness." For alligators, it had been their barrel roll meant to throw attackers off their back. She'd learned to balance through it, to let it happen and allow the animal to tire itself out. Then the capture was easy.

In fact, she'd been instinctively doing that since she'd arrived on the island. Running downhill away from Camocroc because its strong legs had no balance going downslope. Diving into the lake because there was no way Mutant Mantis's deadly appendages would allow it to swim. Even jumping over the whip and turning on a dime to escape the stronger, faster *T. rexes* because they couldn't change direction as quickly.

So, what strengths did her enemies possess that could possibly be their downfall? Lumas—his confidence to control every situation. Glaser—his persistence fueled by intense anger. Mutant Mantis—those whipping arms and how it could see her better than any other dinosaur. Finally, Fangtooth—its ability to read every action or intention.

Each had different strengths, but every one of them had a single desire in common: to destroy Oakley.

Somehow, she had to come up with a plan that would fool Lumas into overconfidence, anger Glaser into making a mistake, disarm Mutant Mantis, and trick Fangtooth with something it wouldn't see as a threat. A tall order.

She and Raptor stayed up well into the night discussing

different strategies and possibilities. Once, she glanced over at Auburn. Her eyes were closed, but that didn't mean she was sleeping. Why had she even come here? Lumas had locked her out of the sanatorium, but she could have gone back later. She probably still would. Whatever plan they settled on, the whole of it would depend on Auburn. If she alerted Lumas to the possibility of a plan, it would fail.

—

ERMAN POINTED to the rundown shack, one of the few wooden structures around with an intact door. The early morning light made the weathered gray boards of the walls seem almost pink against the dark wood of the door. Only that door stood between Lumas and his prize ... or prizes, depending on how many he could capture.

"What's the play here, mate?" Erman whispered, shifting his backpack on his shoulders. "There's likely to be too many in there for a frontal assault."

Of course, he was right. But stealth always trumped strength. So, how to get Penna to come out? She was the one he truly needed. In so many ways.

Keep this about business. Auburn had gone as far as she could with the somatic gene editing. He needed Penna's genius. The way she managed to create was the genetic equivalent of Mozart. The genes seemed to reveal their song to her, and she would recombine the notes into a unique symphony. No one else could do what she could.

The fact he also wanted her back in his bed didn't make this personal. Taking Penna would probably mean taking Teagan as well. A bonus, and yet, the girl was a threat. The whole idea of her manipulating his mind unnerved him. When Penna had set out to create someone to understand and communicate with her autistic son, she'd succeeded and then some.

He wrangled his thoughts back to the problem at hand. This adrenaline pod had a way of causing all his neurons to fire constantly, scattering his ideas like sparks shooting out from a sparkler. Now, how to get Penna?

"First step, we need to lure some of the men away."

"What about a nearby fire?" Erman asked.

"Could be hard to start one in the moist jungle."

"True."

"Although …" Lumas walked around the corner to peer at the back side of the building and then returned to Erman. "We could use a directed fire to smoke them out. This place has ventilation slots in the back."

If only they had something to contain the fire so it didn't burn itself out. Lumas searched in a circle until he found an old plastic container that had apparently held mac and cheese at some point.

Inside it, he shoved the driest vegetation he could find. "I'll light this and place it near the vents. You be ready to grab Penna and maybe Teagan too."

———

AUBURN ROLLED OVER, let out a cough, then tried to go back to sleep. Just as her eyes drifted closed, the urge to cough again was overwhelming. As isolated as she was at the lab, she hadn't had a virus in years. Wouldn't it be ironic to come to the jungle to face fearsome creatures, only to be taken down by a cold or the flu? What would Cane say about it? Some sort of hogwash about never having control of our fate in the first place.

She coughed as quietly as she could. No need to wake the others. Oakley and Raptor had been up most of the night plotting. They kept their ideas centered on how to bring Dad to the authorities, but one thing was clear—Oakley wasn't happy about it. She wanted to kill him.

No matter what they said he'd done, Auburn couldn't sanction that.

Dad was controlling and single-minded and set on fulfilling his own ideas, but he wasn't a monster. Cane's mom had threatened his work. He might have had reason to want her out of the way, but that didn't mean he killed her. And he might have frightened Eric, but he never would have hurt him. Whatever Dad had done, he'd done because he thought it necessary. Was that any different from Oakley wanting to kill him right now? Or any different from why Penna had left her alone with him in the first place?

She sought out Penna, who lay on a cot with her leg bandaged. Teagan slept on the floor at her feet. Could Teagan's declaration that Dad had bought land to create his own society be believed? Maybe it was meant to be a home base for the peacekeeping force he'd always talked about.

Another cough racked her body. She rolled over toward the window. Curls of smoke drifted in through the tightly fitting slats. A fire outside?

She coughed again. This one began to wake some of the others. A few more people began to cough.

She sat up and instinctively found Oakley. She'd ponder why at a later time. "Smoke is coming in. We have to get out."

Oakley's eyes went wide. "Everyone evacuate," she called to the group.

A dark-skinned man whom Auburn didn't know began helping the injured lady that Oakley had called Neve.

Wells came over to check on Penna. "Can you walk?"

"Slowly," Penna answered.

Wells slipped under Penna's arm and then nodded at Teagan. "Take her other arm."

Auburn let out a small sigh of relief. She should probably be helping Penna too, but anger still tightened her gut. Forgiving fifteen years of abandonment wasn't easy.

She followed as they went out into the surrounding jungle. Wells led them to a log where Penna could sit.

Auburn hung back, keeping an eye on the trees for dangerous creatures. The guys had gone behind the shack and returned with a half-melted plastic container. This wasn't a natural fire.

Movement drew her gaze to the area behind Penna. Before she could say anything, shots rang out from the completely opposite direction.

Her head whipped around. Kaleo, Cane, and Oakley took off in the direction of the shots. The dark-skinned man stayed with Neve about twenty feet away on another log. He was speaking softly to her.

Auburn swiveled her head back to Penna, and her heart galloped in her chest. Wells lay unconscious on the ground. Teagan was in the process of slumping to the ground. And Erman was scooping an unconscious Penna into his arms.

She almost cried out. Almost.

But if her dad had his end goal—Penna—maybe he'd stop hunting everyone else. This could all be over without any more bloodshed. At one time, Penna had agreed to stay with him … with them. What did it matter if she was forced to keep that promise?

Erman briefly locked eyes with her. He tilted his head to indicate she should follow him, then he ran into the trees. But she didn't move. Like her feet had snaking vines wrapped around them, chaining her to the dirt. This was her chance to reunite with her father. So why couldn't she make her feet move?

"Hey! Help me." The dark-skinned man shot her a glare. He came running over to Wells and Teagan.

She couldn't blame him. She was standing here like a statue, caught between two worlds, unable to decide for herself where she belonged. She wrapped her arms around her torso and stayed frozen while he worked to revive the women. Maybe if she didn't move, she wouldn't have to choose.

Little by little, reality seeped in. Erman would tell Dad she hadn't followed. In his mind, she'd already made her choice.

But if she'd made a choice, it was the most noncommittal choice ever. She hadn't rejoined Dad, yet she hadn't kept him from taking Penna. Did Penna deserve protecting? The woman had rejected her.

Auburn looked down at Teagan's still form. For better or worse, Penna had been there for her biological daughter. Sweet, innocent, fifteen-year-old Teagan didn't deserve to lose her mom like Auburn had.

With a low growl, she ran after Erman.

She caught up to him only a few minutes later. He had to move slowly because he was still carrying Penna. "Don't do this."

He stopped and looked over his shoulder. "Follow or don't. It doesn't matter, but I'm taking her back to Lumas."

She flipped one of her poisonous quills from the back of her neck. "No, you're not."

Erman scowled at her but said nothing. He bent over and softly laid Penna on the leaf carpet. As he stood, he reached for his gun behind his back.

She let the quill fly, aiming for his center body mass. If she could hit any part of him, he'd be dead in seconds. Except this was the first time she'd ever tried to kill anyone.

He moved faster than she'd anticipated. And she hadn't accounted for the fact he might roll to the side.

His chest twisted, bringing his body sideways and causing her dart to sail just past his right bicep.

As he rolled, he squeezed the trigger.

The bullet hit her in the stomach with the force of a charging bull. She fell to the ground. Suddenly, her aching arm seemed like a paper cut compared to the pain in her abdomen.

Erman calmly replaced his weapon in his back waistband and picked Penna up again. With a last *I told you so* glance, he took off and disappeared into the trees.

Blood seeped onto her T-shirt, turning the oatmeal color an odd shade of dark purple. Lots of blood. Too much blood. This was bad.

Coldness enveloped her. She shivered as she lay back in the leaves. They were a soft pillow.

She should get up. Go search for help. But she couldn't summon the energy.

Her vision closed in. Before darkness claimed her, she frowned at her desolate last thought: Had Erman taken it upon himself to protect the objective or had her dad given him permission to eliminate her if necessary?

Chapter Twenty-One

"TOO MANY PEOPLE getting shot around here." Wells's shaky voice broke through the haze of Auburn's aching head.

Why did her head hurt so much? And why was she having such trouble opening her eyes?

Wells. Something had been wrong with her. Oh yeah. Erman had drugged her and Teagan. Auburn had gone after him. Penna—

A groan escaped as a flash of pain lit up her left side.

"How is her pulse?" Wells asked.

Someone pressed on her right wrist.

"Thready." Was that Oakley's voice? Auburn had never heard that note of panic from her.

The pain forced another groan. It wasn't a flash this time. It was a rabid dog using its teeth to rip and tear the flesh from her stomach. If only she could scream to let out the pain, but she didn't have the energy.

Her heart fluttered, and her head rolled to the side.

Open your eyes!

But her body wouldn't respond.

A wave of awful chills cascaded over her.

"She's crashing!" Wells yelled. "Oakley, you need to—"

The chills took over, swept her away. Auburn's hearing diminished. Everything was muffled. She couldn't fight the darkness.

⎯

"JUST A SHORT BURST," Wells instructed, "directly over her heart."

Oakley placed two fingers on the side of her sister's chest. She swallowed hard and then let a fraction of her electricity flow through her cells.

Auburn's body flopped with the current. Hopefully, she didn't pull out the stitches Wells had just placed in her side after removing the bullet.

Wells placed her fingers on the inside of Auburn's wrist. She shook her head. "Again."

Oakley shocked her for a second time, adding a little more juice.

Wells checked and frowned. "Again."

She repeated the process.

Another check; Wells shook her head. "More current."

Oakley gathered her anxiety and confusion about the woman lying on the table, now pale with blood loss. Who knew where Auburn's loyalties lay, but Oakley couldn't let her die. It was more than their biological connection. Deep down, on some level she couldn't name, they were the same. Always pushing through, always digging for the truth, always messing it up.

The shock rocked Auburn's torso into the air. It flopped back down with a thump.

Wells didn't even check her pulse, just told Oakley to do it again.

She gave it her all, then had to catch Auburn before her body flopped right off the cot.

Wells grabbed the wrist to check. A grin burst across her pixie features. "Weak, but steady."

Auburn's eyelids fluttered.

As Oakley stepped away to allow Wells to continue working on her, she rubbed her two fingers against her palm. A wave of relief crested inside her, and she let out a small smile. Cane caught her eye and winked. He'd picked up on what she was feeling. This was the first time her power had been used to save someone.

Chapter Twenty-Two

OAKLEY POUNDED a fist against one of the wooden planks in the wall of the shack. "We can make all the plans we want, but if we don't know where they're located, we won't accomplish anything."

Last night, their plans had centered on the fact that they held all the cards, and Lumas had none, which meant he would have to seek them out, probably at the bunker. But he'd found them here, and now he had Penna. How would they figure out where he had taken her?

Both Raptor and Kaleo gave her empty stares. Raptor had an idea for how to lure Glaser into a trap, not Lumas. And Cane hadn't even participated in the conversation. He hovered near Wells, helping with small tasks and praying over each patient.

Neve spoke up from the corner cot. "He might go back to the sanatorium in the hope you will come looking for Penna and he can capture all of you."

"Maybe," Oakley said. But it didn't sound right. Yes, Lumas might like to have her, Auburn, Cane, and Teagan, but he wouldn't be stupid enough to risk losing Penna in the process. He'd hide and take what he wanted when the opportunity presented itself. Like he had in the wee hours of the night.

Auburn's voice was hollow, almost childlike when she spoke. "There's another bunker on the island."

Seriously? Oakley just stared at her, afraid to break the spell with a question.

After a long minute, Auburn continued, "It's different. Not underground."

"Where?" Kaleo asked.

She turned sad eyes to him. A strange pang of empathy hit Oakley. How many times had Auburn flip-flopped on which side to choose? At least Oakley had never had to question who deserved to be protected.

"It's in the main level of the ruins of a church in Cartago." She focused on the wooden slats on the ceiling. "Dad, um, Asperten put bars around the open windows and concreted over the missing roof of one of the spires in the church. But there aren't any tunnels in or out of this one."

"Same keypad entrance?" Oakley asked.

"Yes, same code, 5975."

Teagan let out a little gasp. "Mom's birthday."

"What if he's changed it?" Oakley asked.

"Why would he? As far as he knows, none of you have that code. It's used for remote sites with Asperten-only access where the keypad won't support a twelve-digit code. I'm the only other one who knows it, and Erman will tell him I'm dead." Auburn pushed up to her elbows. "I'm coming with you."

Wells must have heard because she rushed over, followed by Cane. "I just dug a slug out of your gut. I don't recommend any kind of travel for a week."

Auburn shrugged. "You said it didn't hit anything vital."

Oakley suppressed a smile. In some ways, they were more alike than different.

While Auburn continued to "discuss" the issue with Wells,

Cane drew up next to Oakley. "Is this a capture or kill situation?"

She firmed her jaw. "Whatever is necessary."

"The problem with having these powers—"

"Is that we have to decide how to use them. I know." She folded her arms across her chest. "What about 'You are more than the sum of your choices'?"

He pinched his lips together before responding. "That's true, because the past is the past. But your choices do matter. They reflect who you are right now."

"Well, if you come along and bring Little Miss Lumas-is-just-misunderstood, then more people will be advocating for capture."

He barked out a laugh at her challenge, though the waves of anxious pheromones rolled off him. He didn't want to do this. Neither did she.

Even Kaleo must have sensed it, because he clapped a hand on Cane's shoulder. "You can sit this one out."

She resisted the urge to push soothing pheromones in Cane's direction. He'd only scowl at her when he figured it out.

Finally, he shook his head. "No way."

Oakley kneeled beside her sister's cot. Wells must have given up arguing because Auburn was putting her boots on. "Do you have an exact location on this bunker?"

Neve rolled over on the cot next to Auburn. "I know where the ruins are. Just a couple of blocks inside Cartago from the east."

They spent some time discussing the layout of the church and the city, then moved on to what obstacles they might face coming in from that direction. Neve was a wealth of information.

Now that she had a picture in her mind of the area, Oakley turned to Kaleo. They needed to tap his memory again. "What traps can we use in that area?"

"There's one on the outskirts, but we didn't set up traps in the city."

"Why not?"

"Some dinosaurs hang out there, but the biggest threat in the abandoned cities are humans."

Of course, other gangs would use the buildings for shelter. This could quickly become complicated.

———

OAKLEY WAITED IMPATIENTLY while Raptor returned to the bunker specifically for his backpack and Wells wrapped Auburn's midsection tight to allow her to travel.

As Wells finished the last turn of the gauze, she put her fists on her hips. "I'm going with you."

"No," Auburn and Oakley said at the same time. This expedition didn't need more members.

Oakley glared at Auburn before responding to Wells. "That's not necessary. You're needed here." *And I don't need one more person to feel responsible for.*

"What are you going to do if Auburn rips her stitches out and starts bleeding everywhere?"

She didn't have an answer for that one.

Wells pointed to Auburn. "If she's going, I'm going."

Oakley turned her glare again to Auburn, who gave her a sweet smile. "You heard the woman. I guess we're both going."

She let out a frustrated grunt and left the shack. On the way out, Kaleo raised his eyebrows, asking if she wanted him to come. She shook her head. She just needed to be alone for a minute and the others were still getting ready to leave.

With slow, quiet steps, she circled the shack in a long path of pacing. The manic jungle actually soothed her. Birds tending their nests, monkeys hanging on branches, and geckos streaking up the sides of trees. An occasional dinosaur screech in the distance. So normal and uncomplicated.

Was it really that she didn't want more people to protect? Or was it because she'd issued the challenge for Cane and Auburn to come while expecting them to decline? More eyes on her meant more scrutiny for how she handled Lumas. Even though she'd agreed to capture not kill him, it didn't sit well with her. He deserved to die for what he'd done. And he deserved to die for what he was planning to do—make more genetically altered people.

But those thoughts were exactly the ones that bothered her. She'd become so comfortable with her role of judge, jury, and executioner when she probably deserved the same punishment. She'd once had the innocence that she saw in Wells's eyes, the conviction to do what was right. But she couldn't figure out right from wrong anymore.

A faint rustling stopped her in her tracks at the corner of the front side of the shack. She wasn't hidden by any means, but she wasn't exposed either. She could dart behind the building, then disappear into the tree line or circle around to the front door.

The leaves of a tree swayed at about the height of a man. If there would have been a breeze, she would have missed it.

Was this a dinosaur predator? Or had Lumas come back? She'd been working under the assumption he wouldn't try anything more because he'd lost the element of surprise and he'd gotten what he wanted.

Maybe Raptor had returned for something he forgot. She was half hidden in shadow, but there wasn't any more shadow to retreat into. At this point, if she moved, whoever or whatever was there would be more likely to see her through the leaves. So, she held her breath and waited.

Several seconds ticked by with no movement.

Just when she'd convinced herself the predator had moved on, a human form wearing a gray T-shirt broke through the leaves. His T-shirt reminded her of Kaleo's, but this wasn't him. *Wyatt.* His gaze zeroed in on her.

The man who typically guarded the front entry of the Cazador gang compound stood with his arms at his side, a rifle hanging from one hand. His eyes nearly bugged out of his head as he stared at her. She couldn't blame him. He'd thought she was dead … for good reason.

"How are you alive?" Wyatt's deep voice rumbled with anger.

"Just lucky, I guess."

He took a menacing step toward her. "Not so lucky to run into me."

The door swung open, and Kaleo stepped out. He must have come to check on her.

Wyatt's gaze shifted to Kaleo, and then his forehead lifted in comprehension. "You betrayed us." He gave her a scathing look. "For her?"

Thoughts were whirling through Kaleo's eyes. She could read his fear even without the benefit of pheromones. He'd done everything he could to protect his position at the gang's compound, to keep the men from becoming more violent, and to protect Misty. Even though Misty had murdered several husbands, she didn't deserve to be abused by the men in the compound.

Oakley had ruined it all by allowing Wyatt one glimpse of her.

Wyatt raised the rifle and pointed it at Oakley's chest. "You're coming back to the compound with me." He slid an elbow toward Kaleo. "If you know what's good for you, you won't ever come back."

She raised her hands but had no intention of stepping toward him. She ducked and jumped to the side, around the corner of the building.

Wyatt fired. The bullet splintered wood off the side of the shack mere inches from her head.

When she peeked back around, Kaleo's long, nylon whip had wrapped around the barrel of the gun. Wyatt tugged on it, but Kaleo yanked it out of his hands.

It fell to the ground, and Kaleo quickly pulled it to him.

Now disarmed, Wyatt must have realized he had no chance. He took off at a dead sprint into the trees.

They couldn't let him go back to the compound and tell everyone about her. She and Kaleo took off after him, but it would be up to her to catch him. Kaleo couldn't run fast with his barely healing legs.

They darted through vine curtains and around kapok trees, down through creeks and up the banks. Kaleo had dropped back at the first creek. But she caught a glimpse every few seconds of Wyatt, still just ahead of her.

But then a minute later, she couldn't hear the sound of his running up ahead anymore. She broke through the trees to an unexpected sight. A herd of *Ankylosaurs* hovered over their nests with their thick clubbed tails swinging about. One bleated and honked at Wyatt, who lay stunned on the ground. He must have run straight into one of the armored beasts at full speed.

With her appearance, the other dinosaurs began to stir as well. She sent out as many soothing pheromones as she could while slowly creeping toward Wyatt.

He rolled away from her.

The move stirred the mother *Ankylosaurus* near him into a frenzy. It stomped its huge feet on the trajectory of his roll, nearly squashing his head.

He jumped up and began running through the crowd of mothers, apparently thinking she'd be too cautious to follow his crazy path.

He was wrong. She was more lithe and nimble than he was.

Though the mothers were surprisingly fast, she leaped out of the way of their sledgehammer paws easily. Wyatt, on the other hand, received glancing blows every few seconds. Not enough to knock him down, but enough to make him stumble and veer.

At the other side of the clearing, one of the mothers swiped a tail in his direction. He ducked but took the blow of the club on his shoulder. He spun around and fell to the ground.

Fortunately for him, the mother didn't follow up with her attack after he was down.

Oakley made it to him unscathed. He was panting but otherwise unharmed. Still, that hit would leave a nasty bruise on his shoulder. He tried to get up again.

She had to keep him from escaping. If not for Misty, she couldn't have cared less about what happened at the compound. But Kaleo had been Misty's protector. If the gang was angry enough at him, they'd take it out on her. Plus, Misty had helped Oakley when she needed it. The woman didn't deserve to be left at the mercy of vengeful convicts.

Wyatt got to his knees. The nearest mother *Ankylosaurus* reared its head again. If Oakley shocked him now at the edge of the herd, he might be trampled before she could get him out of here. But she'd have to take that chance.

She reached out, grabbed his ankle, and shot a pulse of heat from her core. Electricity poured from her palm, doubling him over and clenching all his muscles. When he fell sideways to the grass, she put her fingers on his temple and sent a more controlled pulse to his head until he slipped into unconsciousness. Had she given him too much? It was a fine line.

She checked his pulse. Steady. Now she had to find a way to get him back to the shack.

She backed away from Wyatt's prone body and circled around the dinosaur nests, all the while sending friendly pheromones to the creatures. They sniffed and huffed in her direction in a curious way, but they didn't seem to have much of a problem with her.

On the other side of the clearing, she found Kaleo and told him what happened.

"Do we need to go back and get more help?" she asked.

He frowned for a minute. It had to frustrate him. The powerful gang leader who couldn't run or carry or protect. Finally, he tapped his back where the hilt of his whip would be. "Let's see if together we can rope him and drag him."

They circled back around the mother *Ankylosaurs*. As they came to where they had a clear shot of the far end of the clearing, her steps slowed.

Wyatt wasn't there.

Maybe she'd misjudged where she'd left him? She kept walking until she reached an area of flattened grass. No mistaking it. This was where he'd lain, apparently not as unconscious as she'd thought.

A cold chill swept down her spine. "Misty."

Chapter Twenty-Three

"I'M SORRY," Oakley said to Kaleo in a low voice as they pursued Wyatt. "Your life at the compound is over."

Was she really sorry? She hadn't wanted them to be apart, but it would have been better if it had been Kaleo's choice to leave the compound. A flush of guilt swept over her. Here she was worrying about their relationship when Misty was in danger.

There had been no time to run back to the shack to let the others know. As soon as Wyatt informed the gang, they'd be looking for people on whom to vent their anger. Oakley and Kaleo had to get to Misty first. Problem was, if they couldn't get this done quietly, it might end up being the two of them against a gang of about thirty ruthless criminals.

Several minutes later, Kaleo still hadn't responded. What was he thinking? He'd had a good thing going before she'd arrived. Did he wish she hadn't come here? Ridiculous. He'd never given her a reason to think it.

As they reached the compound, he motioned for her to go to the south side ladder. Alone.

"What are you doing?"

"I'm going around the front. If I show up and talk with them, they might not believe Wyatt."

She shook her head. "It's too risky."

He cupped her cheek and looked deep into her eyes. "Even if it doesn't work, it will give you a distraction and time to get Misty out."

It was obvious in the firm lines around his mouth and the tightness of his eyes. His mind was set. Still, she argued with him until he leaned forward, his lips open and inviting, and then all her fight dissolved.

She closed the distance between them fast and forceful, making it a kiss he would remember. One that would inspire him to fight for his life—for their life together—no matter the odds.

As he walked away, she gripped the bottom rung of the rope ladder. He gave her an exaggerated wink before he disappeared around the side of the resort. She swung her foot up and began climbing. The only other time she'd snuck into the resort was in the middle of the night. Now, in the heat of the day, she was exposed and vulnerable. Fortunately, the guards were usually focused on the front entrance. Their biggest threat was dinosaurs. None would attack from the steep drop offs in the rear of the resort.

As she flipped her leg over the balcony railing on the third floor, she listened for any disturbance. Nothing. Either Kaleo hadn't made it to the front yet, or she couldn't hear what was going on in the rest of the compound.

Quickly, she searched for Misty in her work area—more accurately, a greenhouse.

Empty.

Where did Misty sleep? She couldn't remember. Probably nearby.

Oakley began with the closest room. Nope.

On her way to the next, she heard raised voices coming from deep within the resort. Shouting could mean he was getting his point across. In fact, if they were still yelling, probably no one had died yet.

The next room was empty as well. Hopefully, Misty wasn't downstairs getting lunch.

Finally, she found Misty asleep in the last room in the hall. Not wanting to scare her, Oakley crept to the side of the bed. Just before she reached for her, a hand shot out, armed with a syringe.

Oakley jumped backward, barely avoiding the sharp needle.

Misty rolled over and peered at her. "Sorry, dear. Not wise to come in unannounced."

"I thought you were sleeping."

She gave a crafty smile. "I was. Until you arrived."

Okay. Got it. Misty is a light sleeper. "We have to go. You're not safe here."

"What happened?"

Oakley briefly explained the situation, and for a moment, Misty looked like she wouldn't get out of bed. But then, she flipped the covers back to reveal that she was fully clothed. Did she always sleep like that?

"I need to grab some things before we go."

"I'll help. We have to hurry."

They went back to the greenhouse room where Misty grabbed a backpack and began shoving items inside. She pointed to a workstation near the windows. "Grab all those vials for me."

Oakley reached out, then pulled her hand back at Misty's next words.

"Ah, use the gloves, please."

Oakley slipped on the gloves sitting next to the vials, then placed the vials in the backpack, followed by the gloves. When they again entered the hall, more raised voices boomed through the walls.

She ushered Misty to the balcony. Misty went wide-eyed and backed away.

"This is the safest way out of here."

Misty shook her head.

"If Kaleo doesn't win in there, they will kill anyone associated with him, starting with you."

Misty pushed her rowdy gray hair off her forehead.

"Let me take that." Oakley grabbed the backpack before looking into the woman's eyes. "You could die every day by handling this stuff, which means you are one of the bravest women I know. You can do this." Oakley swung her leg over the railing. "I'll go down first so I can make sure your feet are secure on every rung before you move down."

Finally, Misty nodded.

Slowly, they traversed rung after rung. Oakley only had to stabilize Misty once in the middle. Otherwise, the older woman was surprisingly agile.

When they reached the ground, Oakley gritted her teeth. From the lower level, the shouting inside sounded even louder. This wasn't going the way Kaleo wanted. But at least no gunshots had gone off yet.

―――

IT TOOK a long half hour to get Misty tucked away in the tree house, then another twenty minutes to return. As Oakley approached the rear of the compound, all was quiet.

She hesitated at the rope ladder, the only clandestine way into the compound. If Kaleo had finally won his case, her presence would be proof of his deception. But what if they hadn't believed him? He could be injured somewhere, needing her help. Or they might have killed him. If so, she had to know.

She ascended the ladder and then crept down the hallway on the third floor. It should be deserted up here, but it would only take her three-quarters of the way through the resort before she would have to drop down to a lower level. Even so, she trod softly, the same light footstep Kaleo had taught her in the jungle.

At the end of the hallway, she pushed open the stairwell door and listened. Voices rose from the floor below, and footsteps stomped on the stairs.

She silently ducked inside an empty room, leaving the door ajar as she'd found it. Two men slammed open the stairwell door and walked right past her hiding place.

"I don't know what to think," one of the men said. "Kaleo's always been good to us. Fair, you know."

"But if it's true?" the other man asked. "What's fair about keeping a hot girl like that to himself, then making sure the rest of us don't get a chance when he's done?"

Their voices faded down the hallway. Were they going to check on Misty? Oakley might only have minutes before they realized she was gone. They probably wouldn't take kindly to another missing woman, even if Misty scared most of them.

Why couldn't those men have said where Kaleo was? At least they seemed conflicted about whether Wyatt's story was true. That was a good sign. Now she just had to keep from giving them proof.

She slipped out of her hiding place and into the stairwell. No one else was coming up. She quietly descended to the first floor and cracked open the door.

The hallway was deserted.

If Kaleo was still in charge, or if the others had enough doubt to keep from challenging him, he'd be in his room. If his room was empty, then she'd have to search for where they were holding him captive.

She kept to the side of the hall as she walked swiftly to the closed door of Kaleo's room. Knocking would draw too much attention. She tried the knob. It was unlocked.

In one swift move, she swept the door open and closed it

behind her. The drapes were drawn, and the lights were off. Just enough sunlight came from behind the curtains for her to see a large form lying in bed. The tension eased from her tight muscles. Kaleo must have talked his way out of Wyatt's accusations. She opened her mouth to whisper his name but then snapped it shut.

This person wore a gray T-shirt just like Kaleo had, but instinct told her it wasn't him. Something about the outline of the body or the position of the person on the bed was off.

And if it wasn't Kaleo, it had to be the one other person she'd seen in a gray T-shirt today—Wyatt.

She grasped the door handle. Voices came from the hall. Not a good time to leave. She stood frozen as the man in the bed rolled over. Wyatt focused his eyes on her until they were predatory pinpoints. All her blood pooled in her feet.

He slid out of the bed and stalked toward her. He was the de facto hunter of the gang for a reason.

She had to make a choice and both options were awful: deal with Wyatt alone, or run and try to evade the rest of the gang.

Chapter Twenty-Four

KALEO STRUGGLED against the ropes tying him to the chair. So much for all the trust he'd tried to build with these guys over the years. Of course, they weren't trustworthy guys. And then there was the fact that he was feeding them a load of deception. Better for all of them to stop the lies. He could see that now. If only they weren't going to kill him for it.

He'd gotten one leg free, but the other was tied tightly.

One of the ropes on his wrist gave a little. He slipped off his shoe, hiked his knee up, curled his big toe inside the rope, and yanked. People underestimated how strong toes could be. The gap widened just enough, and he shimmied his wrist out. But as he did so, the chair rocked back on the wooden floor and made a scraping sound.

The door flew open. Orion entered with Kaleo's whip in his hand.

Kaleo tensed for a blow, but Orion merely leaned his back against the door, crossed his feet, and stared at him. The silence turned uncomfortable.

When Orion still didn't say anything, Kaleo went back to trying to free himself.

Several minutes later, Orion spoke in his deep voice. "Do you remember the *Oviraptor*?"

"Yeah."

That day a few years ago, they had been hunting without much success. Orion had found a nest of *Oviraptor* eggs. The creature's name meant "egg thief," and although those dinosaurs didn't steal eggs from other animals, they were serious about protecting their own. Orion had just picked one up when an *Oviraptor* jumped out from the bushes and latched on to his finger. Their toothless beaks had amazing crushing power. Not only had Kaleo pried the animal off Orion's finger and brought him to Misty for a splint, but he'd also made up a story about it being crushed by a swipe from Red Grizzly's tail. It had been one guy helping another.

With a wink, Orion dropped the whip on the ground and kicked it over to Kaleo. Then, he left and engaged the dead-bolt from the outside. The man had given him a weapon and time.

Five minutes later, Kaleo freed himself. He snatched up the whip and debated his options. Unlocking the deadbolt from in here and fighting his way out seemed like a bloody path.

He went to the full-length window. This room had a faux balcony about six inches wide. Fifteen feet below, a ledge of rock sat just above the cliff to the ravine. His whip could easily get him down to the ledge. Except if he missed, he'd plunge straight into the ravine a hundred feet down.

He didn't take long to decide. The guys might not trust him anymore, but he'd spent too much time protecting them to turn around and kill them now.

He wound the whip around the balcony railing several times without tying it. This was where an actual woven whip would've come in handy. The vinyl would be harder to remove from below, but as long as he had enough of a tail at the bottom, he could manage it. He flipped one leg over the railing and put some pressure on the whip. It slipped a little until the slack was gone and then held tight. He grabbed the vinyl—made soft through use—and lowered himself hand by hand.

About ten feet down, he looked between his feet. He was coming down a little too far out. He lowered himself a few more feet, then twisted his body to swing like a pendulum. At the apex of the swing, he dropped to the two-foot-wide ledge.

A small chunk of rock broke off and went careening down the slope. Thankfully, the rest of the ledge stayed intact and held his weight.

Because he was underneath the balcony, he had to lean over and shake the whip several times before it let loose of the railing. It came rushing down at him, then draped into the ravine below. He gathered it, folded it up, and tucked it into the back of his jeans.

With any luck, Oakley and Misty would be waiting for him at the tree house. He slid along the ledge toward the head of the ravine. Along the way, he passed the remains of a fallen, tattered rope bridge. The bridge hung from its support poles on this side, and its slats stretched down the side of the ravine. The end of the bridge twisted among the branches and vines at the bottom of the cliffside.

He'd just reached the shadow of the balcony of his former room when he heard a grunt and a loud gasp. A high-pitched squeal quickly followed, like someone trying not a scream. A shiver ran down his back. It sounded like a woman.

⸻

OAKLEY HELD in another cry as Wyatt pushed her up against the glass door to the patio. She couldn't afford to bring any of the other guys in on this.

He'd cornered her first near the bathroom, but she'd run over the bed to the door and tried to open it. Not that she'd have anywhere to go once outside. This room was on the main floor in the front, but the rear opened to a ravine.

He held her by the shoulders and let his gaze roam over her body.

Disgust crept down her spine. She either had to get away from him or kill him, a possibility that was seeming more reasonable by the second. She closed her eyes and summoned a bit of electricity, then she grabbed his bicep.

He let out a loud yelp and released her.

She darted away from him, but he snatched her arm again, shoving her into the other panel of the sliding doors.

"What was that?" he asked.

She stood to her full height. "Something I can use to hurt you."

He gave a cocky smile. "Not if I hurt you more."

She gathered the energy simmering in her core and reached for him again.

"No more unless I say so." He swiped her hand down and pinned her arms to her sides. He stuck his face into her hair and sniffed. "You smell fantastic."

It probably wasn't shampoo he was smelling since she hadn't showered for a while. Curse those stupid pheromones.

He began trailing kisses down her neck. His hold loosened slightly.

She twisted in his grip. She only needed to get one finger on him.

A cool breeze blew over her right arm from behind, and as she pulled away from him, the material had give to it. The glass panel connected to the door had been replaced by a screen. If only she could get through it.

She wrenched her wrist as far as it would go toward him. Her little finger grazed the material of his jeans, stretched taut over his thigh. She let her electricity flow.

He froze for a brief second, his muscles involuntarily

seizing up, then he seemed to regain control as her contact with his jeans wavered. He shoved her backward.

The screen split at the edges where it contacted the door frame. She fell onto the concrete by the edge of the pool, hitting her head hard. She lay there for a second, stunned.

When she lifted to her elbows, Wyatt was nowhere around. Relief flooded through her, but it was as fleeting as the smack to her head. He was somewhere either getting a weapon or gathering the men to prove she was alive. She had to get out of here.

The haze in her pounding head broke when she heard a flapping sound on the balcony. She looked over, half expecting a large bird. But the reality was even better.

The end of a vinyl whip wrapped around the railing. *Kaleo!*

But how could he be at the bottom of the ravine? His whip wouldn't reach that high.

She pushed to her feet and ran to the edge. He smiled up at her from a narrow rock ledge below.

After he tugged on the whip, he said, "Come on down. It held me just a minute ago."

She didn't need more of an invitation. She swung her leg over the railing and began climbing down as fast as she could. It wouldn't take Wyatt long to figure out where she went when he came back.

Three-quarters of the way down, a shadow darkened Kaleo's form. She looked up. Wyatt pointed an arrow down at her. The angle had him stretching over the railing, most likely balancing on one foot.

She doubled the speed of her descent.

He let an arrow fly. It sailed past her left shoulder.

Good thing he hadn't wanted to waste bullets because he'd be much more accurate with a gun. His next arrow sliced through her T-shirt and cut into the skin on her side. Probably a flesh wound.

Before he could nock another arrow, Kaleo helped her stand on the ledge. But now they were a bigger target.

"This way," he directed her toward the center of the resort.

Shouldn't they be trying to get away from the resort? Wyatt could just follow them from room to room, shooting until he hit the mark. Then Kaleo stopped her and pointed to the edge. A weathered and broken rope bridge dangled down.

He couldn't be serious.

Another arrow flew toward her. She ducked just in time.

Okay, she could take a leap of faith.

She hung on to the first board as she dropped her legs over the cliff, searching for a foothold. Kaleo held her arms firmly until she found it.

She moved down from board to board, trying not to acknowledge the hundred feet of air between her and the bottom of the ravine.

As Kaleo climbed onto the rope bridge, she clung to the sides. It swayed under his weight. Another arrow sailed through the air, and he let out a loud grunt.

"Are you hit?" she yelled.

"Just keep going," he responded.

That meant yes. But he was right. They couldn't do anything about his injury until they reached the bottom. Her heart gave an unsteady flutter. Hopefully, this went to the bottom.

About a hundred wooden planks later, her feet came to the end. Frayed ropes dangled another ten feet, but they died out twenty feet above the rocky floor of the ravine. Too high to jump. How could they descend farther?

That was when it hit her. Kaleo had left his whip up there. His single most useful tool was gone.

"Now what?" she asked.

He clung to the rope bridge with one hand. She mimicked his posture and scanned the ravine bottom along with him. An intermittent stream had created this ravine, and it wasn't flowing right now, but that didn't seem to hinder the plant growth. Mounds upon mounds of dark green and flowering plants scattered the area between rocks. Many of them had sharp branches and several species probably had thorns.

"Over there." He pointed ten feet off to the right. "Purple shield plants. No thorns. Plus, they don't grow directly on rocks, and they can reach five feet tall. These look a little shorter, but I think it's our best bet for a soft landing."

The patch of purple leaves spanned only five feet in width. It would be a small area to hit. She shrugged. What choice did they have? They couldn't stay up here forever.

She shimmied down the dangling rope until the threads started to shift in her hand. With a deep breath, she heaved against the cliffside to start a pendulum motion.

Two more pushes off the cliff, and she was close to the necessary arc.

Last one. She shoved off with as much force as she could.

At the peak of her swing, she let go, keeping her body as flat as possible. She held her breath.

Free fall took over, and her stomach flipped.

She hit the patch of purple shield plants nearly horizontal.

She skidded along, and leaves bunched up in the back of her shirt. Her tailbone hit a small rock, but then another mound of leaves became trapped between her legs, stopping her momentum.

Slowly, she pushed herself to standing and gave Kaleo a thumbs-up. "Not too bad."

He repeated her actions with only marginally similar results. Not only had she already pushed down some of the leaves, but he came in with much greater momentum. He landed with a loud grunt.

"Are you okay?"

He groaned. "Help me up."

She reached down. He took her hand and pulled her on top of him. She landed on his chest with a surprised yelp.

The purple leaves cocooned them like they'd jumped into a pile of fall foliage. He caressed her cheek. She leaned into him and brought her lips to his for a sizzling kiss.

Electricity crackled over them as they parted. For a moment, life seemed almost normal.

Then he moved his arm and winced. She examined the injury. The arrowhead had torn through his shirt. Just a scratch on his skin, though. He'd be fine.

He noticed the rip in her shirt. It was her turn to wince under his probing fingers.

"It's nothing," she said. "But I think we need some more clothes."

That earned her a frown, which she kissed away. If only she could stay here forever with him. Just the two of them. No dinosaurs. No angry gang members. No Lumas. But life didn't work that way. She pushed herself up again with a stab of regret. They needed to get going. It would take hours to hike out of this ravine and find their way back to the tree house.

Chapter Twenty-Five

MISTY FUSSED over them when they returned to the tree house. Oakley couldn't blame her. On the way back, they'd had to hide from several predators—since they had no weapons—and skirt around two nesting grounds. By the time they saw the tree house ladder, the setting sun had started to blanket the jungle in shadows. Being so close to the equator meant sunset rarely shifted and came every day around six o'clock.

Misty wrapped her arms around Kaleo the moment he climbed up. Rightfully so, she'd worried that they hadn't made it out of the compound.

"We will stay here tonight," Kaleo said.

As anxious as Oakley was to return to the shack, she agreed with him. Traveling through the jungle was risky to begin with, much less doing it in the dark. They couldn't drag Misty along and take the chance she would fall or attract a predator's notice. Besides, Kaleo's legs had to be shot from all the activity.

After she and Kaleo had their wounds bandaged from a kit they found in the corner and ate a dinner of dinosaur jerky,

Misty implored them to tell her where they'd been. Oakley recounted the events of the past week.

Misty furrowed her already wrinkled brow. "We have to leave early in the morning. Wyatt knows about this place. He won't easily give up looking for you."

Hopefully, Wyatt had spent the rest of the day fruitlessly searching for them at the mouth of the ravine. They hadn't seen any sign of him on the way to the tree house.

"And he doesn't even have to track us from the ravine," Kaleo said. "He can just head back to where he saw us today, which will lead him straight to the others."

Had any of them gone searching for her and Kaleo? Surely, they would have turned around when the tracks led to the gang's compound.

Misty curled her finger toward a small table in the corner. "I've got something that might help with your dinosaur problems or even your human problems if you wish to go that route."

They followed her to the table where a small vial rested. She lifted the vial and swished the liquid inside. "It's Komodo dragon venom."

What? Misty was famous for her poisons, but this one was out of place, at least according to Oakley's former Geography of Reptiles teacher. "Where would you get it on Extinction Island? They're native to Indonesia."

"There used to be a zoo near here, back when this was Costa Rica. They kept a Komodo dragon for an exhibit. When the civilians evacuated, they must have figured the reptile deserved to live with other reptiles. They left it behind."

"What does the venom do?" Kaleo asked.

Misty nodded to her, so she answered, "Raises blood pressure, prevents blood from clotting, and induces shock. The prey can't escape or resist, and then it dies."

"Can it kill a dinosaur as big as Mutant Mantis?"

Misty fielded that one. "From what you've said, that's a big lizard, but if you use enough of it, yes. Do you have a trap you can put this on?"

He slowly nodded. "There's one on the outskirts of Cartago." He snapped his fingers. "The one you sewed from the palm tree."

"Oh yes." She filled Oakley in. "It's a dead-drop trap where a rectangle of wood falls on the animal that triggers it."

That didn't seem deadly. "Does it smother the animal?"

"No. It pierces them with long spikes from the Chuga palm tree. I wove them together like a net. They stab the animal, leaving behind deadly bacteria, which causes them to either die from blood loss or a bacterial infection. But you need something that will act faster." Misty held up the vial of Komodo Dragon venom again. "That's where this helps out."

If they painted it on the spikes, they could kill at least one of the dinosaurs that had been hunting them. Sounded like a good plan.

Misty winked at her. "Maybe you could even use it on the agent who's been stalking you."

The familiar tug of war tightened Oakley's chest. To kill or not to kill. It was a morbid question. She turned away and walked to the window. The slats were closed, since Misty had a candle burning and didn't want to attract attention, but Oakley imagined what the dense dark forest looked like. Shadows and dangers everywhere, unending.

Kaleo put his hands on her shoulders. "What's wrong?"

"There's always someone or something more to kill. How do you stand it?"

"It's necessary."

"I know that. And I know I'm supposed to be programmed to kill. But sometimes, it doesn't feel like enough justification."

A soft sigh leaked out of his mouth. "If you can justify killing and feel good about it, then something is wrong. I try to remember there is one important distinction between me and the other killers on this island. Even though I have power over life and death, I know that doesn't make me God."

She glanced back at him. This was the first time he'd ever mentioned God to her. "Now you sound like Cane."

"I'll take that as a compliment." He slid his hands down her arms. "You listen to him most of the time."

True. But she and Cane had their disagreements. Despite her mixed feelings about killing, it seemed wrong to let Lumas live when he'd ordered so much death or to let Glaser live when he'd tried to kill Neve. Then again, maybe they both deserved to spend the rest of their days on this island running from death.

He leaned closer until his breath was hot on her ear. "You know, Neve has your tracker. Agent Brooks is gone. There's still a chance for you to leave here and disappear."

She shook her head. "If Glaser gets back to the mainland, he'll tell his superiors I didn't get tagged. Then, Raptor will be on the hook again, and I'll be hunted down and executed wherever I end up."

All of that was true. She'd left out only one thing. She couldn't imagine leaving Kaleo forever. If she ever had a real chance to leave, it would be the hardest decision of her life.

⬛

THE OCCUPANTS of the shack slept soundly while Cane kept watch at the front window. Where had Oakley and Kaleo gone? And why hadn't they come back before dark? He took several deep breaths and turned his eyes heavenward, trying to ease his anxious spirit. The Lord knew where they were even if he didn't. His worrying did nothing except wear himself out.

Someone came up behind him. He didn't turn around. It had to be Wells. She was almost as perceptive about his moods as Oakley. No need to add to her worries either. She already took care of everyone here with no complaints.

"If they don't come back, will we go ahead with the plans tomorrow?" she whispered.

He gave a small smile. That was one of the things he appreciated about her—she dealt with practical matters first. "We can't leave Penna to her fate with Lumas. We're already taking a chance by assuming he wants Teagan too and therefore hasn't left with Penna. I think we have to act."

"Good. Better to do something—"

"Than to sit around growing armpit hair," he finished for her.

She laughed softly. He'd asked her so many times to rest and relax that they had turned her response into a game. The last time she'd said it, he'd answered it was better to do something than to sit around calculating square roots in your head. It was the most boring thing he could think of. But he'd fallen off his cot laughing when she told him she used to do that for fun as a kid. To prove it, she rattled off the first twenty square roots for the factor of two—in descending order. This woman might be more than he could handle.

"We're sitting around now," he grumbled.

"Only because it's smart to wait until daylight."

He turned around to face her. "And it's smart to leave essential people like doctors behind the front lines."

"I'm not staying here. Someone might get hurt." She took a step toward him, leaving only inches between their bodies. "You might need me out there."

Yeah, he was pretty sure he did need her. But what if this attraction was all in his head? Just a bond between them because they'd survived a harrowing situation together?

She tilted her head, and her platinum curls shifted and bobbed. His gaze met hers and held. There was only one way to find out if this was real.

He leaned toward her just a few inches. She came the rest

of the way, meeting his lips with surprising force. But he didn't mind as a rush of desire swept him away. He cupped the back of her head and pulled her in for a deeper kiss.

This was happening so fast after his heartbreak with Oakley, but it was also so different. All the attraction. All the desire. None of the guilt. This just felt right.

When they finally parted, he rested his forehead against hers. His heart still raced, and his body shivered from her closeness.

"We should have done that ages ago," she said.

He laughed. As usual, she was right. If nothing else, this was something good that had come out of the repeated disasters of late.

Chapter Twenty-Six

EARLY THE NEXT MORNING, Oakley, Kaleo, and Misty returned to the shack. Everything seemed normal. No sign that Wyatt had come back during the night, but he couldn't be far behind. They had to get everyone out.

After a short recap of what happened and a discussion about where they should go, they split into two groups. Cane and most of the people here would go to the main bunker. As long as they blocked the tunnel's entrance, they would be safe. Since Oakley couldn't return there for fear Glaser would be waiting for her, she, Kaleo, and Auburn left for Cartago to ready the trap.

Teagan had wanted to come with them as well, but Oakley convinced her it was better to keep the details of the plan secret from her. Otherwise, they couldn't use the trap with Fangtooth because it would know what was coming.

Before they left, Neve grabbed Oakley's arm and pulled her aside. "Try to reason with Glaser before you do anything else."

"What do you mean?"

"Convince him to take Lumas into custody and go back to the mainland like nothing happened."

"He shot you, Neve."

She swept her long hair out of her face. "It's all forgiven. If he can put his grudge against you away, then his mistake never has to come to light."

"Very generous of you, but I'm not sure I can support that."

She placed a cool hand on Oakley's cheek. "It's easy to lean in to violence and vengeance. Remember the friend and enemy inside you. Choose to listen to the friend. Choose the way of peace, Oakley."

A sarcastic retort bubbled up—something about Glaser resting in peace instead—but she swallowed it. Lumas's violence had devastated lives. Her violence had brought almost as many consequences. How could she defend it now?

"I'll try," she eked out.

Now, as she took step after step closer to the end of her problems with Lumas, that promise felt like an anchor around her neck. One way or another, it would be over soon.

After gathering some items, the others would meet them at a children's park on the outskirts of Cartago. Cane would bring Agent Brooks's tranquilizer guns and zip ties to capture all three men: Lumas, Glaser, and Erman. When Raptor came, he'd bring the backpack with the microscopic trackers. Glaser wouldn't be able to resist following, and as long as Lumas was in that bunker, he would be lured out and distracted by the possibility of capturing Teagan.

Assuming Wyatt didn't follow them, that left only one man to worry about—Erman. She hadn't promised to bring him in alive, but Cane would probably want her to.

Halfway to the second bunker, a familiar rustling captured her attention. Cody bounded out of the bushes and rubbed his rough head against her leg. "Hey, buddy. Good to see you."

He gave her an almost chiding look.

"I know. It's been hard to track me down. I'm sorry."

She absently patted him on the head as she walked,

earning a rumbling coo from him. Hopefully, he'd stay out of the way once things were set in motion.

A hundred feet from the trap, they peered through the trees. All quiet.

The trap was built into an old carport attached to a sagging shanty house. Behind the house, buildings rose up to proclaim the city of Cartago. Over top of what looked to be an old restaurant, gray stone ruins stretched to the heavens, marking a church that had never been restored. According to Neve, Dios Sangre Church had been destroyed three times in the seventeenth century. When a final earthquake damaged it beyond repair in the 1800s, the residents left it as ruins.

They slid through the trees silently, coming toward the trap from the rear. Even Auburn walked quietly. The only sound came from Cody's bobbing feet and clucking tongue. If anyone in the town heard, hopefully they'd chock it up to a roaming solitary dinosaur.

As they crept around the corner of the house, she spied the splayed-out carved lines marking a trap cut into a piece of siding.

"Who built this one?" she asked.

"I did," Kaleo replied.

An ingenious design. The trap used the supports for the carport as a base. Another long branch leaned against those supports, balanced on a flat rock. On that branch, a cross piece had been nailed in and draped with what looked like a fuzzy coat. A closer look confirmed that the coat wasn't fuzzy but was instead covered in six-inch-long spikes. Any disturbance would bring the branch crashing down, along with the dangerous coat. Plus, the back of the carport was open, making for an easy escape once the person led the dinosaur into the trap. Even Auburn looked impressed.

Time to make it more dangerous.

"Keep an eye out, okay?" Oakley said to Auburn.

"Sure." She moved to the tree line at the end of the house closest to the city.

Kaleo put on a pair of old gloves he'd found at the janitor's shack. Oakley gathered some banana leaves to wrap around the vial so that she wouldn't get the venom on her hands if it spilled over. He used half a banana leaf to dip into the venom and spread it on the spikes, concentrating on the ones that would hit the trunk of the body.

Twenty minutes later, they stood back to survey their work. Job well done, except for one problem. This trap would work perfectly for a Fangtooth-sized creature, but it was questionable for something as large as Mutant Mantis. If that gangly predator showed up, they'd have to improvise.

Preferably, this confrontation would stay between the people. She'd learned her lesson from last time with Adler— no using her pheromones to call dinosaurs.

She turned to tell Auburn they were done, but the corner of the house was vacant. Perhaps she'd gone into the thin row of trees to keep an eye on the buildings beyond. Oakley searched but to no avail. A heaviness settled on her chest.

Auburn was gone, probably warning Lumas at this moment.

⌁

TAYE LED the group toward the children's playground. Cane followed behind, trying to keep his focus on the task at hand but not needing to since Taye knew this area of the jungle better than he did. His mind wandered like a bumblebee searching for just the right flower and landing on none. Because none of this was right.

And yet, they had to stop Lumas. Would this be the final confrontation with his father?

The thought seeped into his mind like black tea, coating everything it touched. His father had ordered the death of his mother, created deadly adaptations inside his own children for profit, kidnapped multiple people, and tried to sell Oakley. And those were just the things Cane knew about. He might have been better off not knowing his father at all.

Better to know the truth with sad eyes than to wear a blindfold forever. That's what Neve would tell him. The Costa Rican people had a proverb for everything. At least she would be safe with the other cave members watching over her in the main bunker. She'd already sacrificed enough for Oakley and Cane's crazy search for their origins. A search that had come full circle from the way it began two weeks ago on the floating lab—with Lumas Verret kidnapping someone.

The world might be a better place without his father in it, but he wasn't qualified to judge a life. God would have to make that determination. This place had taught him that, if nothing else.

Behind him, Wells placed a footfall incorrectly and snapped a twig. Everyone froze to listen.

He glanced back at her, and she gave a sheepish shrug. The city girl hadn't learned how to travel silently yet. When this was over, he should teach her, assuming she stayed for a while. Spending lots of time alone with Wells sounded like a good idea. If she learned a thing or two in the process, so much the better.

When no sounds of pursuit came and Raptor nodded the all clear, Taye again led the group west. Since Taye had the front covered and Raptor the back, Cane kept his head on a swivel, checking their flanks on their march toward the city. He avoided the cities as much as possible for several reasons: other gangs took shelter in the empty buildings, there wasn't much cover if you were chased, and the area wasn't devoid of dinosaurs. Fewer dinosaurs spent time in the concrete jungle, but many had adapted to use the buildings on the outskirts as housing for nests or as dens for devouring prey at their leisure. Too many predators, no easy escape.

He'd never visited the church ruins, though he had a vague idea of where they were located. At least they wouldn't have to travel too far into the city.

A few minutes later, the orange plastic railing of a children's slide came into view. The end of the slide had vines creeping over it. Five feet behind it, a tall swing set and a climbing wall had almost been reclaimed by the jungle. Trees grew from the middle, drawing the swings up and entwining them in branches. Vines snaked over the wooden slats of the climbing wall. A seesaw had lost its balancing board, which lay sideways on the ground, and an old roundabout sat rusting in the center of the playground.

Wells came around to his left. She stumbled over something, and he reached out to steady her.

She probed the ground with her feet, bringing up sand from between the blades of grass. "A buried sandbox. Weird."

He agreed. This deserted half-swallowed playground was the creepiest thing he'd seen yet, which was saying a lot.

The men dropped to the ground to sit while Teagan and Wells sat on the edge of a rusty bench to wait.

Not long after, Kaleo and Oakley approached from the trees.

Cane got to his feet. "Where's Auburn?"

"Gone," Oakley said.

That didn't bode well. She could expose all their plans to Lumas.

Oakley nodded at his unspoken communication. "Yeah. We may want to adjust. Give them a few surprises. Neve said there was an old gaming store on the opposite side of the bunker."

"What did you have in mind?"

She motioned for him to sit again. "First of all, we're going to go in from the back side."

228

HIDDEN in the shadows of an old coffee shop doorway, Auburn stared at the remains of the Dios Sangre Church. Why had they named it God's Blood Church? Seemed kind of morbid. Hopefully, no more blood would be spilled today.

The front of the ruins looked like the remnants of an old castle, with two turrets on either side. The second bunker was located in the north turret, as evidenced by the bars over the windows. It would have a concrete roof to replace the missing one and a door with a keypad that could only be accessed from inside the surrounding stone walls.

She shifted on her feet and bit her lip. She'd needed to get away from Oakley and Kaleo because she needed space to think. Space to figure out what to do. But she only had two courses of action: warn her father or disable his security measures.

Neither of those things felt right. How could she betray him after so many years together? But how could she continue to let him act in ways that betrayed the peace he claimed to want?

He'd raised her to have discipline, to sacrifice for an ultimate goal. But her sacrifices had all been for his goals. What did she want out of life?

Not to make more humans like me.

The thought shocked her with its clarity. She clutched her phone until her knuckles turned white. This island was overrun by "special" people, and it was too much. The world didn't need any more.

The ghost of Adler's voice whispered agreement in her ear. He'd tried to kill Oakley. He might have told her to kill everyone here. Would she have done it to please him? Probably not. But she'd finished the kill switch program shortly before his death. As much as she'd condemned Oakley for her murderous ways, she'd been going down the same road.

It was time to find her own way.

Better yet, it was time to let her father face the consequences of going *his* own way. He'd killed an FBI agent with one of her own darts, if Cane was to be believed. And Cane was the one person she trusted on this island. Her dad had indisputably committed murder because he'd asked for one of her quills as they'd entered the bunker. He needed to pay for his crime.

She turned on her phone and searched for the wireless network signal that should be coming out of the bunker. After connecting, she searched the network for her laptop. Yes! Dad had found it and brought it with him.

First, she had to take care of the defense system. She hadn't told the others, but this bunker was built more for defense than hunkering down. To deter a gang of convicts or a ten-ton dinosaur required high-powered ammunition, triggered automatically using solar power systems. Turning off the sensors might alert Dad to trouble, but it would also render the remote weapons useless.

A few clicks later, she'd turned off the security measures but left on the lights and other powered features. Maybe Dad wouldn't notice if only part of the system went down.

She then typed in the operational code for her kill switch program. Part of her itched to destroy it, this power born out of fear, but another part of her grasped for the control it gave her. What guarantee did she have that Oakley wouldn't kill Dad instead of arresting him? He deserved to pay for his crimes, not die for them. A twinge in her gut clued her in to her hypocrisy. If Dad didn't deserve to die for the things he'd done, neither did Cane or Oakley. This program was worse than holding a loaded gun to their heads. She should have never created it.

Her phone pinged at her.

Null reference error.

What in the world? She typed in the command to display the entire code in the simple program. The list came up— much too short. Half her code was gone.

She let out a string of curses. Maybe she'd lost the wireless connection in the middle of the listing? Not likely, but she was grasping at straws.

With tentative steps, she slid her feet out from the shadow of the door and onto the cracked sidewalk. No one was around. She dashed across the street and crouched behind an overgrown bush about five feet from the barred window. She was exposed to anyone coming down the street, but this would be as close as she could get without being seen by people in the bunker.

She woke her phone and tried again.

Null reference error.

It was true. The code activating the microbots via satellite was gone. Only one person from Asperten could have even seen it, much less taken the code—Glen, her father's computer expert. If he had noticed the program, he would have immediately informed her dad. No doubt about it. He had moved the functional parts of the program to a place where her dad could access it but she couldn't.

Fear churned in her gut. Dad could eliminate Oakley or Cane with a keystroke. She ground her teeth. But this wasn't finished. Glen had the computer science degree, but operating systems were like old women—unique and full of scars and warts from days gone by. She had grown up with this system. Time to show him she had a few tricks up her sleeve as well.

Her fingers flew over the miniature keyboard. She found the backup from a month ago. He'd wiped it clean. She went back week by week until she found the backup from a year and a week ago. Most of her code was there. Leave it to Glen to only go back a year because he didn't realize the system rerouted older versions to a different folder.

Just a few keystrokes and she'd restored the program. A few more keystrokes, and she'd completed the code in the way she had before Adler died. Now she just needed to search for the whole program within the rest of the system to find out where Glen had hidden it for her father, then she'd send a command to delete all copies.

"Step over here with your hands up," a gruff voice ordered.

Her gaze darted to the street. A man with short dark hair, tanned skin, and an overbearing attitude held a gun on her. Her mouth dropped open. This was the man who'd wanted to kill her outside the sanatorium. He was some sort of government agent.

His mouth swung open too, like it was on a hinge. "You again. Where the hell is she?"

Should she admit to their relationship? He'd probably already guessed. "I'm her sister."

He didn't look surprised. "Then you probably know where she is. Give me the phone."

She complied.

He threw it to the ground and smashed it with his boot. "Now take me to her."

Chapter Twenty-Seven

"OAKLEY LAVEAU." The commanding voice came from the edge of the tree line nearest the city.

Oakley's heart skipped a beat. *Glaser.*

Of course, he would come in from the west when they'd been trying to lead him in from the east. He pushed through the foliage with his gun pointed at someone.

Auburn gave her a sheepish look.

"This girl says she's your sister."

Oakley glared at her. "Yeah, but we're not close. A dysfunctional family dynamic. I won't bore you with the details."

He didn't respond to her sarcasm, just took a few steps closer, dragging Auburn with him.

"I didn't kill your partner," Oakley said.

From the corner of her eye, she saw Taye flinch. He'd reached down for something, probably his bow and arrow set, but it wasn't there.

Glaser tightened his grip on the gun, which looked awkward in his unsteady left hand. He kept his eyes on Taye as he spoke to Oakley. "I propose a trade. You for—What's your name, girl?"

"Auburn."

"Right. You for Auburn."

"What do you plan to do with Oakley?" Kaleo's hands were at his hips. He had to be itching to reach for the whip he would normally have tucked in the back of his jeans, but it was at the resort compound dangling from a railing.

"I'm carrying out her sentence one way or another. If not on Oakley, then on Auburn here."

"She's never been convicted of a crime," Cane said.

He rolled his eyes. "It's a crime for her to be on this island."

Oakley pasted on a disinterested look. "Okay, tell me why I should care. I'm not even sure whose side she's on."

Auburn visibly winced. Her barb had hit its mark.

A prickle of intuition niggled at the back of Oakley's mind. There was something about the situation she should have noticed but hadn't. Slowly, she swept her gaze over the group on the playground.

That was it. Teagan and her pheromones were missing.

Well, at least Teagan wouldn't be accidentally injured if things went wrong here. She returned her attention to Glaser.

Auburn trained her gaze on the gun. "Don't we all deserve to die for the awful things we've done? But death doesn't make anything right. That's part of the reason why they built this place. To give people a chance."

Glaser's raised eyebrows indicated that her words weren't having an impact. But they might still be able to reason with him.

"What if you could make a legitimate arrest to bring someone to justice who has committed many crimes?" Oakley asked.

"Including the murder of FBI Special Agent Noah Brooks," Auburn added.

Wow. Auburn was really putting the truth out there. Maybe there was hope for her sister, after all.

The revelation created a chink in Glaser's armor. "Agent Brooks is dead?"

Auburn nodded. "My fath—um, my employer killed him."

"How?"

That was the tricky part. Oakley shot her a warning glare to keep her from revealing too much. Glaser recently found out about Oakley's ability, so he might be able to guess her sister had some sort of one.

"With poison," Auburn replied.

Suddenly, a fresh rush of pheromones assaulted Oakley's senses. Fear. Coiled tension. Anger.

But it wasn't coming from Auburn. The source was behind her.

"Drop the gun." Teagan's firm tone was harsher than Oakley had ever heard. "I have an arrow aimed at your back."

No doubt Teagan was sending biological impulses to Glaser's brain to convince him what she said was true. His gun hand gave a slight tremor.

Teagan closed her eyes and wrinkled her brow. She was pushing into his brain, urging him to give up.

He lowered the weapon and released Auburn's arm.

Taye jumped up to zip-tie him as Auburn rushed away. From the looks of it, Taye had to strain to tighten the zip tie over Glaser's wrapped arm.

Teagan relaxed the bow, and the nocked arrow fell to the ground. She glanced over at the group. "I'm sorry. By the time I sensed his biological signals, I didn't have time to warn you."

Oakley went to her and gave her a hug. "You did good."

───

TWENTY MINUTES LATER, everyone except Taye slipped down the cracked and dirty sidewalk a block from the Dios Sangre Church, moving as silently as a large group could.

Shadows of movement behind windows put Oakley on edge. The last thing they needed was to deal with more people.

Kaleo led the way since he was the only one who'd been in the city before, other than Taye, who'd stayed at the playground to guard Glaser. One man captured, two to go.

Kaleo cut down a cross street to bring them along the back of the ruins. The massive stone walls of the roofless church rose up on the other side of the street, only separated from them by a small cemetery. The building had been built in a long rectangle, flat in the back and with two rounded spires in the front. Auburn had said the bunker was located in the north spire.

Halfway along the block, they ducked into an old gaming store. Cords lay strewn about the floor. The broken remains of a computer sat inside a shattered glass display case. The one advantage this building had was several life-sized cardboard cutouts of game characters in the front windows. Perfect to hide behind.

Once they were safe, Oakley couldn't take it anymore. She rounded on her sister. "Why did you leave?"

Kaleo went to the windows to keep watch. Cane took a position between the two of them. The others scattered to separate points in the room as if trying to escape any fallout.

"You sure you want to know the truth?"

"It would be nice for a change."

Auburn scowled. "The feeling is mutual. I left because I don't trust you."

"Me? You don't trust *me* when you're the one holding some sort of kill switch over my head?"

"You'd like to kill my father. And you have a history of doing whatever you want. I don't trust you not to hurt him." She swiped a loose strand of her much-too-similar hair from her face. "You're so worried that Dad and Penna made you a killer. But stop blaming them. Your own choices are making you that."

Oakley swallowed hard; her sister's words were going down like a bitter pill. Then, the echo of Cane's wisdom came to her again. *You are more than the sum of your choices.* Somehow, Cane and Auburn were both right. Deep down, she had a spirit that transcended her mistakes, but every day she acted in ways that revealed who she believed herself to be. If only she could get those two things aligned.

She swiped the thoughts away for later and focused on the issue at hand. "Did you warn Lumas?"

"No. I thought about it, but he needs to be stopped." Auburn clenched her fists. "Promise me that you won't kill him."

Could she make that promise? Lumas had high-priced lawyers to sway legal proceedings in his favor. If she let him go, he might get away with the deceit, the kidnapping, and even the murder of Cane's mother. But she had already promised to *try* not to kill him, and the time had come to change things for herself. She nodded firmly. "What did you do, then?"

"The bunker is protected by automatic weapons. I took their defenses offline." Auburn hung her head and stared at her feet. "I also tried to delete the kill switch program."

"Tried?" Cane asked. "As in, you weren't able to do it?"

She didn't look up. "My father and Glen must have discovered it. They deleted parts of my program and moved other parts. I was able to restore it so I could search for working versions on their servers to delete the whole thing, but I didn't get the chance before Glaser destroyed my phone."

Sparks of fear jostled down Oakley's spine. "Lumas has access to my kill switch? And Cane's?"

"Why hasn't he done it?" Cane asked.

"Leverage," Oakley replied.

Auburn finally looked up. "He has Penna, his primary objective. He has nothing to lose by going for his secondary objective—Teagan. If he can make contact with us, he will try to force you to give her up."

Teagan sat in the corner on an overturned plastic display case. Oakley caught her eye, and she gave a shaky thumbs-up.

Oakley returned her attention to Cane and Auburn. The situation was all too familiar: Lumas hiding in a bunker with someone they wanted to free. But this time would be different. This time, they would make sure he didn't get what he wanted.

Chapter Twenty-Eight

"ARE YOU CRAZY? He has access to the kill switch." Kaleo grabbed both of Oakley's arms and peered into her eyes.

She shook off her fear. She had the same misgivings. But she was the only one who could easily get under Lumas's skin. With a pointed glance at her sister, she said, "I'm the one he can't control. I have the best chance to distract him and possibly push him into making a mistake."

"Put me out there," Teagan said. "He won't kill me."

"No, he'll just take you and run. Besides, we need your skills elsewhere."

She rose on her tiptoes and planted a tender kiss on Kaleo's lips. The others turned away to give them some privacy. As she pulled back, she smoothed a hand down his stubbled cheek. "I have to do this."

To his credit, he didn't argue any further. "Then I'll be backing you up."

He meant from the trees. Kaleo and Raptor were to hide in the scattered trees growing inside the ruined outer wall of the church. Their tranquilizer guns would be trained on the metal door of the bunker.

"What should I do?" Wells asked.

"Slip through to the front and make sure nothing comes at us from the jungle side," Kaleo answered. The front of the church was only two blocks away from the ever-encroaching trees. "Raptor and I can watch for anything or anyone coming through the back of the church grounds."

With the plans settled, Oakley picked up a small blogging light that still had an intact circular lightbulb. She borrowed a knife from Kaleo to cut off the plug and then the lowest inch of the outer plastic casing to expose the wires. "Ready."

"Let us get into position first. Ten minutes," Kaleo said.

He, Raptor, Wells, and Cane filed out one by one. Cane would climb a tree to get to the top of the ruined wall, traverse to the concrete roof of the bunker, and take up a position there, mostly as a lookout, but also in case they needed him to use a little of his hydrogen cyanide. Oakley would do everything she could to keep that from happening.

After ten minutes, Oakley, Teagan, and Auburn quietly left the gaming store. Oakley crossed the rutted road with her skin prickling as if a hundred eyes watched her every move. They walked through the small graveyard attached to the back of the church, dodging headstones while furtively scanning the area.

"On the south side. I sense a lot of people. Mostly curious," Teagan whispered.

"Hopefully, they won't interfere," Auburn said.

Her sister hadn't been on Extinction Island long enough to know better. Of course they were going to interfere. It was just a matter of when.

Stepping through the double-door opening in the thick stone walls brought a sense of seclusion, if not security. Their footsteps were muffled by thick grass. The church had been abandoned for so long a soil layer had formed over the broken floors.

Once inside, Auburn and Teagan split off to hug the north outer wall, searching for a hiding place near the bunker door. Oakley kept on a straight path through the middle of the old sanctuary. The walls rose up thirty feet on both sides, then stopped, as if someone had cut the roof off using a scythe.

Every so often, her feet would step on a hard tile. This had probably been a paved path through the church when it was a tourist destination. She gripped the light tighter the farther she traveled.

About a dozen full trees dotted the inside of the church. She tried to pick out which ones held Kaleo and Raptor, but no luck.

At the front of the church, the stone walls circled together as if the two sides had joined hands. The only openings on this side were barren windows overlooking the sidewalk on the front. The original front door had probably been stained glass but now was boarded up with weathered plywood.

To the right, the southern spire sat empty. She peered inside. The arched doorway led to a small antechamber. Beyond that, another doorway, this one rectangular, opened to a larger circular room. Assuming the northern spire was set up the same way, Penna would probably be in that back room.

Oakley turned to face the northern arched doorway, enclosed by a metal door with a keypad embedded in it. This bunker didn't have the circular, submarine-type lock.

She waited a few minutes to see if anyone would spontaneously come out. Nothing happened.

Finally, she picked up a broken piece of stone with her free hand and threw it at the door. It clanged when it hit.

"Lumas!" she yelled. "Come face me!"

Several minutes passed. Maybe they had miscalculated, and he wasn't in there. Had this been a waste of time?

By the time a click sounded at the door, she'd already started to leave. The door opened painfully slow. Finally, she spied Lumas's dark hair, graying at the temples, as he looked around. He took one step out and shut the door. He stood rubbing his completely gray goatee with one hand while holding a pistol in the other. Then he reached for something in his back pocket. He pulled out a cell phone and, using the pinkie of his gun hand, tapped something on the screen. Perhaps he'd triggered the adrenaline surge Auburn had warned them about.

He stayed in the shadow of the overhang. Could Kaleo or Raptor get a good shot off? And how would the adrenaline affect the tranquilizer dose? She clasped the light in both hands and stood with her feet shoulder-width apart, in case she had to run.

His focus strayed to the trees and the partial stone walls nearby. He suspected a trap.

She had to draw him out. "You know how I found you?"

He scoffed. "Auburn, of course."

So, if he thought Auburn might lead them here, why had he come? The answer had to be Teagan. He was hoping to double his haul. A niggling suspicion colored her thoughts. Had Auburn and he set this up? Was Auburn delivering Teagan to him on a silver platter?

Their motives didn't matter. Teagan would do anything to get her mother back. This was their only play.

"I told Lillian that you were dangerous." He clucked his tongue. "Your mother wouldn't listen, and it cost her her life."

She held her breath. *Don't let him get to you. He has no idea what your mother tried to do.*

"Did you ever wonder why Lillian and Marcel agreed to split you two?"

Of course, she had. It must have been at Lumas's insistence. Her dad hadn't been strong enough to stand up to him.

"Poor little Oakley. No one tells you the truth." His mock concern galled her. "Well, at least I didn't lie to you. I just didn't tell you at what age they agreed to split the two of you up."

"What does that have to do with anything?"

"It's the answer to everything. Why I risked your life to send you here. Why I'm willing to sell you to the highest bidder. Why your dad was willing to do anything to help Eric but not you. Even why your mother tried to murder you."

She shook her head in confusion. He did know what her mother had tried to do to her. Which meant Dad had told him. The extra layer of betrayal cut as deep as a knife to her gut. But no matter what he said about Dad, Lumas had been the one to bring them to this point.

He raised one brow. "You and Auburn weren't separated at birth."

"So?"

"You were separated when you were both three years old." A malicious grin spread across his face. "For Auburn's safety."

"I don't understand."

"At three years old, you tried to kill your sister over a stuffed bear toy. The electric shock put her in the hospital for a week and damaged a portion of her heart."

"What?" The word was a whisper of turmoil and heartbreak. Had she really done that? She didn't remember any of it.

"There's no denying it, Oakley. You only hurt those around you."

She backed away from him as emotions swirled inside her gut. Finally, he started to move toward her and away from the bunker. But he shifted behind a tree trunk, not exposing himself to the open area.

If she could only get him out a few more steps, even if Kaleo and Raptor couldn't hit him, Teagan and Auburn might be able to sneak inside. She fidgeted with the light and dove into the internal pain. "I was three. I couldn't have known what I was doing."

He took a cautious step toward her. Was that her doing, or was Teagan influencing him to move? Either way, it would make room for the women.

"That's the point." He'd mastered a compassionate yet condescending tone. "You were a killer before you knew how to spell the word. No different from Adler. Your aggression can be useful, but you have to face the truth. You're not like the rest of us."

The truth? What was the truth? Killer, sister, daughter, friend, girlfriend. Who ... no, *what* was she? She took another step away from him. Lumas didn't define her, but neither did Kaleo or Cane or her dad. She was the only one who could. And she believed all the horrible things Lumas said.

━━

TAYE LEANED his back against a tree at the edge of the playground, trying to listen to the sounds of the jungle above the tossing and thrashing of Agent Glaser. After the group left, Taye led the agent over to sit on a spinning piece of play-ground equipment with the chipped letters *Whirligig* painted on it. The roundabout was out in the open and easy to guard, but that didn't stop Glaser from fighting to break the zip ties. Except the man didn't realize Taye had a loaded tranquilizer gun in the back of his pants, just in case. Zip ties weren't infallible.

Good thing somebody from the group had taken Glaser's pistol—Kaleo maybe, or Raptor. Otherwise, Taye would have struggled to honor Neve's wishes of forgiveness. If only he could cave this guy's skull in for daring to harm her. Then again, Taye had been a part of the plot that ended up getting Special Agent Jack Fischer killed. It didn't make them even, but it made it easier to let things lie.

Glaser stomped a foot on the patchy grass. "You know, when I get free, I have the right to carry out your sentence immediately. Interfering with a federal officer in performance of his duty is the same as choosing execution."

Taye let the corner of his mouth tip up. "Funny thing is, you weren't in the performance of your duty. You were in the middle of threatening a civilian and attempting to kill an inmate who had no knowledge of your partner or his death."

Glaser just grumbled under his breath.

Taye's mind wandered to the main bunker where he'd left Neve. What he wouldn't give to be cuddled up with her right now. He'd missed his opportunity to tell her of his feelings on the night they'd been alone before she was shot. Why hadn't he tried to talk to her since then? Fear of rejection, that was why. His cowardice sickened him.

He turned his head to keep one ear trained on the jungle and one eye trained on Glaser. Something was rummaging around out there. Still quite a distance away but drawing closer.

Could be coincidence. He should find out in a few minutes. Most predators would veer in random directions, searching around and hoping to surprise their prey. The predators that came through the forest in a straight line ... well, those locked on to your scent.

As he listened, he formulated an image of the creature. Not much bigger than a man since few of the thicker, larger branches cracked during its approach. Definitely not Mutant Mantis because that dinosaur's gait was distinctive. This one was fleet-footed and agile, like most raptors.

Several more minutes of focused concentration cemented his fears. The animal was moving faster and coming right at them.

A cold wave of dread started at the base of his neck and traveled down his body. Only one raptor would have tracked them down so systematically. Oakley's, Teagan's, and Cane's scent was all over this playground. They had to leave now.

He hurried over to Glaser, flipped out a knife, and cut the

zip ties. "I'll give you the same chance I gave your partner. Run!"

Glaser opened his mouth to say something, but Taye wasn't listening.

Fangtooth sprinted into the playground at full speed.

Both men circled around the roundabout, sending it spinning. Taye stumbled for a second when his knee hit one of the metal supports.

Fangtooth caught its foot on the same wooden edge to the sandbox that Wells had stumbled over. It flew forward on its belly and slid over the sand, dragging the covering of grass and vines with it.

Glaser snatched the tranquilizer gun from Taye's waist. He headed for the slide and began to climb.

Fangtooth had gotten to its feet.

Taye didn't have time to get the gun back from Glaser. He sprinted to the other side of the slide and ducked behind a wobbly toy horse.

Though the thing was covered with vines, Fangtooth wasn't fooled. Footsteps scratched through the debris toward his ridiculous hiding place. This dinosaur always seemed to know exactly what its prey would do.

"Shoot it!" he yelled up to Glaser.

No reply. The man wouldn't even give him a second's worth of distraction to work with.

Fangtooth had to be just on the other side of the toy horse by now. What was he going to do? Then it hit him. If this dinosaur could predict his moves, the only way out of this was to be completely unpredictable.

Without conscious thought, he sprang up from his crouch and leaped on top of the toy horse.

Fangtooth reared back in surprise.

Using the springs under him as a trampoline, he vaulted at an awkward angle over Fangtooth's head.

The dinosaur swiped at him with its mouth, missing his calf by an inch.

While still in the air, Taye grabbed the handholds on the slide and used them to swing himself in a half circle. His momentum propelled him to the ground in a roll.

Fangtooth spun around to pursue him.

Taye scrambled to get traction on the ground. *Shoot.* He'd landed in the sandbox. Blindly, he kicked and scraped with his hands to get up.

Sand flew at Fangtooth's face. It yelped and gagged, rubbing its face on the ground.

Perfect, he'd gotten sand in its eyes. He took off into the trees comprising the short expanse of jungle between him and the city, running in an erratic sprint, zigzagging around trunks, doubling back around vine curtains, and leaping over bushes. If Fangtooth was going to follow, he wouldn't make it easy for the creature.

Too soon, he popped into the open onto broken concrete. Bushes thrashed behind him. Fangtooth hadn't given up. Now he either had to hide or speed up.

He pushed his legs hard for a block while dodging the remains of old outdoor furniture and cars. He was headed vaguely in the direction of more dangerous territory. Years ago, he'd been questioned here by a rival gang. Better to stay away. He looked around for an option.

A bright color to his right caught his attention. Blonde curly hair next to a bush. He angled in that direction but overshot it.

As he passed the bush, Wells reached out to grab him. He let her tug his momentum in an arc so he could drop down next to her. Hopefully, it would look to Fangtooth as if he'd pulled a magic trick and disappeared. But if what everyone said about this dinosaur was true, that was a false hope.

He peered through the openings between the leaves of the bush. Gray-green scales flew by. Maybe they were in the clear?

Taye held his breath.

The scratching of claws on concrete, coming to a halt.

More fear flooded his system.

The claws scraped out a longer pattern.

It must be turning around.

Bile rose in his throat. He'd endangered Wells for nothing, and now both of their lives were at stake.

Chapter Twenty-Nine

CANE FIDGETED on his perch on the top ledge of the spire. Oakley was confronting Lumas as much as she could, and that only made him more anxious. Right now, he could see her, but Lumas had moved beneath a supporting beam, out of sight.

Even though Cane had promised Auburn he wouldn't hurt Lumas, he might not be able to keep that promise if Lumas tried to hurt Oakley.

The familiar bark of a dinosaur came from the front of the building where Wells should be hiding. He carefully slid his feet along the ledge to peek over the side.

His stomach clenched. Wells and Taye crouched behind a clump of bushes. Beyond them, Fangtooth scanned the ground in circles in the middle of the street.

The dinosaur raised its head and slowly turned it in their direction.

Cane had to do something. But what? If he went charging down there, his pheromones would draw the animal in his direction for sure. But maybe if he could sneak down, he could let out a little poison and force Fangtooth away.

The dinosaur took a step toward the bush. Better see if he could distract it first.

He snatched a fist-sized piece of stone, hefted it, then, using his little league pitching form, threw it as hard as he could. It plunked off the building across the street.

Fangtooth went to investigate.

Cane swung his leg over a beam girding the outside of the spire and came down to the same ledge on the other side. Twenty feet off the ground. Too high to jump. But he spied another ledge eight or nine feet down.

Hanging by his fingertips from the upper ledge, he searched with his toes for the lower one. It was still too far away.

He'd just have to trust.

After a shaky breath, he let go. His feet hit the ledge and slipped off. His knees collided with it instead, sending pain shooting through his kneecaps. He grabbed a protruding stone to steady himself.

Whew. A quick glance down the side of the church showed Fangtooth hadn't retuned yet.

He repeated the process of hanging by his fingertips. His arms shook from being stretched to their limit. This time, he'd have to roll when he hit to mitigate the effects of gravity.

He let go. His stomach barely had time to lurch before he hit the grass and flipped more than rolled.

After he stopped, he stayed low and raced over to Wells and Taye. She placed a hand on his cheek, but her gaze was troubled. He had no time to reassure her.

He squeezed into the space until he sat in front of both of them, then he spread his arms out to push their bodies behind him. He'd lost the height advantage, but he still held one he'd forgotten about: since Fangtooth was a modified dinosaur, he could sense its pheromones almost as well as it could sense his.

He took a long deep breath. Alarm tingles shot to the base of his skull. The dinosaur was close.

He slipped a hand halfway through the bush and relaxed

the pores between his fingers. Releasing the mist brought the familiar burn and vague flapping sensation.

Huffing sounds came from the other side of the branches.

Wells tried to pull him back. She didn't understand what he was doing. What a way for her to find out about his power. He resisted her pull and pressed his other hand through an opening, doubling the hydrogen cyanide. The compound probably wouldn't kill Fangtooth in the same way it wouldn't kill modified humans, but sucking the oxygen out of a space should make the creature retreat.

A snort came, as if Fangtooth was trying to expel the fumes. Had he given the dinosaur enough to force it to leave? He pushed more of the poison out of his pores.

The crack of snapping teeth. Good, he was making it frustrated.

Something yanked on his arm.

Sharp, fierce pain flashed up to his right elbow, then disappeared just as quickly. His heart rate spiked, and his breathing became shallow. His arm was going numb. What was happening?

Taye grabbed him around the waist and hauled him backward. No! He hadn't shut off the valves yet. He might kill Taye. He closed his eyes and focused on stopping the gas. His left arm tightened up as the tiny valves flapped shut. His right arm wouldn't respond.

Someone, probably Taye, coughed. Had the gas been too much for him?

Better question, had it been enough to repel Fangtooth?

He opened his eyes at the sound of a shirt ripping. Wells was kneeling close to him while tearing off a piece of Taye's shirt at the bottom. Had Taye been hurt?

Cane tried to sit up. How had he gotten to the ground?

Wells put a hand on his chest so forcefully he stopped moving. Wait, she wasn't kneeling close to him; no, she was kneeling on his right bicep.

She shifted one knee off his arm, then tied the strip of shirt just below her other knee. He twisted to look. Blood darkened the pavement in an amorphous circle.

What the—

Wells bent quickly to kiss him. Her soft lips soothed his anxiety.

"It's okay." She frowned. "It's going to be okay." Her attention went to Taye, suddenly all business. "Help me get him to that building."

Her change in demeanor confirmed what he'd seen. It wasn't a mistake. His arm below the elbow was gone. Hopefully, Fangtooth would choke on it.

━━

OAKLEY'S MIND spiraled into a darkness so deep it coated her every neuron. *You're not like the rest of us.* She pinched her eyes closed. Was there any light inside her? Any hope for redemption from who she was?

The spark started as a flicker on the back of her eyelids. It built to a tiny ball of flame, hovering in her mind's eye. This electricity formed the core of her. It also infused her every cell. She could either let the darkness snuff it out or allow it to grow into the spark it intrinsically was. Neve had been right. She had a friend and an enemy inside. It was time to choose. Which one would she cede control to?

Her eyes flew open. She slid her hand down the length of the cord to grasp the exposed wires. She imagined throwing the ball of light from her fingertips.

The blogging lightbulb illuminated on the highest setting.

Lumas grunted as it blinded him.

Behind him, Auburn and Teagan took the opportunity to sneak to the door. Auburn punched in the code.

To cover the click of the door, Oakley shouted, "I won't let you mess with my head anymore!"

Lumas lifted the cell phone in front of his eyes as a shield. "I'm only showing you your real self."

But this time, his words had no effect on her. "If I'm so terrible, why take the chance of making another me? Why have Penna continue her work?"

He gave her a patronizing smile. "She might modify more embryos for the future, but I want her to focus on other research avenues."

"Like somatic gene editing?"

He blinked in surprise.

She'd completely outed her sister as the source of that information. No going back now. Plus, she had to keep him talking. "How many people will you experiment on to satisfy your desire to control the genome?"

He didn't answer. He swiped at a layer of sweat on his forehead with a shaky hand, then he squinted and leveled the gun at her. "Too bad you won't be here to see the results of her work."

Her light dimmed as she braced for a shot.

But he didn't pull the trigger. He focused instead on his phone. Could she rush him and get the gun?

Then the horrible reality hit her. He hadn't shot her because he was trying to activate the kill switch program.

━━

AUBURN STOOD in the alcove and peered through the glass panel of the door into the main area of the bunker. Penna was nowhere to be seen. Erman sat working on a laptop. *Her* laptop. A gun rested on the desk next to him. Her blood boiled. There was only one way he could have gotten past her computer's security. Dad didn't have the skills. Glen must've helped them.

"Can you tell what he's typing?" she asked.

Teagan shook her head. "Glass is an insulator. It's hard to

read any electrical signals through it."

"So you can't influence him from here, then?"

"Nope."

"I guess we will have to get closer."

She gently pulled down the lever with a stealth borne of many nights sneaking around the headquarters with Adler. A pang of longing hit her. Adler would have known how to handle this situation.

The door opened about a foot before the hinges creaked. Erman glanced up at the sharp sound. He scowled at her, got to his feet, and picked up the gun.

"Teagan?" Auburn croaked.

For a second, Erman stayed focused on her, but then his head swiveled, almost robotically, toward Teagan.

"No need for that," Teagan whispered.

Erman's hand shook. A frown crossed his face briefly. His jaw clenched as he carefully put the gun in a desk drawer.

Teagan blew out a breath. "So much hate."

"Is there a back way out?" Auburn asked.

"Not that he knows."

"Can you make him leave?"

"Yes," Teagan answered, "but then I won't have control over him."

Good point. He would alert Dad and cause more trouble. "Just hold him for a minute."

She nodded. Auburn hesitated, torn between retrieving her laptop and finding Penna.

She sat at the chair he'd vacated. His livid eyes could have burned holes in her, but he didn't—or couldn't—move.

Oh no. The laptop was open to her program. Glen must have given them access. She checked the signal. Dad's phone was connected to the computer. He'd already entered the kill switch code, and her sister's six-digit identifying number. Before she could do anything, he hit Enter.

Auburn's breath hitched. He'd sent a microbot heading

straight to Oakley's heart. She would have a few seconds to a minute to live, depending on where in her bloodstream the bot was located right now.

Auburn typed in the word *Abort*.

By the time she received the confirmation for the abort code, Dad was typing in Oakley's number again.

She quickly moved the cursor to the top and disconnected his device. Then she turned off wireless access so he couldn't connect again. Thank goodness he hadn't taken the time to download the program onto his phone. Hopefully, she'd canceled the command in time to save Oakley.

Flipping the laptop closed, she turned to Teagan. Before she could ask, Teagan pointed to a small door in the opposite end of the room. The girl had probably gleaned the information from Erman's mind, plus it was the only place left to look.

Penna lay on a small cot inside. She was groggy, but stable. Time to get her out of here.

Given that there was no other way out, they would have to go with the original plan. Not ideal, but it was the only plan they'd come up with.

She supported Penna under the arms as they came into the main area.

With a flick of her wrist toward Erman, she said, "Send him out."

Chapter Thirty

AFTER TAYE HELPED Wells get Cane into the nearby building, she'd asked him to go to the gaming store for her larger first aid kit. The smaller one wasn't enough for this wound. He left and slid along the building, on the lookout for trouble.

A dinosaur screech resounded from a distance, but on this street, all was quiet. He came to the corner of the church, the place they'd last seen Fangtooth. The rough stone scraped his back through his shirt as he peeked around the corner.

No Fangtooth.

Had the chemicals coming from Cane's arms put it out of commission? He could only hope.

He crossed the empty street, hugging the overhang of the buildings across from the church. Half a block later, he heard running feet coming from the jungle. There was no cover here, and it was too late to duck back around the corner. He plastered himself to the wall.

Wyatt, Orion, and several other members of the gang ran down the street, dragging Glaser with them. Wyatt held a pistol, and Orion held a rifle. Many of the others held knives and spears.

They spotted him almost immediately. Rather than run, he stood tall to face them. When Glaser saw him, he glared his fury but didn't draw attention to himself.

"Taye." Wyatt's tone spoke of disappointment. "You knew Oakley was alive?"

He didn't respond. Nothing he said for explanation would dispel their anger.

"Where is she?"

With a resigned shrug, Taye nodded and began walking. As expected, Wyatt and the others followed blindly.

Taye marched down the street to a two-story building on the left. This was a place he'd spent two days as a captive. He plastered on an innocent look and gestured to the door.

Wyatt peeked into the blackened windows. Probably couldn't see anything. He shoved Orion's shoulder. "You go in first."

Orion balked. Then Taye jumped back as the door banged open. A man in grungy jeans and a scratched leather jacket walked out, carrying a rifle. Another man came out behind him. And another, and another. All carrying some sort of handheld weapon. Taye swept his back to the side of the door, almost like a butler introducing gentlemen callers. *Cazador gang, meet the Cartago gang.*

FOR A SECOND, an odd shot of electricity had vibrated in Oakley's left arm. But it shut off just as quickly as it sparked. Lumas tapped his phone insistently, as if it wasn't responding. Could she have gotten a reprieve? If so, it had to be due to Auburn.

She almost smiled. Her sister had helped her.

Lumas growled and marched toward her with his gun raised.

The door to the bunker swung open. Erman came out, but

Lumas didn't seem to notice. Auburn exited behind Erman. Penna and Teagan stood in the doorway.

Oakley retreated, trying to electrify the light once again to stun Lumas so Kaleo or Raptor could get a shot off with their tranquilizer guns. Raptor also had Glaser's weapon, but he wouldn't use it unless absolutely necessary.

A dart whizzed by, grazing Lumas's arm. Near miss. It probably hadn't discharged at all.

He kept coming.

A second shot stuck in his leg. He lowered the gun to quickly yank it out. Rather than raise his firearm again and pursue her, he seemed to appreciate the additional danger. He retreated to the shadows but showed no signs of passing out.

Finally, she lit the spotlight again. But instead of just keeping Lumas from firing, it blinded everyone behind him as well.

Oakley shifted the light to the left and waved at the women to go.

Auburn ducked her head and ran out along the wall, dragging Penna and Teagan behind while Oakley eased backward down the center of the path. The light flickered. Her strength was waning. She couldn't keep the charge steady.

When Teagan darted away, Erman shook his head as if waking from a dream. He looked from Lumas, who was now unsteady on his feet, to her. His eyes narrowed.

She'd better get out of here.

She dropped the light and turned to run just as Erman snatched the pistol from Lumas.

As she flew across the grass-covered stones, the flick of flying tranquilizer darts competed with the sound of Erman's wild gunshots. She glanced back. None of the darts had hit Erman.

She picked up the pace. Erman was now out of range of the tranquilizer guns. Kaleo and Raptor would have to climb down before they could help her. If they had any darts left.

A horrid screech stopped her in her tracks.

Erman caught her and pressed the gun to the back of her head. But the situation had changed. Neither one of them was safe now.

Mutant Mantis blocked the exit door, its long arms crossed and wobbling on the grassy stone pathway. She recognized its unique attack posture.

"What the …" Erman dragged her backward with a hand on her chest, not soon enough.

The two appendages lifted off the ground in a slicing motion. On instinct, Oakley kicked her feet out and slid through Erman's grip, landing on her backside.

The arms snapped at Erman's head with the precision of two swords slicing off each other.

Oakley rolled away as his body dropped.

No time to consider the horror of it. She took off toward one of the gaping open windows before Mutant Mantis prepared to attack her.

A roaring screech sounded as she dove through the window and landed on the grass near the sidewalk. At least she didn't have to worry about the others. Mutant Mantis would only pursue her. Somehow, she had to find a way to end this.

Chapter Thirty-One

OAKLEY SCRAMBLED through a group of men spilling from the sidewalk into the street. Wyatt punched a stocky man over by an old restaurant. Why was he here? He must have followed their trail. Not much farther away, Orion flipped another man over his back. She'd landed in the middle of a gang war. But then what were Taye and Glaser doing here?

Behind her, Mutant Mantis dropped its screech an octave to an angry growl. The creature barreled out of the same massive window it had likely entered through.

She took off down the street while keeping an eye on the creature. Men scattered, trying to avoid its slashing arms. One gang member didn't move fast enough. With the sound of crunching ribs, Mutant Mantis swiped him to the side. A glancing blow to the head knocked Glaser to the ground.

When the creature got close to Taye, Oakley intervened. "Hey! I think you're looking for me!"

The fearsome dinosaur turned to face her. The two yellow ridges above its eyes flared as if it was raising bony eyebrows.

She ran along the side of the church, hoping the grass would make it stumble. No such luck. It was gaining on her.

Its long legs meant it took one step to her three. Her only

chance was to get to the trap in time. She'd have to make the smaller trap work for the large dinosaur.

But it was eating up the distance between them. She'd never make it.

Something to her left moved.

Kaleo shot through an empty window. He rolled on the grass and jumped out of the roll in practically one movement. Then, he leaped at the dinosaur.

What was he doing?

In a football tackle, he took out one of Mutant Mantis's legs. Both of them pitched into a row of rusty bicycles. Bless him. He was buying her time. But would the creature harm him before it returned to pursuing her?

Still in a dead run, she twisted at the waist to gauge the situation. Mutant Mantis flailed, trying to get to its feet. Its back legs found an area without bicycle parts to steady itself. Those black eyes searched, lasering in on her half a block ahead.

She faced front and pushed her legs harder. One more block to the right. She veered in that direction.

Pounding stomps sounded behind her with the telltale hitch in the gallop from those terrifying front arms. The creature was all in.

Another dinosaur came out of the bushes of a side street. This one didn't run at her. Instead, it angled to run beside her.

Bad timing, Cody. Oh, please don't let him get hurt.

At the last city block, she darted into the trees. If she could come at the trap from the rear, maybe Mutant Mantis wouldn't realize the threat until it was too late.

The dinosaur crashed through the trees behind her. Her sense of direction hadn't failed her. There was the house with the carport attached to the side.

With Cody following, she darted in, slid under the trap, and waited in a low crouch on the other side. She conjured a burst of electricity, flaring heat in her hands. That and her scent should be sufficient bait. Cody settled next to her.

Mutant Mantis broke through the trees at a gallop, then put the brakes on hard. It stared at her and Cody briefly before turning its attention to the leaning structure situated between it and them. It hesitated. Were her pheromones giving it some sort of hint at the trap? Or did it have an innate aversion to avoiding the spines?

"Come on," she coaxed while sparking her electricity again.

Finally, the creature kneeled and spread its front legs flat out in front. Taking its ten-foot-tall frame down to four feet, it shuffled its way through the trap. Impressive, if she weren't trying to kill it.

What now? It was almost out, and it hadn't triggered the trap. It snapped at her with its jaws.

She could trigger the trap herself, but she wouldn't have time to get over there before Mutant Mantis was clear. Still, she jumped to her feet. Cody let out an angry honk.

"Keep him busy for me," she told him.

Suddenly, Cody began his own version of snapping at Mutant Mantis's hard legs and then the sharp tapered ends of its feet. In another spot, the creature would have taken Cody's head off. But it was vulnerable while crouching.

No blood came from the cuts Cody gouged in its mantis legs, but the dinosaur howled in either pain or anger. It tried to bite Cody but couldn't. He darted in and out of range too quickly.

She made it to the pole on which the trap balanced. Mutant Mantis was inches from knocking into the pole and bringing the trap down. So close, but not quite there.

"Out!" she yelled at Cody.

He didn't understand what she'd said, but he jumped back and stopped to look at her. Perfect.

She smacked the pole. The blanket of spikes attached to

the plywood came crashing down on Mutant Mantis hard, piercing the leathery skin on its back. But would that be enough?

Cody jumped at the impact, then circled behind her.

Mutant Mantis gave a high-pitched wail. It rose up, trying to throw off the painful apparatus.

As the creature freed itself, she ran backward. The plywood flew through the air as the dinosaur tossed it aside. Chunks of spikes stuck out from Mutant Mantis's back in patches. No blood came out, though, so had the compound gotten into its bloodstream?

If possible, the dinosaur looked at her with even more hatred than before, its dark eyes mere slits of fury.

"Time to go," she said to Cody, but he was already halfway down the driveway, his bravado gone.

She ran, looking over her shoulder as Mutant Mantis struggled to its feet. It shook its body like a wet dog. She ducked as a group of spikes sailed over her head.

A quick glance to check on Cody. The clump had missed him.

Mutant Mantis took one unsteady step, then another. It appeared to shake off the effects of the poison ... until it faltered and dropped to one knee.

Its head bobbed up and down like it was attempting to catch its breath. Then, in the middle of the driveway, it heaved a foul-smelling mixture of rancid meat, acid, and something foamy.

Finally, the creature collapsed onto its stomach, still alive, but not for long. The rogue beheader wouldn't swipe at anyone else's head. She gave Mutant Mantis a saucy salute and ran off to find the others with Cody following at her heels.

CANE GROANED AS HE AWOKE. Why had he been asleep? They were supposed to be capturing Lumas today. Had the others left him behind? He tried to open his eyes, but his eyelids were glued to his eyeballs. His mouth stuck together like he'd had cotton soup before bed. Except he wasn't on a bed. The structure under his back was hard and unyielding.

A great pressure in his right arm distracted him. If only he could look to find out why. Wait, something teased him at the edge of his consciousness. He already knew why. Remembered pain crippled him for a moment. But there was no pain now. Only pressure.

He gritted his teeth and forced his lids to open. A fuzzy picture of someone with wild hair greeted him. He blinked to clear his vision. Wells.

She placed a hand on his forehead. Her touch was cool and soothing. "Welcome back."

"Where did I go?"

"Good question. How do you feel?"

Confused. Curious. Scared. That last one gave him pause. He wasn't normally scared. God usually gave him courage.

He reached up to touch her face, but the pressure wouldn't relent in his right arm. He glanced down.

She quickly grabbed his cheek and turned his face away. But she was too late. He'd seen the stump of his arm, the blood coating the end of his frayed sleeve.

It all came rushing back like the ocean swamping a rowboat. Fangtooth had taken his arm—the pain—and Wells had given him a tourniquet, trying to stop the blood—the pressure. Had it worked, or was he in the midst of bleeding to death? It would explain the panicked look in her eyes, though the rest of her demeanor was professionally calm.

"I'm going to check on it. You keep your eyes focused over here." She pointed to the left of the building where large picture windows looked out over the street. "I don't need you going into shock again."

He obeyed. It wouldn't help anything to stare at his injury anyway. At least he knew she was safe. How were the others doing with Lumas? He should be out there helping.

Wells untied the tourniquet, then let out a little gasp.

His gaze shot to her face. "Bad?"

"No, actually. The bleeding has stopped. Quite surprising, but not as shocking as this." She gently raised his stump, so he gave it a quick glance. "This tissue here on the end is some sort of collagen scaffolding."

"Strange tissue would not be so strange for my body." No sense pretending anymore. Trying to poison a dinosaur had already blown his cover.

She gave him a look that said *duh* before continuing, "This tissue appears normal. It's the kind that forms after an injury."

He quirked his mouth at the corner. "Normal tissue would be strange for my body."

She scowled at his sarcastic humor. "Except deep wounds heal from the inside out. This type of tissue is the last of the outer skin to close over a wound." She shook her head in astonishment. "It forms several weeks after a deep injury." Her breath whooshed out of her. "It's been half an hour max since this happened. Come to think of it, I sent Taye for first-aid supplies, and he hasn't returned."

Cane frowned. Taye was nothing if not reliable, especially in life-or-death situations. "I need to go find him and everyone else."

Wells helped him sit up. Once he was sitting, his head stabilized. The effects of adrenaline had left him weary, but he couldn't rest. His friends were out there, and he was ready to continue the fight.

Chapter Thirty-Two

THE BRAWL HAD TAKEN over the width of the street from the old businesses to the church. Oakley slowed her steps as she tried to make sense of the chaos. Trash, parts of bicycles, and chunks of concrete from the road were all being used as weapons. Good thing no one wanted to waste their ammunition on killing people.

Taye had one man by the throat against the wood siding of a building. No worries there.

Where was Kaleo?

Orion glanced her way, scowled, and went back to sparring with the burley gang member in front of him.

There was Wyatt, under an overhang. He stood over another man who was trying to get up—Kaleo!

She weaved through the groups of men fighting. Wyatt hadn't seen her yet. Kaleo did and put up a hand to tell her he had this.

He didn't have this. He clutched one arm tight to his side, and his legs shook as he pushed himself up.

Wyatt lifted the remains of a bicycle frame over his head.

She picked up the pace. Anger sparked inside her. No time

to meditate to ramp up her charge. Wyatt would get whatever came out.

As she came at him from the side, he attempted to lean away, but he couldn't fend her off with his hands holding the bicycle. He threw it at her instead.

She crouched and slid beneath it, then grabbed his knee while expelling the fastest charge she could muster. His body seized with muscle cramps.

He shook for a few seconds. When she let go, he slumped to the ground. Probably not dead.

She shot to her feet to check on Kaleo. His handsome face drooped, and his eyes were weary. The injuries were starting to take a toll.

A gang member ran past them and into the shelter of what had to be their hideout, fleeing Taye. He approached them and said, "Let's get out of here."

They'd just begun to run down the street when Kaleo tugged on her arm. She glanced back. Cane and Wells were running after them. She waved for them to follow through the window of the ruins. They needed to get back to Lumas. Had anyone cuffed him while he was down?

After they all climbed through, Oakley took in Cane's pale face. Wells had helped him through the window. He had blood coating his shirt, and he kept his body angled away from her. She stepped around to see all of him.

"Oh God," she whispered.

"This wasn't God. Just Fangtooth." He gave an awkward one-armed shrug. "And I'm fine."

He was most definitely not fine. The memory of the alligator taking her left two fingers raked through her mind. The wide, gaping jaws. The dagger-like teeth. However this had happened, the loss would haunt him.

But they had no time to help him grieve. She led the group through a few trees and onto the path. Along the way, she saw the handle of a dark object. A tranquilizer gun. The chamber was open and empty.

As they approached the bunker, her stomach twisted in knots. Matted grass displayed the outline where Lumas had lain.

The quick dose of tranquilizer hadn't kept him down for long. She ran to check the bunker.

"Let me." Taye pulled out a knife.

She punched in the code, then he crept inside. A minute later, he returned, shaking his head. "No one."

Lumas must have gone after Penna, Teagan, and Auburn. Since they hadn't seen Raptor, she could safely assume he'd followed the plan and gone with the women to the rendezvous point. Hopefully, they were all still there.

A familiar screech sounded about a block over. Fangtooth again. Thankfully, the cry came from the west.

She led the group to the north-side windows to avoid the gang altercation. As they climbed out onto the opposite street and turned east, she gave a quick glance to the sky. If there was a God up there, surely he'd help a teenager and her mom escape a controlling sociopath.

FROM THE CRACKED window of a ransacked store, Gabe Glaser growled in frustration. He'd been dragged into this mini gang war when he should have been pursuing Oakley. The battle was winding down, but he needed to stay hidden until they all left.

His vantage point gave him a perfect view of Oakley as she disappeared inside the mammoth ruins of a church. He'd been close so many times, and yet, she continued to evade him like a slippery eel. An electric eel. He'd seen what she did to the gang member who was beating on her friend. One touch was all it took. The man froze like he'd stuck his hand in a light socket.

She was something else all right. Her conviction for electrocution suddenly made sense. And Jack's death too. She'd probably shocked him and left him for the dinosaurs to eat. No matter what the others said, she'd never left the island. They were all covering for her.

The men began to disperse, and the local gang returned to their hovel. The other gang limped back down the street. Several members of both gangs lay on the sidewalk or in the street immobile. Dead or injured really didn't matter. They were on their own.

Gabe stepped around the broken glass of the door and into the shadow of the overhang. One man moaned to his right.

He ignored them all. His obligation was to carry out Oakley's sentence. And he would track her to the end of her days. Even though she'd surrounded herself with people who could protect her. Even though she had some sort of unusual deadly power. Even though she'd benefited from a boatload of luck so far. He wouldn't give up. Failure only came to those who gave up too soon.

———

LUMAS MADE himself comfortable while his targets stayed inside the Lankester Botanical Gardens shelter. He had found a hiding place within the hollow opening created by several dead trees surrounded by strangler figs. The roots of the parasitic plants grew from the top down. Once they reached the soil, they deprived the host trees of nutrients and slowly strangled them until the whole structure formed a hollow woody shell. Perfect for covert surveillance.

He couldn't confront them now. He held his pistol close,

which he'd reclaimed from Erman's body, but he was alone. Plus, when the group entered the hideout, Raptor had been holding a pistol as well. If Lumas managed to get in there, it would be a standoff. Raptor would never give up the women voluntarily.

He fiddled with the adrenaline settings on his phone, then administered another slug of the drug. His heart raced, making him feel strong and virile. His toes tingled, and he bounced on the balls of his feet to mute the sensation.

This strategy went against his nature. Wait and see if something changed wasn't his style. But he was smart enough to know patience sometimes brought reward.

He stopped bouncing and dug his heels in. He would wait until some advantage came his way.

Chapter Thirty-Three

THE BOTANICAL CENTER sat quiet as the group of five approached. Taye had done a cursory job of tracking, which told them several people had traveled this way. But they didn't have time for him to be more precise. Raptor and the women were probably inside. Safe? Or battling with Lumas? Oakley strained her ears. No sounds of struggle.

They might be better off drawing closer from the back side where an arched bridge spanned the little creek that ran behind the structure. Although it was probably still blocked by the skeletonized bones of the *Triceratops*, it was worth a try to pick their way through the bones and draw close unnoticed. Plus, circling around would allow them to search for signs of Lumas outside. She wrapped a hand around Kaleo's arm and pointed in that direction.

He nodded. She moved to grab Taye's arm.

Before her hand could close around his bicep, he was tugged away from her and around the side of a large tree.

She circled around the tree and gasped.

Lumas held a gun to Taye's temple. "You didn't think I'd be stupid enough to grab you, did you?" His gaze flicked to Cane. "Or him."

Her electricity flared within her. She took several calming breaths. There was nothing she could do right now.

"I'm a reasonable man."

"When did psychopathic become reasonable?"

He glared at her. "I'm tired of this back and forth. You come after me. I go after you. I just want to be out of this country with the people I need."

"Like who?" she asked, though she knew the answer.

"Penna and Teagan."

Not Auburn. Interesting. "Why don't you let them decide for themselves?"

He gave a cunning grin. "Oh, sure. As long as they decide to come with me."

She clenched her sparking fists. "So you can brainwash Teagan like you did Auburn?"

Not even a flinch. "You already know that I won't hesitate to kill anyone who gets in my way."

Cane's mom. Monica. Agent Brooks. Yeah, he'd proven his ruthlessness.

Lumas backed several steps toward the building, dragging Taye with him. "Call for Penna to come out."

The gun barrel dug into Taye's temple. Rushing at Lumas would only get him killed. What choice did they have?

She sucked in a breath and yelled, "Penna, we need you to come out here!"

───

EVERYONE inside the visitor's center heard the shout plainly through the open-air section between the roof and the walls. Auburn went to the dirt-encrusted window. The sight outside sent an icy shiver through her veins that went all the way to the spiky needles on the back of her neck.

Dad had one arm wrapped around Taye's neck, and with the other, he held a gun to Taye's head.

Raptor had come up to peer over her shoulder. "None of you are going out there."

"I know how to talk to him without agitating him," Auburn said. "He will listen to me."

But would he? Looking back over the years, Dad's pattern emerged clearly. He listened only when it was in his best interest. Had he ever asked her about what she wanted out of life? Her hopes and dreams weren't valid unless they were logical. And the only logical dreams were his.

"It's me he wants," Penna said. "If I go out there, maybe he will take me and leave Teagan alone. He's always known when to cut his losses."

Teagan stepped up beside her mom. "I'm the one who might be able to get him to change his mind."

Raptor blew out a frustrated sigh. Auburn couldn't blame him. His only goal was to protect them. But they were not going to hide from this.

"Stay behind me, then," he said.

He stepped onto the concrete just outside the door, gun pointed at the ground. Probably didn't want to risk shooting Taye since Lumas was using him as a shield.

Auburn came from behind Raptor to stand on the gravel that edged the path. She opened her mouth to speak, and what came out was a surprise. "Dad, do you really own property in Paraguay?"

"Auburn, honey, it doesn't matter where we go. For our work to continue, we need Penna and Teagan." His eyes were bright, earnest, almost glistening. "We will be responsible for foresighted evolution."

Before coming to this island, she would've swallowed his lines like a fish swallowing a lure. Now, everything she'd seen swirled in her head in a jumble of confusion.

"Come to me, Auburn." He gave a fatherly smile. "We can be a family again, the way it used to be."

But the way it used to be had been based on lies. She glanced back at Teagan.

"He's taking that stuff again," Teagan whispered. "His mind is so chaotic."

Penna shifted to catch her attention. "Don't go."

She had to. Because he would do anything to attain his dream, which meant killing Taye and kidnapping Penna and Teagan. Her mouth went dry as she took a step toward him. She had to talk him down. But could she?

This was no longer about her deciding between going her own way or following him. This was about stopping him before he sucked other people into his web, drained their free will dry, and cocooned them in his control.

———

A STRANGE FEELING came over Oakley as Auburn walked slowly toward Lumas—protectiveness. Not that it was unusual for her to feel it, but having it directed toward her sister was unprecedented.

Lumas was balancing on a knife's edge, his desire to have Penna and Teagan was so strong he might be capable of anything. But he must know that if he shot Taye, Raptor would kill him before he could shoot anyone else.

Auburn's every step ratcheted up Oakley's tension. Then Penna and Teagan began to follow. No, she wouldn't let them give themselves up. Her core simmered and roiled like a pool of lava. A cooling breeze blew over her neck from the trees, a balm to her sparking insides.

Raptor raised his gun, pointing it at Lumas's head as best he could since Lumas was antsy.

Auburn stopped five feet from him. "Dad, they don't want to come with us."

"It's the only way."

"No, we all have choices here."

He frowned in a profoundly sad way. "You too, my dear? I thought you'd never leave me."

"I haven't left you." Auburn turned to look at Penna and Teagan, who stood a few yards behind her. When she spun back around, her face held a calm resignation. "In fact, I'll go with you. You don't need these two. We can go to Paraguay or wherever. We can continue where we left off."

Oakley slid several steps backward while Auburn kept him distracted. If she could get to the cover of the trees, maybe she could circle around and creep up behind him. But then what? If she shocked him, his gun hand would seize up, and he'd shoot Taye.

Auburn closed the distance between her and Lumas. She put a hand on his arm. "I want to fulfill your vision. Let's just go."

"Prove it," he growled.

"How?"

He nodded downward. "Take my phone."

Oakley took another small step toward the tree line. Where was he going with this?

Auburn tugged the device out of his back jeans pocket and presented it to him.

He gave her a challenging look. "Reconstruct the kill switch program." When she hesitated, he said, "I know you can do it in minutes. Use the program to kill Oakley, and then I'll believe you're with me."

"Why?" Auburn asked in a whisper.

"She's different from you. Always has been. You think and plan. You're methodical. She's out of control. You've seen what she does with her power. Don't you want to honor Adler's memory?"

A flicker of pain crossed Auburn's face. How could she still care so much about losing a killer like Adler? He must have had other sides to him. Auburn cared about the parts of Adler that she experienced, and some of it must have been good. Did she feel the same way about Lumas?

Oakley could think of only one way to end this standoff. She glanced over at Cane first. Her next move put him at risk as well. He didn't speak, but his eyes gave her permission.

"Do it," Oakley said. "Give him the program."

Auburn glanced at her with regret-filled eyes. Oakley merely nodded.

Auburn put her head down, and her fingers flew over the phone's screen. Oakley crept closer to the trees. Who knew what kind of range the program had? Maybe she could get far enough away. Or maybe he'd even chase her and forget about the others.

Penna began moving toward Lumas. Teagan followed but stayed in the shadow of her mom. No, they couldn't give themselves up.

Raptor arced in a circle, moving away from the women so he could keep his gun trained on Lumas.

While they waited, Lumas nodded to Cane. "You have nothing to fear from me."

Cane merely blinked at him. Did the father-son connection mean something to Lumas? What did it mean to Cane?

With a heavy sigh and a grimace, Auburn handed the phone back to her father. "I won't push the button."

"No problem. I'll do the honors."

He released Taye's neck and switched to holding him with the phone hand looped through his arm and the gun pointed at his abdomen.

Auburn stared first at her feet and then back at Penna. She looked everywhere except at Oakley.

Sweat beaded on Oakley's forehead. After all the times she'd almost died in this jungle, now it would come at the hands of Lumas and her sister. Would it hurt? Her heart being torn apart from the inside sounded painful. But maybe it would lead to a quick heart attack.

Lumas glanced at the phone with a smile, then he looked at her. She should run, see if she could get out of range, but that wasn't likely. Instead, she turned away from his triumphant expression and locked eyes with Kaleo. If this was to be her last image, it would be of his strong jaw, his shadow of stubble, and his caramel-colored eyes.

The seconds dragged on, seeming to slow into a thousand milliseconds. Kaleo mouthed *I love you*. She loved him back, but what did that matter if she was going to die? They would be forever separated.

A shiver ran along her spine. Unless Cane was right, and there was more after death than just nothingness. But she had no more time to think on that.

"Goodbye, Oakley," Lumas said.

From the corner of her eye, she saw him dramatically stab his finger down, pushing a digital Enter button. She sucked in a shallow breath—her last?—and fought the urge to close her eyes. Only seconds separated her from the end. She wouldn't waste them behind closed lids. *Focus on Kaleo.*

When Lumas let out a heavy grunt, she didn't look. She stayed focused on Kaleo's profile as his eyes turned to Lumas. Shock registered on his face. Even though she tried hard not to, her gaze finally rotated in that direction.

Lumas still held the gun, but his other hand had released Taye and now clutched his chest. Taye quickly backed away.

Lumas fell to his knees, then leaned back onto his heels. His mouth turned up in a pained grimace. Sweat gleamed on his forehead. The gun rested on his thighs. "What did you do?"

"*You* did it," Auburn said logically. "An overdose of adrenaline."

His upper lip sneered. Without raising the gun, he twisted it sideways and squeezed off a shot at Auburn.

"No!" Penna screamed and dove in front of her.

At almost the same time, Raptor shot Lumas in the head.

Penna's eyes rolled back in her head as she hit the ground. The bullet had penetrated the center of her chest. Auburn and Teagan screamed and collapsed next to Penna.

Oakley could barely fathom the events. She tensed her legs to join them, but a hand clamped over her mouth from behind, and a bandage-clad arm circled her waist. Caught off balance, her body was dragged into the surrounding trees with barely the swishing sound of parting leaves.

Chapter Thirty-Four

WHEN OAKLEY RECOVERED from the shock enough to struggle, the person behind her slammed a fist into her back. Pain radiated down her spine and through her shoulder. She barely managed to keep from falling to the ground.

A piece of plastic wrapped around her right wrist. No, no, no. She would not let this person bind her.

She thrashed her other arm out.

A masculine growl, followed by another hit to the back.

She echoed his growl.

The man wrapped his hand around her middle again and dragged her farther into the jungle.

She twisted, trying to get a hand on him. He avoided her touch by keeping her on her heels struggling to stand.

It had to be Glaser, given the wrapped arm. He was six inches taller than her and strong. The harder she fought, the more he used her momentum against her. But if she gave up, he'd cuff her with the zip ties.

When they were about a hundred yards away, he stopped and stood her upright. Before removing his hand from her mouth, Glaser whipped out a knife and held it to her neck. "Scream, and I'll just cut your throat and run."

With his other hand, he slipped the plastic around her right wrist again. When he went for the other one, she brushed one of his fingers and let out a shock. He grunted and dug the knife into her skin.

If she didn't comply, maybe he *would* slit her throat right now. She allowed him to capture her other wrist and secure both in front with the zip ties.

Once she was bound, he seemed to relax.

She looked at him over her shoulder. "At the risk of getting what you ask for, I have to question, why not kill me now?"

He shoved her in the direction he had been dragging her. If she screamed now, would he gut her like a fish?

Just when she'd given up hope of an answer, he responded with, "You will have the same fate as Jack."

Did that mean he was going to feed her to a dinosaur? Her body didn't have enough of her own adrenaline left for another life-or-death situation. But staring into Kaleo's eyes a few minutes ago had strengthened her resolve. She would fight to live, if for no other reason than to be with him.

"I last saw your toothy little friend near the playground. Hopefully, he's still around that area."

Clearly, he didn't mean Cody, whom she'd lost track of during the gang battle. Her soul jerked at the dawning realization of his intentions as if a bucket of ice water had been thrown on her innards. He was going to feed her to Fangtooth!

They broke from the trees and into the clearing of the playground. He walked past the slide and dodged the displaced board of a seesaw, stopping her a few paces in front of the large spinner. She imagined children pushing each other until their sides split with laughter and their heads swam with dizziness. This innocent site would be her grave because surely Glaser would leave her here to rot. Maybe someday Kaleo would come upon her and grieve, if there was even enough of her left to identify.

Glaser pulled out another zip tie and fastened her to one of the metal safety bars. Then, he used his knife to cut off a section on the bottom of her long-sleeved T-shirt.

"Can't have you yelling in case someone is out looking for you," he said while he tied the cloth around her mouth as a gag. "Don't worry. I'll be up there"—he pointed to the slide—"watching the whole time."

He gave the roundabout a shove. She held on as dizziness mingled with her dazed fear.

Every swishing branch and stirring leaf could be Fang-tooth coming for her. Was it already too late to mask her pheromones?

———

AS SOON AS Kaleo realized Oakley was gone, he enlisted Taye to track her. They had left the others to deal with the fallout from Penna's and Lumas's deaths. Raptor had wanted to search too, but Kaleo insisted he stay to watch over Teagan, who refused to go inside and leave her mother's body.

The signs indicated Oakley had been dragged for quite a distance into the jungle. Taye had no problem following that trail. But now he stopped and examined a ten-foot radius of ground. Kaleo recognized the indicators of two tracks.

"This person has training," Taye said. "He's doubled over his tracks. I can't tell which ones are coming or going or how many people traveled them. We should split up and follow both."

Kaleo let out a grunt of acknowledgment.

Taye veered to the left, so he took the right. Before his friend disappeared into the foliage, Kaleo gave him the signal for twenty minutes: two fingers held up to his forehead. If they didn't find anything in that amount of time, they'd return to this spot to reassess their plan.

Kaleo weaved his way through the trees, following broken

branches, cracked sticks on the ground, and freshly fallen leaves. It was nearly impossible to eliminate your own path through the jungle, but it was much easier to confuse it. He backtracked once when he'd been misled by a game trail.

About fifteen minutes later, his trajectory became obvious. The playground was up ahead.

At the clearing, he paused behind tree cover and surveyed the area. His heart did a stutter step. Oakley was tied to the playground spinner like bait on a spit. Glaser sheltered at the top of the slide. The monster was going to watch her be eaten by something.

Fierce anger boiled in his veins, followed by a fear so deep it threatened to smother him in a quicksand of dread. He'd rather face a five-ton roaring dinosaur than the possibility of losing her, but he sucked in a shaky breath and wiped sweat off his forehead. He had to keep control of his emotions. He couldn't act rashly.

Glaser flipped a knife back and forth, the blade glinting in the sun. He probably knew how to throw it. Unfortunately, Kaleo had lost his knife in the gang fight, and he hadn't brought Lumas's gun because it had no more bullets. He could go get Raptor's gun, but he'd lose too much time backtracking.

At least he didn't need a knife to free her. Those zip ties would give under the pressure from a sharp rock. He searched around his feet until he found a skinny chunk of basalt that would work.

Now, how could he distract Glaser?

A series of huffing sounds came from the far side of the clearing. His gut hardened into a tight ball. She'd attracted a dinosaur already. Certainly, that qualified as a huge distraction.

Problem was, he had nothing to help fight off a dinosaur. He needed a weapon, fast. He searched around and found only sticks and vines.

The dinosaur stuck its snout into the clearing. *Fangtooth.*

His terror increased a notch. Of course, that freakish creature would find her. A crazy idea came charging into his mind. Fangtooth had experience with his whips. It was risky, but a bluff was the only move he had left.

He quickly filled his pocket with rocks until it bulged, then he grabbed a long, thick vine. He stripped the leaves from it with one swipe. Holding the vine behind his back with one hand and his cutting rock with the other, he entered the clearing just as Fangtooth decided it was safe to do the same.

The creature and Kaleo stood at the same height. He probably weighed more, but Fangtooth made up for that with its firepower of claws and teeth. The two protruding teeth shook as it worked its jaw. Sizing him up, or anticipating a meal?

From behind his back, Kaleo whipped out the vine in the same way he would have brought out his vinyl seatbelt whip. He envisioned his vinyl whip, imagining it in detail down to the nicks and cuts brought by use, and even the stains left from the times he'd drawn Red Grizzly's blood.

Fangtooth shifted from foot to foot. It glared first at him, then the vine.

But Kaleo didn't look at the vine at all. He clung to the image of his whip. This dinosaur might see more than others did, but Kaleo could still control what it saw.

"Close your eyes," he said to Oakley. He couldn't let her biological signals ruin the effectiveness of his counterfeit weapon.

"Why?"

"Please trust me."

She didn't argue further, so he assumed she complied. He slowly took a few steps toward her, though he didn't dare take his eyes off Fangtooth long enough to look at her.

The creature took the same amount of steps toward her at practically the same speed. Fortunately, Kaleo was closer.

When he reached her, he flipped the vine up and rolled it toward the ground, mimicking the movements he would have made with his actual whip. It didn't give a satisfying crack like it should, but he imagined the sound.

The movement made Fangtooth take a step back.

With his right hand, Kaleo leaned down, stuck the rock inside the middle zip tie, and yanked the tie toward him. If he'd had more time, he would have been kinder. As it was, the action probably cut her wrists.

She was free from the spinner, though her hands were still tied.

"Keep your eyes closed," he reminded her.

Fangtooth danced near the end of the pretend whip. It was starting to suspect something was different.

Glaser let out a low growl as Kaleo cut the last zip tie binding her wrists. The man was trying not to draw attention to himself since that could be a death sentence. Well, Kaleo was going to shake up that strategy.

He drew Oakley to her feet and shoved her behind him.

Fangtooth let out an angry screech that his primary prey was gone.

Kaleo took a step backward, pushing Oakley with him, not toward the jungle but toward the slide. He kept the creature at bay with the vine for several more seconds … until the tip of it hit Fangtooth on the foot.

It realized the whip had no bite.

Fangtooth screeched louder and dug its feet into the grass, readying a charge.

"Okay, eyes open. Time to move now."

She clutched his T-shirt as she peered around him. He pushed her backward, faster this time. Just before they were to duck down between the slide's ladder and the metal chute, he grabbed the rocks from his pocket and threw them with his wrist flipped backward as if doing a reverse layup on the basketball court. The rocks clattered along the rusty chute.

Fangtooth winced at the loud noise and looked up.

Kaleo and Oakley ducked beneath the slide and around to an angled climbing wall, out of sight. They peered through the vines covering the slats in the wall.

Fangtooth twisted toward Glaser, almost as if recognizing him.

Glaser screamed curses at them, somehow forgetting he'd been the one trying to lure a dinosaur here. Kaleo wrapped his arms around Oakley and hunkered down. They weren't out of danger yet.

Fangtooth circled to the end of the slide and tried to climb it. Glaser held his knife out in front of his body, tracking the creature's movements with the blade.

After a few feet, it slid back down.

The creature went to the side of the slide and jumped, not quite making it to the top. It jumped again, an astonishing vertical of more than four feet, propelling its head up to Glaser's arm height. It snapped at him.

Glaser swiped the knife at the animal, catching it across the shoulder.

Undeterred, Fangtooth leaped again, this time snapping more aggressively.

Glaser leaned away to avoid the bite. He teetered on the edge and then began to fall over. As Fangtooth descended, Glaser switched his momentum to slide down the slide.

At the bottom, Glaser took a crouching stance with the knife out. His fierce expression had probably worked to intimidate common street thugs, but attitude wouldn't help against a true predator. In this case, Kaleo's money was on the dinosaur.

Glaser circled around, trying to keep the slide between him and the creature.

After Fangtooth passed their hiding place, Kaleo nudged Oakley. This was their chance to escape.

They crept toward the jungle. Only ten feet from the safety of the trees.

They sidestepped the broken-down seesaw. Now five. Almost there.

"Oakley!" Glaser yelled.

Fangtooth and Glaser seemed to forget each other. They both ran at Kaleo and Oakley. Kaleo had nothing to hold them off except his fists, but he could allow her to get away.

He pushed her toward the trees. "Run!"

The two predators passed the end of the slide, coming at him almost as one body. He took his own crouching stance. He'd tackle Fangtooth like he had Mutant Mantis and maybe shove the creature into Glaser.

"Duck!" Oakley yelled from behind him.

He crouched further. Her body spun next to him. A long wooden board sailed over his head. From the seesaw?

With impeccable timing, she smacked the board into Fang-tooth, catching the animal around its neck, and followed through by propelling Fangtooth and the board into Glaser's head. The weathered board splintered under the strain.

"Now run!" she yelled.

They took off into the trees.

A quick glance back. Glaser was down, but Fangtooth was already getting to its feet.

Chapter Thirty-Five

AT FIRST, Oakley led the way through the trees. Then, Kaleo passed her. She focused on blocking the release of her pheromones as much as she could while running.

They zigzagged through the jungle, but their ultimate destination needed to be the shelter at the botanical gardens. They had to get inside and hide until Fangtooth gave up. Then they could sneak out later.

As they came close to the garden grounds, she heard thrashing in the jungle about ten yards behind and to their right. Fangtooth was in full on pursuit.

When they broke through the last of the foliage, nothing had changed at the botanical gardens from when she'd been abducted. Two bodies lay on the ground. Teagan hovered over her mother. Auburn stood off to the side, halfway between the bodies. Wells and Cane stood close. But Taye was missing. There was one other difference: Raptor now had his gun trained on the direction of the thrashing jungle.

Her heart pounded at the sight of them. This had been a mistake. She and Kaleo had led Fangtooth to a human buffet.

The creature sprinted from the jungle, then skidded to a

stop when it realized it had overshot its targets. It pivoted, putting itself between them and the path to the front door.

Raptor took aim and fired. The creature bobbed to the side. The bullet missed it completely.

He aimed at its head and fired again, but it crouched at the last microsecond and received only a scratch. It growled at Raptor and advanced a step.

The whole group moved backward toward the rear entrance. But getting inside unscathed would be a challenge. To keep from getting stuck in the mud, which would leave them as easy targets, they had to get across the bridge. Going over the bridge meant climbing over the *Triceratops* skeleton obstacle course.

A third shot went wide as Fangtooth spun in a circle.

Raptor shot another bullet almost instantly and another one after that. The last one managed to carve a chunk out of the dinosaur's shoulder. Rather than run, it screeched and advanced another step.

Fangtooth truly had Teagan's abilities. No dinosaur could have outmaneuvered those bullets unless it could sense when and how the person was going to shoot.

Raptor pulled the trigger again. The gun gave a harmless click.

Kaleo and Cane spread their arms wide, herding the others toward the bridge. It was their only option.

Fangtooth rushed at Raptor.

"No!" Oakley yelled.

Raptor spun to the side like a star quarterback evading a rush, then raised his leg to deliver a round-house kick to Fangtooth's side. The creature had antici-pated the move and turned at the last second, but Raptor's kick still connected with its belly. Fangtooth brought its leg up at the same time and swiped a claw along Raptor's thigh.

He grunted, but he didn't go down. He switched his

weight to one leg and faced Fangtooth again with blood seeping from a hole in his pants.

"Hey!" Teagan yelled from beside Oakley. How had she worked her way past the men? Then again, this was Teagan.

The dinosaur immediately focused on her. Had she captured its mind with her ability?

She put a hand up like some sort of dinosaur whisperer.

Fangtooth stared at her with one corner of its mouth lifted and its head tilted to the side. Scrutinizing her? Or pushing back against her signals? Only Teagan knew.

"Get to the bridge," Teagan said to everyone.

Kaleo tugged on Oakley's arm. She shook her head. "Help Raptor. I'm not leaving her."

He circled around the women with both hands out in an innocent gesture, but no one else moved.

Seriously? Teagan had just told them to go.

Well, since it looked like they were doing this together, Oakley gently took Teagan's arm and slowly moved backward. The rest of the group moved to accommodate them.

After a few more tense steps, they were about even with the bridge. Now if only the members at the rear of the group would start to go over.

Oakley peered behind and nodded for Wells to begin navigating the maze through the *Triceratops*. But as soon as she took one step that wasn't matched by the group, Fangtooth let out a horrific screech and sprinted to cut her off.

Wells zipped back to Cane's side, and the whole group pivoted to keep Teagan facing Fangtooth. *Ugh*. Now the dinosaur stood between them and the bridge. It bobbed on shifting feet and pierced Teagan with a penetrating glare.

How were they supposed to kill this intuitive dinosaur? If they even came up with a plan, Fangtooth would know the instant they formulated it.

Unless she could confuse it while it focused on Teagan.

Her heart skipped a beat. Of course! This thing read

biological signals … electrical signals! Oakley had enough electricity sparking in her veins for ten people.

She leaned close to Teagan and whispered, "Close your eyes."

"What?"

"I'm not crazy. Trust me."

Teagan gave one quick shake of the head before she obeyed.

With her eyes closed, she wouldn't be able to give away whatever plan Oakley came up with. Now she needed a plan.

She glanced at the bobbing and stomping dinosaur. It stood in front of the weathered skeleton's leg bone, which was right next to the skull. There might be some weapons on hand, after all. A flicker of an idea surfaced, but before it could fully form, she imagined it sparking and catching fire like a firecracker exploding in her mind.

Fangtooth shifted its gaze to her. Its two yellow head ridges flipped up and down as if it was furrowing its brows. Good, she was about to give it more to be concerned about.

She delved deep into the emotional center of her mind, pulling forth everything that had impacted her: her father's subtle fear of her, harming her sister as a kid, putting her mother in a coma, coming to Extinction Island, Kaleo's kisses, disappointing Cane, fear for Eric …

All her experiences bubbled and flickered through her blood and crackled in her synapses. She pushed a heavy slug of it at Fangtooth.

The dinosaur pushed its shoulders back and shuffled its feet away.

Perfect.

She whispered in Teagan's ear, "Make it walk backward."

The girl nodded. She pinched her face tight and bit her lip.

Fangtooth arched its head as if trying to fight the suggestion. Shuffling feet. But no backward movement.

"Try again," Oakley said.

Same results. Only a stomping dinosaur.

This wasn't working. Plus, the high level of electricity in her blood was hard to sustain. She couldn't keep this up much longer, and yet they both needed to ramp up the pressure on the dinosaur.

Yes, exactly! Pushing thoughts wasn't her specialty. It would take both of them.

"I'm going to touch you," she said to Teagan. "I want you to take the energy I give you and push it into Fangtooth's head."

Without waiting for a response, she grabbed Teagan's elbow. She delivered the spark at a tolerable level first. Best to start small.

Fangtooth responded with a squawk. Its leg muscles tensed in twitchy bursts. They gained a few inches of backward movement but not much more.

This wasn't going to work either unless they pushed harder. They needed to shove it backward. She sent apologetic pheromones toward Teagan for what she was about to do.

To get an extra punch of electricity, she sought out Auburn. Her sister's face brought a chaotic mixture of pain caused by her longing for connection and the sadness at so many missed years. She shoved the electrical slug of heartache through her hand.

Teagan jerked with the pulse. Her head slumped forward, and her eyes pinched tighter.

A little more. She gasped and shook as Oakley pushed harder. Thankfully, she didn't seize up.

Fangtooth yelped and backpedaled.

Its feet hit the dead dinosaur's long leg bone. The bone rolled, sending Fangtooth's feet scrambling like a frantic cartoon character.

It couldn't find purchase and fell backward.

Fangtooth's body twisted and thrashed almost in slow

motion as it shifted and tried to keep from falling. The trunk of its body landed squarely on the *Triceratops* skull. The skeleton's horn came through the side of Fangtooth's chest with a sluicing sound. Blood splattered from the wound, then dripped in a thin line.

Fangtooth didn't screech again. It let out one low breathless growl before it stopped moving.

Oakley collapsed to the ground, followed quickly by Teagan. They each put an arm around the other and blew out relieved breaths.

At the edge of the clearing, the trees parted one last time. Oakley barely had enough energy to turn her head to look. The corner of her mouth lifted at the sight of Taye walking into the clearing dragging a zip-tied Glaser behind him.

Chapter Thirty-Six

OAKLEY HELPED GET Teagan settled on a cot after Wells gave her a shot of something to calm her. They'd retreated to this building since it was much larger and no one could threaten them here anymore. Wells had taken Kaleo and Cane into a room she'd decided was the medical bay to check them over.

"Can I talk to you for a minute?" Raptor called to Oakley from a back room in the original bunker.

"Shouldn't you get your leg checked and rewrapped first?" she called back.

Raptor's leg had been hurriedly wrapped at the botanical center before they'd left.

"In due time. This is important."

A wave of fear swept over her at his serious tone. What now? He was supposed to have been delivering his explanation of the deaths of Special Agent Brooks and Lumas Verret to Brooks's superior. Come to think of it, he'd been in there a long time. Was the government asking too many questions about her?

When she joined him in the back bedroom, he closed the door and gestured to a nearby cot. She perched on the edge.

He sat across from her and clasped his hands in front. "You have some decisions to make."

Well, that was better than *The government wants me to execute you immediately*.

"Is this about Glaser?"

On the trip back to the bunker, they'd told Glaser the woman he'd shot was prepared to testify against him. Neve's testimony would carry weight because she wasn't a convict and she wasn't on the island illegally. Plus, they still had the bullet they'd dug out of her as proof. To ensure that information never came out, Glaser agreed to file a report saying Jack Fischer's death was a tragic dinosaur attack and no one else was involved. He'd also agreed never to return to the island.

"No. Going back on our deal would likely send him to prison or land him here, so I don't think that will be a problem." Raptor lifted his brows as he continued. "Agent Brooks was a better FBI agent than even I realized. He took my claims of your innocence seriously and began looking into your case. Not only did he think the evidence against you was light, but he found indications of jury tampering. And as it turns out, a strand of hair was found in the bottom of Monica's tub. The prosecutor never had it tested, but Agent Brooks did. It contained unknown male DNA. The exact DNA didn't generate a hit, but the sequence suggested a relative was in the system—Michael Calais."

"Adler's father," she whispered. Agent Brooks had proof Adler Calais had been there, but now both men were dead.

"Taking into account what he found on Lumas's laptop, Brooks wrote up his findings and sent a recommendation to the federal prosecutor the night he died." Raptor grabbed one of her hands and held it between both of his. "He recommended setting you free."

Her gaze shot to his face. His brown eyes held joy. No way. He was serious. Her heart beat as if it had wings and was trying to escape from her chest. She opened her mouth to speak, but nothing came out.

"The prosecutor agrees. They are releasing you with no plans to try the case again." His eyes misted. "You can go home."

A flood of sparkling joy bubbled through her. Her name had been cleared! She wouldn't have to get another tracker. "Wait. Does that mean the tracker can be taken out of Neve?"

He smiled. "Yes. Wells has authorization to take the newly installed tracker out of"—he made air quotes—"'your' arm."

She gulped in a breath. She could go home to Dad and Eric. But how could she go back to her old life as if nothing had happened? How could she pretend she'd never met Kaleo and Cane?

Raptor released her hand and gave her a knowing look. "Take some time to process this. If you decide to leave, you know there's always a job for you at the Lazy Lizard. The 'gators at the swamp tour have missed you."

He stood. She impulsively jumped up and hugged him. "Thank you for everything. You never lost faith in me." She gulped past her thick throat. "Even when I did."

After giving her a hard squeeze, he pulled back to look at her. "I've always known who you are. You are the same person now that you were five minutes ago, before you knew the world had exonerated you."

He was right, but she continued to sense a battle inside her. She'd been seeking the truth about how she'd been created. Now that the truth had come out, it hadn't brought her peace.

"I'll give you some time alone." Raptor quietly closed the door as he left.

After a few minutes, the silence overwhelmed her. She needed to walk.

Raptor merely raised his brows again as she passed to the

front door. The other protective men were either being attended to by Wells or visiting Neve, in Taye's case.

But Auburn ran up to her side. "Going out for a coffee?"

"Something like that."

Oakley didn't give her permission to come, and she didn't ask. As they both stepped out into the bright sunshine, Raptor propped the door open with his foot.

"Hey, I found this in a back storage closet. Thought you might be able to use it." He tossed a long length of pipe at her.

She caught it with a smile. This would be her new metal pole. "Thanks."

"Your friends give you strange gifts," Auburn said with a wink.

They walked in silence for several minutes until they came to the edge of a clearing full of small dinosaur eggs. Several *Coelophysis* worked near the nests, piling grasses around the eggs. One bounded toward them. *Cody!*

So this was where he spent time when he wasn't with her. She rubbed his head while he nuzzled her leg.

A relatively clean fallen tree lay near the nesting grounds. The *Coelophysis* didn't seem to mind their presence, so she sat and tucked the pole beneath her feet. Auburn settled on the other side. Cody leaned on her legs. Auburn's arm looked like it had been freshly bandaged. They all had their own wounds, the price of the struggle for freedom.

Oakley glanced at her sister out of the corner of her eye. "Thank you for not allowing Lumas to kill me. That must have been hard to do."

Auburn's voice cracked when she spoke. "I needed him to choose peace like he'd always talked about." She brushed stray hairs off her face. "Deep down, I knew he wouldn't."

Oakley nudged Cody over between them so Auburn could pet him as well. "He might not have been serious about peace, but we can be."

Auburn nodded, and they lapsed into silence for a few moments.

Finally, Oakley said, "I can leave this place. They are expunging my conviction."

"You don't seem excited."

"I am, but I don't know what to do."

Auburn didn't answer right away. Eventually, she turned to her with pursed lips. "You've got a hardness inside."

Oakley drew in a long breath. Would her sister always think negatively of her?

"I don't mean that as it sounds. You've got the hardness inside to make hard decisions, to face the hard things, to love the hard people. Instead of trying to be something you're not, you need to embrace your hardness."

Huh. Not such bad advice. But did that mean she should stay here? Or make the hard choice to go? No one could make the decision for her. They had their own lives to live. And Auburn's life would be her own for the first time. "What are you going to do?"

"At one point, Dad said he'd left the company to me if anything ever happened to him." Auburn's eyes welled with tears but none dropped from her lids. "I think Asperten needs to go in a different direction. Genetic research can enhance people's lives for good reasons, not selfish ones."

Oakley bumped her with a shoulder. "Penna would be proud."

"Do you think Teagan will come with me?" Auburn asked.

"Not likely. This is her home. And her mom is here." They had buried Penna in a grave near a stunning patch of purple orchids with rounded petals.

Auburn bumped her shoulder in an echoing gesture. "If you decide to stay, I think Asperten could find room in the budget for another dinosaur behaviorist, one with a primary residence on the island." She hooked her thumb over her shoulder in the direction of the bunker. "You could have a safe place to live with better sanitation than a cave."

Oakley's jaw dropped open. Her sister would do that for her? Her throat was dry when she answered. "Thanks. I'll let you know."

WHEN THEY RETURNED to the bunker, Kaleo sat by the door as if he'd been waiting for her, his arm now in a sling. He adjusted the strap around his neck. "Turns out it's a little hard on the shoulder to tackle a dinosaur."

Oakley laughed. "Go figure. How are your legs?"

"No worse than before."

"Good." She ran a hand over his stubbled cheek and gestured for them to go to a quiet corner to talk.

Before she had the chance to sit, he grabbed her wrist with his good hand, pulled her toward him, and covered her mouth with his. She melted into him as he wrapped his arm around her waist. A rush of electricity sizzled beneath her skin, then burst from her lips. He moaned as he absorbed the shock. Between kisses, she sighed against his mouth. This ... She needed more of this.

He pulled away much too soon and rested his forehead against hers, causing him to hunch over. "Raptor told me. I'm happy for you." Yet, tears brimmed his eyes. "I will miss you so much."

"No, you won't."

He drew her into another passionate kiss. She was getting better at controlling the electricity between them, but this time, she had a tenuous hold on her emotions as tears welled in her own eyes. When tingles sparked her lips again, he gave another satisfied grunt and didn't release her.

Finally, they parted, both breathing hard.

"Well, I like it," she said, "if that's the way you're trying to prove you would miss me." She tugged him down to a chair and sat across from him. "But you won't because I'm not leaving."

He started to protest. She put her hand on his mouth to stop him, but he spoke through it anyway. "You should go. There's nothing for you here. I don't even have a place to live."

He was right, meaning he couldn't go back to the gang's compound, but also so wrong when he said there was nothing for her here.

"This isn't all about you." She scooted her chair closer until their knees touched. She'd been trying hard to channel Cane's and Neve's philosophies while making this decision. "I want my life to be more about *who* I am than about *where* I am. I love reptiles. I love the jungle. I love Cody." She placed a hand on Kaleo's strong jaw. "And I love *you*. If I was to leave so many things I love, I'd be denying who I am."

She watched his expression carefully. It morphed from frustration to confusion to disbelief.

"But the struggle? The danger?"

"Everyone is struggling to survive on the mainland too, just in a different way. Here, I feel alive."

"You really want to stay here?" he asked.

"Yes, I'm staying here." She gave his cheek a light slap. "Deal with it."

"Hook." His voice was a raspy whisper that stirred her deep inside. His good hand slipped behind her neck and pulled her toward him for another deep kiss. Careful to avoid his injured arm, she gave in to his tug and landed on his lap. He kissed her until the electricity pulsed from her in waves. When he released her this time, she fanned her face with her hands.

Teagan walked into the room, and Oakley jumped to her feet. Perfect timing. She gave Kaleo a wink and said, "I'm going to go see how Cane is doing."

He kissed her hand before he let her move away from him. Wow, that man knew how to be irresistible.

She entered the back part of the bunker and came to the medical bay just as Auburn was speaking.

"I told you that you didn't want to find out this way."

"Find out what?" Oakley asked.

Auburn looked to Cane for permission. When he nodded, she answered, "Find out about his other ability, the one his twin gave him." She pointed to his right side.

One glance sent a shock of surprise through Oakley. What in the world? Not only had his arm stopped bleeding, but a lumpy mass had begun to project from the severed stump. "What's happening here?"

"Fascinating, isn't it?" Wells said from the other side of the bed.

Auburn circled a finger in the air near his missing appendage. "Those are special stem cells called radial glia. They are helping to regenerate his arm in the same process seen when a leopard gecko regrows its tail." A subtle cough. "Just don't try it with anything other than your arms and legs. It won't turn out well."

He grimaced. "I don't plan on it."

Auburn grinned, then left.

"I need to go check on Neve," Wells said. "I'll be back."

Cane gave her a tender smile before she left. Finally, he was coming around to what Oakley had recognized at first sight. The two of them would make a sweet couple.

He turned his attention to her. "Need the keys to the boat?"

Apparently, Raptor had informed everyone she'd been exonerated. She shook her head. The boat they'd taken to the floating lab last week ended up beached after a dinosaur attack. "I'm never going on a boat ride with you again."

"I'm a good boater ... minus the bloodthirsty dinosaur aboard."

"Of course, you are. But a boat won't be necessary. I'm not leaving."

He did a double take. "No?"

"I'm trying to walk in love like you. There are too many things I love here. Besides, who best to keep me from abusing my abilities than people who understand what it's like to have them."

"What makes you think you'd abuse your power?"

She twisted her hands together. "It's natural that people with power abuse it."

He reached out to still her hands. "These hands may have made mistakes. But they also saved Auburn. You are responsible for the choice."

His words resonated inside her. Up until this point, she'd been living a life she hadn't chosen. Now she needed to take control. "I agree. I want to embrace the friend that's living inside me, rather than the enemy, like Neve says."

"Good idea. You know," Cane said with a bright smile, "God can be that friend, if you'll let Him."

She laughed at his eagerness. Always a pastor. She rolled her shoulders as she sat on a nearby cot. A higher power. A higher purpose. Both of those things sounded more comforting now, not so constricting. "Okay, about the God thing … let's talk."

Dear Reader

I hope you enjoyed this final tooth-and-claw-filled adventure with Oakley. As a child, my two dreams—if you don't count my crazy "I'm going to be a pop star"phase—were to be a writer and a paleontologist. Writing about dinosaurs has been a perfect blend of my two loves. May you have as much joy slaying the (metaphorical) dinosaurs in your life as I have had in these books.

If you enjoyed this series, I would truly appreciate it if you would consider leaving a review on Amazon or Goodreads. You opinion matters, to other readers of course, but especially to me.

To explore more of the Jurassic Judgment world, including dossiers on characters, a special author interview, exclusive bookmark/postcard files, and info on how all the special abilities in these books are based on real animals, visit the **secret** Jurassic Judgment Junkie page (link: https://janiceboekhoff. com/jurassic-judgment-junkie). Note: you cannot access this page from the menus on my website, only from the back of this book or by typing the above link into your browser.

If you're interested in learning about my new releases and book recommendations, I'd love to connect with you, so please sign up for the quarterly newsletter on my website (https://janiceboekhoff.com).

For some fun Execution Island facts, flip to the next page …

Blessings,
Janice

Execution Island Fun Facts

- Kaleo means "voice" in Hawaiian. I thought this would be fitting for him because he is often the voice of reason for Oakley.
- Ogden Greene's name has the same initials as Owen Grady (Chris Pratt's character) as a nod to *Jurassic World*.
- Costa Rica is a big country! To keep my characters from having to walk for days in between locations, I took inspiration from interesting areas in Costa Rica, but I shrunk down the scale to allow the characters to travel quickly from one to the other.
- The inspiration for the decapitating dinosaur, Mutant Mantis, came from the mantis shrimp, which is neither a mantis nor a shrimp. These animals can use their mantis-like claws to smash at the same velocity as a .22 caliber rifle. They can crack the glass in an aquarium. Plus, they are the only documented species that sees a special kind of light called circularly polarized light. I made this dinosaur villain a *Dilophosaurus* because that is my son's favorite dinosaur.

- Cody, Oakley's pet *Coelophysis*, is named after my pet Vizsla—I bribe him with chew toys so he won't demand more compensation for using his likeness.
- To keep track of all the characters in this series, I have a list of their names and characteristics (including the dinosaurs), and if they die, I turn their name red. It was so hard for me to turn Red Grizzly's name red in the end, perhaps because I love *Utahraptors* or maybe because Red Grizzly started out the series with me.
- The Lankester Botanical Gardens truly exists and is not abandoned as suggested in the book.
- The ruins of the Dios Sangre Church were based on the Cartago Parish ruins built in 1575 by the Spanish. I moved this to the outskirts of Cartago— it is actually closer to the middle of the city—and added a cemetery. This church was rebuilt many times after earthquakes until finally being abandoned in 1841 after another earthquake left it decimated.
- The abandoned prison exists on San Lucas Island in the Nicoya Peninsula, and it was known as one of the harshest prisons in Costa Rica before it was abandoned in 1991. The island was designated as a National Park in 2020.
- The sanatorium was based on the abandoned Duran Sanatorium near the Irazu Volcano, built in 1915. It served as a hospital for tuberculosis patients until 1960 and then became an orphanage and finally a prison. It was shut down in 1973.
- As far as bringing dinosaurs back to life goes, scientists can't yet accomplish this, but every year more soft tissue is found in dinosaur bones. Someday, maybe …

Acknowledgments

This is one of the few times when words seem to fail me. I cannot possibly convey how grateful I am to be living this author life with so many wonderful people by my side, but here goes:

Todd, Zach, Jenna, and Riley—you all are my greatest joy and an endless source of encouragement (and entertainment). I truly appreciate how you patiently wait for laundry to get done while Mom decapitates people with her dinosaurs. I love you for that … and so many other things.

Crystal Joy and Amelia Judd—this last book is dedicated to you because this series wouldn't be what it is without your talented input. Thank you for embracing the dinosaurs and death that I brought into your lives.

Carol Brandon, Donna Feld, Lisa Lee, and Mary Johnson—you've stuck with me for the whole series, and your insightful comments have made a Jurassic-sized world of difference. Thank you for being the best beta readers around.

Kim Mesman—you've done it again! If people judge my books by the covers, I'm set! I am truly thrilled to have you for a cover artist. Thank you.

Linda Yezak—I am so grateful for your editorial talent! You make my prose tighter, remind me to describe more when I'm being lazy, tell me when I'm flat-out not making sense, and most of all, you encourage me to keep writing. I'm so glad God brought us together.

Amazing readers—I'm beyond blessed to have spent this

entire series with you! My prayer is that you have had some fun, enjoyed a little fear, and caught a glimpse of faith. I hope to spend time with you again whenever my next series comes out.

Happy reading!
Janice

About the Author

Blessed with an insatiable curiosity and a low tolerance for boredom, award-winning author Janice Boekhoff (pronounced Beau-cough) has worked more than twenty jobs ranging from Loan Consultant (important, but mortgage paperwork makes her sleepy) to Landfill Environmentalist (literally her smelliest job) to Research Geologist (the job that gave her the best tan and the most adventures). She began writing as a way to express all the unique ideas colliding in her head. A Midwest native, she now writes from Eastern Iowa where she lives with her hubby, three basketball-loving kids, and one adorable Vizsla.

CPSIA information can be obtained
at www.ICGtesting.com
Printed in the USA
LVHW052157260223
740466LV00014B/693

9 781948 003117